Much Ado About Jessie Kaplan

°

Paula Marantz Cohen

ST. MARTIN'S GRIFFIN

New York

To my sister, Rosetta

www.stmartins.com

Book design by Jonathan Bennett

Library of Congress Cataloging-in-Publication Data

Cohen, Paula Marantz
    Much ado about Jessie Kaplan / Paula Marantz Cohen.
       p. cm.
    ISBN 0-312-32498-7 (hc)
    ISBN 0-312-32499-5 (pbk)
    EAN 978-0-312-34299-5
    1. Parent and adult child—Fiction. 2. Shakespeare, William, 1564–1616—Relations with women—Fiction. 3. Mothers and daughters—Fiction. 4. Jewish families—Fiction. 5. Reincarnation—Fiction. 6. Aged women—Fiction. 7. Widows—Fiction. I. Title.

PS3603.O372M83 2004
813'.54—dc22
                                              2003026481

First St. Martin's Griffin Edition: August 2005

10 9 8 7 6 5 4 3 2 1

Praise for *Much Ado About Jessie Kaplan*

"A brightly comic book . . . [that explores] the redemptive capacity of the literary imagination. . . . Highly literate light fiction."

—*Times Literary Supplement*

"Humorous for those with no Shakespearean background, hilarious for those who have one, and insightful for all."

—*Jerusalem Post*

"Anyone—Jewish or not—who has ever attended a bat or bar mitzvah will find Cohen's take on the preparations and planning for this rite of passage spot on. By the end of this thoroughly entertaining romp, the author convincingly resolves all of Carla's family dilemmas with large doses of humor and heart."

—*Publishers Weekly*

"Cohen scores another hit."

—*Library Journal*

"Comical and entertaining . . . With the substitution of a bat mitzvah for a wedding, Cohen's latest laugh-out-loud novel is reminiscent of *My Big Fat Greek Wedding*."

—*Romantic Times*

And for *Jane Austen in Boca*

"Page-turner of the week . . . Austen never schmoozed by the pool with a pack of bronzed yentas, but her *Pride* plot proves as durable as ever. . . . What's not to like?"

—*People Magazine*

"Utterly charming . . . think *Pride and Prejudice*, but with better weather."

—*Vanity Fair*

"Cohen's wit is sharp, smart, and satirical, and her characterizations are vividly on target."

—*San Francisco Chronicle*

ALSO BY PAULA MARANTZ COHEN

Fiction

Jane Austen in Boca

Nonfiction

Silent Film and the Triumph of the American Myth

*The Daughter as Reader: Encounters Between
Literature and Life*

Alfred Hitchcock: The Legacy of Victorianism

*The Daughter's Dilemma: Family Process
and the Nineteenth-Century Domestic Novel*

Although I draw on facts relating to the life and work of William Shakespeare, this book is an act of imagination and fantasy and not of literary or historical scholarship. In short, a great deal of poetic license is taken with the subject matter. Please note as well that any resemblance between characters in the novel and living people is purely coincidental.

—Paula Marantz Cohen

Much Ado About Jessie Kaplan

*C*arla Goodman WAS WORRIED.

She knew she had much to be thankful for: a nice home, a good marriage, two beautiful children. She even had a close relationship with her mother, whom her husband actually liked.

But lately, there were problems.

First, her husband was coming home from work frazzled and depressed. A gastroenterologist in private practice, he should have been free from worries about making a living. But medicine wasn't what it used to be. "It's one thing to look up butts and get rich," Mark complained wearily. "It's another to do it for nickels and dimes."

Then there was Jeffrey, their ten-year-old, on his way to becoming a fifth-grade delinquent. Each week, Jeffrey's backpack released an avalanche of notes from his teachers. "Dear Mrs. Goodman," one recent note read, "Your son's poking of the girls with pencils is unacceptable. Please apprise him of the dangers of lead poisoning and the fact that several of his victims' parents are lawyers."

If this weren't enough, there was Stephanie, aged twelve, who existed in what seemed to Carla like a perpetual state of PMS. Stephanie's bat mitzvah was only months away, but the unpredictability of her moods—which often revolved around whether she was having a good or a bad hair day—

meant planning this event required the tactical insight and diplomacy of a seasoned military strategist.

But these were all everyday problems, part of the expected stresses and strains of life. The business with her mother was another story. Carla found it confusing, disturbing, even (truth be told) scary.

She had noticed the first sign that something was wrong one evening a few months after her mother had moved in with them. The afternoon of that day had been uneventful—which is to say, no more nerve-wracking than usual. She and Stephanie had spent several hours fighting in a stationery store in an upscale strip mall on Route 73 in Cherry Hill, New Jersey. . . .

Chapter One

*T*his one LOOKS NICE."

"I hate it!"

"How about this one?"

"No!"

Carla and Stephanie were leafing through a sample book in the fancy stationery store, trying to pick out an invitation for Stephanie's bat mitzvah.

Things were not going well.

What Carla liked, Stephanie hated, and what Stephanie liked, Carla couldn't help saying, "Are you sure that's what you want?"— a question guaranteed to drive any daughter crazy.

Carla hadn't thought that picking out an invitation would be so complicated. How hard could it be to choose a good paper stock with a colored border and some curly type?

But she had failed to take several things into account.

For one thing, invitations were not as simple as they used to be. Now, not only was there a dizzying array of paper stocks, borders, and typescripts to consider, but ornamental features like gold leaf, ribbons, and stars; whimsical inserts like confetti, whistles, and gold coins; and high-concept design elements like holograms, taped messages, and scratch-and-sniff panels.

Then, there was the additional complication posed by the bat mitzvah girl herself. Stephanie Goodman was at that highly sensitive and volatile age where choices of any kind tended to stress her out. The many trivial, hard-to-differentiate variables involved in picking out a bat mitzvah invitation were just the sort of thing liable to cause a meltdown.

"What's wrong with this one?" Carla held up a sample invitation with a pink border and a matching pink bow. A little packet of pink sparkles was also included as a "fun feature"—guaranteed to spray out when the envelope was opened, get embedded in the recipient's sweater, and remain there through numerous dry cleanings.

"Too girly," pronounced Stephanie.

"And what's wrong with girly?" asked Carla, succumbing to sarcasm: "You're a girl, aren't you?" In point of fact, Stephanie and her friends liked to advertise their gender—what with the makeup, the tight-fitting tops, and the heavy dousings of cheap perfume that, in the words of Carla's husband, Mark, made the car (when he drove them to their favored destinations, Friendly's and Starbucks) smell like a French cathouse. Yet for some reason, certain tried-and-true artifacts of girlhood had been thrown by the wayside. The color pink was one of them.

"I like the turquoise," said Stephanie, ignoring her mother's remark (in Stephanie's world, mothers weren't allowed to be sarcastic).

"That's nice." Carla tried to sound noncommittal.

"You don't like it!"

"The turquoise is fine."

"You're lying! You don't like it!"

"What does it matter what I like? It's what you like that counts."

"I don't like the turquoise," said Stephanie with sudden decisiveness. "I like this one." She pointed to an invitation with pinkish trim and a pinkish bow, similar to the one Carla had just picked out.

"Lavender is very popular," said the salesgirl diplomatically.

"Yes," said Stephanie, glad to see her choice—in actuality pink—identified as not pink. "I like the lavender."

"So that settles it," said Carla with relief.

"Lisa's invitation had her voice recorded in it," Stephanie noted, not content to close the case so easily.

"We have speaking invitations," said the salesgirl. "They're really neat."

Carla felt like swatting the girl, whose skin-tight jeans and heavy eyeliner—not to mention the fact that she wasn't a day over twenty-three—obviously gave her an unfair advantage. "No speaking invitations," she said firmly. "Everyone we plan to invite knows how to read."

"I was just asking!" said Stephanie. "I wasn't necessarily saying I had to have them."

"Well, you aren't going to."

"I didn't say I wanted them. I was just asking." Stephanie's voice had grown shrill but she managed to mutter under her breath, "You're so mean! I hate you!"

Carla held herself back from responding. All the books said that the teenagers' goal was to get the parents angry and on the defensive. It was important not to let them win—or at least know they had. Carla pursed her lips and handed the salesgirl her credit card.

"Do you have a ballpark figure of how many you plan to send out?" asked the salesgirl sweetly.

Carla sighed and shook her head. The original plan had been for a modest brunch—the modest brunch being the common starting point for all bar and bat mitzvahs, though none ever seemed to take this form. In the Goodmans' case, the brunch had been nixed by Mark's parents, who had argued that they and their friends weren't about to schlep up from Florida to have the event over on Saturday afternoon. Better to do an evening affair, with a nice spread for the out-of-towners the next morning to stretch things out.

Once an evening affair was settled on, other variables followed in inevitable succession: a sit-down meal, a band as well as a deejay, a prima-donna entertainment coordinator with entertainment facilitators in matching outfits—not to mention high-end favors, prizes, and other specialty items that the bar mitzvah marketers stipulated as de rigueur for evening affairs.

"It takes on a life of its own," said Carla's friend Jill Rosenberg, who was still recuperating from her son Josh's bar mitzvah a year ago. "But you don't want to fight it. If you resist, they make you feel guilty, so it's better to give in and go with the flow."

Carla had taken Jill's advice and watched unprotestingly as the guest list grew and grew. Stephanie's list alone drew from three substantial constituencies: her camp friends, her middle-school friends, and her Hebrew-school friends—each group to be treated as inviolable and not to be mixed under any circumstances.

Mark's list was also substantial. He had to invite all the referring doctors in his hospital (or risk never getting a referral again) and those nurses who had dropped hints as to how they'd love to observe this wonderful Jewish ritual (or risk their developing weird scenarios as to what went on when so many Jews got together in one place).

Carla's mother, Jessie, planned to invite large contingents from both sides of her family. This included the highly sensitive Scarsdale Lubenthals—to omit one was to bring down the ire of the entire clan—and the lively but disreputable Brooklyn Katzes, likely to show up with new spouses, a doubling effect in itself.

Carla's in-laws seemed intent on inviting practically everyone in their condominium community in Southeast Florida, including people they frankly detested.

"Invite them," her mother-in-law said. "They won't come anyway and it'll make them feel bad for not inviting us to their grandchildren's."

"But what if they do come?" Carla protested. She had learned from friends that people were unpredictable that way and you never knew when someone might be in the mood to hop on a plane and go to a bat mitzvah. Just the other day she had heard a horror story about a woman who invited her husband's cousins in Venezuela, and had them all show up on her doorstep the morning of the affair.

"If they come, you add a few more tables," her mother-in-law counseled lightly. Carla's in-laws were always making such casual pronouncements, until they saw the bill and were appalled. Carla thought they might be suffering from a rare form of Alzheimer's in which their memory was affected only with regard to what things cost.

Finally, there was the associative principle attached to the invitations. This was the principle whereby asking X meant having to ask Y and Z, who would be mortally offended if they found that X was invited and they weren't. In short, each invitee immediately spawned two or three more, making compiling the guest list akin to the breeding of rabbits.

"How about a five-hundred-dollar down payment?" said the salesgirl, noting that Carla's eyes had glazed over at the prospect of giving an estimate. "We can make up the difference when you have the exact count."

Carla said this would be fine.

"And if you need to change any of the options, we'd be more than happy to accommodate. It's such an important event; we want the bat mitzvah girl to have everything she wants."

The salesgirl glanced slyly at Stephanie and her mother as she spoke. She was close enough to her own bat mitzvah to know that what the bat mitzvah girl wants wasn't always in line with what the mother of the bat mitzvah girl thinks is appropriate. The prospect of a clash of wills filled the air as she saw Carla and Stephanie dart angry looks at each other. It was nice to think that certain things remained the same, mused the salesgirl. Even as you grew older and the world changed around you, others followed in your footsteps and repeated the age-old patterns. That's what rituals were all about, weren't they?

Chapter Two

*C**arla and* STEPHANIE RETURNED FROM THE STATIONERY store just as Carla's mother, Jessie Kaplan, was taking a casserole out of the oven. Ten-year-old Jeffrey was sitting at the kitchen table, drinking a glass of chocolate milk and kicking his foot against the refrigerator.

"Stop kicking the refrigerator," Stephanie ordered her brother angrily as soon as they came in the door.

"I can kick it if I want," replied Jeffrey. "Grandma doesn't mind."

"Well, I mind. You'll dent the refrigerator," said Stephanie, suddenly concerned about the well-being of this appliance.

"Dent the refrigerator?" exclaimed Jeffrey. "That's the stupidest thing I ever heard!"

"Don't call me stupid," said Stephanie, darting forward and punching Jeffrey on the arm.

"She hit me!" screamed Jeffrey. He had jumped up from his chair and gotten hold of his sister's T-shirt, which he was pulling violently around the collar.

"He's stretching my Michael Stars T-shirt!" shrieked Stephanie. "He's ruining it! It cost thirty dollars!"

The two had by now recessed to the living room, where they

were battling each other noisily. The stretched Michael Stars T-shirt had provoked Stephanie to grasp the stiff wedge of hair that stood out on Jeffrey's forehead in the style popular with pre-teen boys.

"Oww, she's hurting me, she's hurting me!" Jeffrey screamed. "She's pulling my hair out. Help!"

Carla, too tired to intervene, had fallen onto the kitchen chair, while Jessie calmly poked the casserole with a fork.

Jessie Kaplan was unfazed by the screams emanating from the other room. In fact, she was unfazed by turmoil in general. She had raised two children of her own: Carla and her younger sister, Margot. Carla was the easy one; Margot was the handful (and at thirty-four, still a handful). Having raised Margot, Jessie was used to carrying on in a climate of mayhem and strife.

Jessica had been living with Carla's family for several months now. For most daughters, this would have been a trial, but Carla counted herself blessed. Her mother was one of those rare specimens: an even-tempered, uncomplaining Jewish woman, who performed household chores with cheerfulness and efficiency. Carla sometimes believed that her mother had been switched at birth and was actually the product of a nice Protestant family who had been saddled, in her stead, with someone who refused to vacuum for fear of breaking a nail.

On this particular day, while Carla and Stephanie had been engaged in the exhausting stationery outing, Jessie had spent the afternoon straightening up and making dinner.

She now handed her daughter a mug filled with a pale yellow liquid: "A glass of mead?" she proffered, as the children could be heard knocking over the andirons in the other room.

"Mead? Is that something you picked up at Whole Foods?" Carla asked suspiciously. Whole Foods was the area's specialty supermarket where one could buy a wide array of "gourmet organic" foods (an ingenious combination that permitted the food to taste like sawdust and still cost an arm and a leg). The contents of the mug looked and smelled like apple juice, but that hardly prevented it from having been sold at an astronomical price as something more exotic.

Jessie didn't answer; she was staring dreamily into space. Carla looked at her mother, then gazed down at the alleged mead.

That was the beginning. Other oddities soon followed.

The next night, Jessie prepared a new recipe for the family's dinner that, upon interrogation, she pronounced to be "venison stew."

"Venison—what's venison?" Jeffrey asked.

"Venison is deer," Mark translated unadvisedly, at which Stephanie jumped up from her chair and bolted from the room. Carla wondered when Whole Foods had begun to carry venison. It certainly wasn't available at the Acme.

Then, later that evening, after Jessie finished stitching up a hole in Stephanie's jeans, she turned to Carla and asked if Mark's doublet needed mending.

"His doublet?" Carla looked at her mother in bewilderment. "What's a doublet?"

"It's the tunic worn over the hose," Jessie answered matter-of-factly.

Carla had tried to react casually: "No doublet, I'm afraid, but you could reinforce the buttons on his dress shirt"—at which Jessie had nodded agreeably and gone ahead and worked on the buttons.

Carla managed to put these strange remarks out of her mind until a few nights later, when Mark was late for dinner.

"Did he stop at the Wild Boar?" Jessie asked in a disapproving tone.

"The Wild Boar?"

"The tavern up the way."

"No-o-o-o," said Carla slowly, "Mark is *not* at the Wild Boar. He's at a meeting with a drug rep to discuss the side effects of a new colitis drug."

She was about to ask her mother where precisely "up the way" the Wild Boar Tavern was located (and how an establishment so-named had managed to escape her notice)—but a phone call from Jeffrey's social studies teacher intervened. It seemed that Jeffrey had pulled down the map of the continental United States, ripping it from its roller and entirely disrupting the lesson on the Finger Lakes. The resulting damage was to the tune of $144.99, for which the Goodmans would be billed.

"Under no circumstances is your child to touch the map, the globe, the worksheets on my desk, the other children's pencils, papers, notebooks, or anything not belonging exclusively to himself," said the teacher, in what Carla took to be an unnecessarily snippy tone.

After this phone call, she might have returned to probe the reference to the tavern—not to mention the earlier references to the mead, the venison, and the doublet—but somehow she wasn't in the mood.

Chapter Three

*H*ow *was* YOUR DAY?" CARLA ASKED HOPEFULLY WHEN Mark finally arrived home that night.

"A disaster," he snapped. "Mrs. Connor lost her health insurance when she was laid off last year and now she comes in with rectal bleeding. And Jack Morris—you know, the guy who sold us our Volvo, nice fellow—finally developed an ulcer and his insurance doesn't cover the cost of an endoscopy; I had to drop that carrier six months ago."

"So what are you going to do?" said Carla, thinking about poor Mrs. Connor and Jack Morris, bereft of medical coverage.

"I'm going to treat them," sighed Mark, "but I'm not running a charity ward. And it doesn't help that some of the others give me a hard time about the twenty-dollar co-pay. You'd think I was soaking them for their life's savings. Not that they'd give a second thought to buying a hundred-and-twenty-dollar pair of running shoes, or paying thousands to the vet to treat their beloved Fido."

He slumped wearily in his chair, and Jessie ran to cluck over him. She had, in the manner of many elderly Jewish women, an enormous respect for physicians, whom she placed on a metaphorical dais above all other human beings. Mark greatly appreciated this attitude. It always gave him a lift to overhear his mother-in-law referring to him reverently as "the doctor," as in, "What do you think the doctor would like to have for dinner tonight?" Lately, with Jeffrey's behavior problems and the screaming fits erupting between Stephanie and her mother over the bat mitzvah, Jessie was about the only member of the family Mark could bear to have around.

Noting that her son-in-law looked especially tired and irritable tonight, Jessie placed her palm on his forehead and inquired solicitously, "Would you like—"

"Some mead?" Carla interrupted, glancing slyly at her mother.

"Some Tylenol?" Jessie continued, appearing not to notice the interruption.

"Tylenol would be great," said Mark, smiling wanly. "And I could sure use a scotch with that. God, what a day!"

Jessie hurried off to fetch the Tylenol and the scotch, leaving Mark to embark on the familiar lament about how thankless the practice of medicine had become.

"How about getting a partner to ease some of the burden?" Carla suggested, launching into the litany of possible solutions they had rehearsed many times before: "Hire someone, or join a group."

"How can I hire someone when I'm barely taking home a decent wage myself?" protested Mark irritably. "And what group am I going to join? I've been competing with the other GI groups for five years, so naturally we hate each other. And besides, I wouldn't want to work with them—they only care about money."

"You care about money," pointed out Carla. It seemed the only thing he ever talked about lately.

"I care about making a decent living," clarified Mark. "But I want to practice good medicine. The two things shouldn't be mutually exclusive."

"Why don't you speak to someone at HUP?" suggested Carla, referring to the area's medical mecca, the Hospital of the University of Pennsylvania, where Mark had done his training. "You could teach and see some patients on the side. You liked doing that when you were doing your fellowship."

"You don't understand," he said impatiently. "You can't just decide to have an academic career. I'm too old. Besides, it would mean a drastic pay cut."

"I thought you didn't care about the money."

"I don't," sighed Mark. "But there's you and the children. We have expenses."

This was true. The bat mitzvah alone had become a fearsome extravaganza, the costs mounting scarily by the day. She could imagine her poor husband doing assembly-line colonoscopies for years just to pay for it.

"I could get a job—a real one," Carla suggested. She knew this was ostensibly the logical course of action. In the lexicon of feminism, instilled in her from her college days, she was not operating up to par. Her college roommate was now a senior vice president at Maidenform, and her sister, Margot, was one of the highest-billing criminal lawyers in Philadelphia. Of course, her roommate was divorced with a fifteen-year-old son already in rehab, and Margot was without the appendages of husband or children. But even as she noted these qualifying factors, Carla scolded herself for stooping to note them. Tallying the failed marriages and delinquent or nonexistent children of high-powered working women was one of the pettier pastimes of the stay-at-home mother. Besides, for every professional woman with a dysfunctional family, there existed a more domestic one whose family was no *Leave It to Beaver*. Her own—she could hear the kids screaming like banshees at each other in the living room—left something to be desired.

But the fact was that Carla was already busy doing what might have counted as several jobs. She supervised the temple book fair and soup kitchen, was secretary of the Home and School Association, helped Mark at the office two mornings a week, and volunteered three afternoons at the Golden Pond Geriatric Center. On top of all this, she shouldered the mundane but labor-intensive tasks associated with running a household of four: shopping, cleaning, and cooking.

The latter was a particular challenge given her family's fastidious tastes. Stephanie, for example, was lactose intolerant, grossed out by tomatoes, and allergic to all berries; Mark wouldn't eat anything orange (an aversion developed, according to his mother, when he was frightened by a Halloween pumpkin at the age of three); and Jeffrey required constant vigilance because he was liable to ingest anything that came within range of his mouth. Just the other day, he had consumed an entire jar of beef jerky, bought at the 7-Eleven with his allowance money, and had diarrhea for three days afterward.

"You do so much already, and I'd hate to see you give up the geriatric center," Mark responded to Carla's suggestion that she get a "real" job. "Not many people can do that kind of work. It's one thing to deal with human beings clinically, the way I do; it's another to help them go to the bathroom and tie their shoelaces."

It was Mark's greatness, Carla felt, and one of the reasons she had fallen in love with him, that he didn't believe that what he did, in having greater social prestige, was superior to what she did. If anything, he admired her more for dealing with the emotional aspects of life that often confused and frightened him.

Mark and Carla had fallen in love during their sophomore year at Boston University. He was pre-med and she was a psych major, which meant that he helped her do the math and she explained to him what the professor really wanted on the exams—a division of labor they had held to ever since. As Carla's sister, Margot, put it: "You had an arranged marriage, only you arranged it yourselves. It's actually kind of disgusting. You even look alike."

Carla protested that this wasn't true. Mark was thin and fair—his parents descended from German Jewish stock, a fact that Rose and Charles Goodman managed to relay by a certain superciliousness of manner that would have bothered a more prickly daughter-in-law. Carla was darker and more robust in the style of her Mediterranean roots—Jessie's side of the family had Sephardic blood. Yet Margot had a point in noting a resemblance between her sister and brother-in-law. It sprang from deeper points of correspondence: Carla and Mark came from basically the same economic background, shared the same religion (albeit with different degrees of piety), and were the same age (with Carla, in stereotypical female fashion, six months younger than Mark). They had been pleased to discover on their third date that they both wanted to raise their kids in the suburbs, preferably a girl and a boy, with the girl coming first to act as a calming influence (future events would accommodate them here in letter if not in spirit).

"Heartwarming!" noted Margot dryly when told of this coincidence. Secretly she was rather jealous of her sister's marriage.

Having now weathered Mark's familiar lament about the dire state of his medical practice, Carla put her hand against her husband's cheek and kissed him. He smiled despite himself. They had fallen in love in college, and they still loved each other—that was something. They had two beautiful if cantankerous children—that was something else.

"Don't worry," she reassured him, "things will work out for the best."

"They'll work out"—Mark sighed in his usual fatalistic tone—"for the best, I don't know, but they'll work out. They always do."

Chapter Four

I won't HAVE KOSHER FOOD, IT TASTES AWFUL!" DECLARED Stephanie.

They were addressing the first hurdle related to the catering of the bat mitzvah: whether or not the meal should be kosher. Carla had assumed that it would be—since in her experience it always was. But she was judging from affairs held when formidable individuals like Grandpa Abe, Jessie's father, were still alive. Abe and his ilk were men of adamantine will for whom many things, the food at bar mitzvahs among them, were as immutable as the setting of the sun.

"There's Uncle Sid to consider," Carla reminded Stephanie. Sid was Jessie's ancient uncle, so old that he no doubt ate very little except pablum. But he stood as the last clear support for keeping things kosher.

"You said Uncle Sid was in the hospital and probably wouldn't come," Stephanie reminded her. For a girl who couldn't remember to put the juice back in the refrigerator, her memory could at times be surprisingly sharp.

"Yes, but he may recover," said Carla. "We wouldn't want to offend him."

"But he's like a hundred," protested Stephanie. "He wouldn't even notice. I don't see why we have to have the food taste horrible just because some dead people want it to."

Though her logic was somewhat askew, the spirit of her argument was sound, Mark thought. He had never been one for the fine points of Jewish ritual and had gone along because his wife's family had found it important. Now that Grandpa Abe was dead and Jessie appeared to care less, he could hardly see the point of holding to the old ways simply for the sake of doing so.

"Your mother and I will discuss it," said Mark, having learned through years of marital tongue lashings not to oppose Carla in front of the children.

"At least we can sample the kosher food," suggested Carla. "It may taste better than you think."

"I know what it tastes like," said Stephanie. "David Schwartz's was kosher. The fake cheese on the cheesesteaks was gross, and no one would eat the make-your-own soy sundaes."

"Well, I'm sure that there's good and bad kosher food, just like everything else," said Carla. "The least you can do is try it. I have an appointment for a tasting with a kosher caterer tomorrow night who comes highly recommended, and if you finish all your homework, you can come with us."

"I'll try it," Stephanie said with a shrug, "but if it's awful I'm not going to have it."

"You'll do what we say, young lady!" said Mark, who, though more on Stephanie's side than her mother's when it came to the food, was more prone to take offense at her tone—probably because he had less contact with it.

Stephanie muttered something under her breath and went off to do her homework.

"I don't see why we have to make the thing kosher," said Mark, once she was out of earshot. "It's not that anyone would care anymore."

"It's the principle," said Carla. "I can't help but feel that a bat mitzvah should be kosher. We're expressing our Jewish identity to our friends and family."

"But we don't keep kosher," argued Mark. "And Stephanie's right—the stuff tastes awful."

"Some kosher food can be very good. Remember my mom's?" Mark had courted Carla in the days when the Kaplan family kept kosher, and he had raved about his mother-in-law's cooking then, as he did now. Though Jessie had let the custom lapse when her own father died fifteen years ago, Carla had remained sentimentally attached to the memory of those earlier times. The image of her grandfather presiding over the Sabbath meal that her grandmother—and later her mother—had scrupulously prepared for the occasion was one of the most compelling images of her childhood. "Having a kosher bat mitzvah is a symbolic gesture," she explained now. "It shows respect for our heritage."

The spirit, if not the subject, of this debate was a familiar one in the Goodman household. Carla was "more Jewish," as the saying goes, and Mark was "less." It was not that Mark had been raised in a lax religious household. On the contrary, he had grown up in a Conservative Jewish home and weathered years of religious training, trudging back and forth to Hebrew school, through snow and sleet, to be drilled in the prayers by aged rabbis with phlegmy voices. But though this intensive training had produced the expected piety in many of his peers, it had had the obverse effect on him.

There were two aspects of his religion (one could say of religion in general) that went against Mark's grain. First, were the supposed charms of repetition. Religion was predicated on repetition—on rites and rituals performed over and over again. But Mark had no patience for repetition. It bored him.

Second was the alleged superiority of one God over many. The idea had never impressed him in the way his teachers obviously felt it should. He could still remember being told what differentiated Judaism from those benighted, earlier religions: "We believe in *one* God," the teacher had said in a hushed tone while the other five-year-olds opened their eyes wide in reverence. But Mark had not grasped the advantage of this singularity. It seemed to him that there were definite benefits to having more than one God; indeed, the more the better, given how much there was to do.

Yet despite the practical and philosophical problems he had with his religion, Mark was not wholly alienated or disenfranchised from it. He identified himself as a Jew, was proud of his heritage, and, after his marriage to Carla, had agreed to join an area synagogue, though only under the stipulation that it be a Reform temple where the services were shorter and the relationship to the deity more metaphorical.

Carla, by contrast, was of a totally different view. She had strong feelings of affiliation and affection for the religion of her ancestors. Her mind was more emotional and impressionistic than her husband's, and she found the prayers and rituals to be enormously compelling and consoling. Judaism, as she saw it, was a vast, complex tapestry from which one might follow any thread to arrive at a profound truth.

She had tried unsuccessfully to convince Mark to join a Conservative synagogue, closer in spirit to the Orthodox one in which she had been raised. In making her case for this traditional affiliation, she relied on all sorts of arguments, and had even put forward the example of the area's notorious Reform rabbi, incarcerated for life for the contract-killing of his wife some years before. The case, when it first made its explosive appearance in the press, had been a source of morbid fascination and impassioned debate for the Jewish community of Cherry Hill. Many had voiced skepticism: "Okay, maybe he had a few women on the side—not a rabbinical thing to do, but it's been known to happen. But murder—Jews, and certainly rabbis, don't do things like that."

There had been a trial (in actuality two, since the first had resulted in a hung jury, obviously possessed of a few jurors of the persuasion that "rabbis don't do things like that"). And while the rabbi had eventually been found guilty and placed behind bars for the remainder of his life, the case continued to be regularly invoked by the Jews of Cherry Hill as an object lesson in any number of things—from the escalating dangers of adultery (said rabbi had dallied with numerous women before taking to murder) to the advantage of an open-office plan (many of the rabbi's trysts had happened in his locked study—specifically, on his cherry wood desk). But Carla might well have been the first to use the case to argue against Reform Judaism as itself a slippery slope: First, it was shorter services and less Hebrew; next, it was murdering your wife.

Such an argument, obviously, did not hold weight with Mark, and Carla had finally given up and agreed to membership in a Reform synagogue. To her surprise, she found that the services were not so different from the Conservative ones she had attended in the area—though they *were* shorter and the cantor *did* play the guitar.

Still, when it came to the bat mitzvah, Carla remained steadfast on certain points that pertained to the traditional nature of the event. She bristled, for example, when told of the *volkschuls* that existed in many affluent suburbs, where educated, highly assimilated Jews staged "special events" in honor of their children's thirteenth birthdays. These were celebrations of ethnic history and creativity in which the children could do such things as write a research paper on Ellis Island or perform a stand-up comedy routine in the style of Jackie Mason or Jerry Seinfeld (stand-up comedy being seen as a form of cultural expression as close to the actual practice of Judaism as one could get in modern life).

Events like these were not to Carla's taste. For her, the bar mitzvah was a sacred marker of the old ways, to be celebrated with all the conventional trappings. And a principal one of these was a kosher meal.

Fortunately, her friend Jill Rosenberg had done the groundwork and sampled the kosher caterers across the Delaware Valley in preparation for her son's bar mitzvah the year before.

"If I have to eat another potato knish, I'll die," Jill had reported dramatically in the midst of this evaluative process. In the end, she had declared that one caterer stood out from the pack and could hold his own with the best kosher chefs on Long Island. (Jill grew up on Long Island and saw its offerings in the way of food, clothes, and household appliances as the measure for all things.) This caterer, she said, was the king of kosher caterers: "His soy ice cream's ambrosia. Josh and his friends practically OD'd on it." What better recommendation could there be?

"At least try the caterer," Carla pleaded with Mark now. "If you or Stephanie don't like the food, we won't use him."

Chapter Five

*A*nd *so*, THE NEXT DAY, CARLA, MARK, AND STEPHANIE prepared to drive out to northeast Philadelphia to sample the handiwork of the Iron Chef of kosher caterers.

Jeffrey was left home with Jessie, who, despite her recent odd behavior, seemed the only person able to get him to sit still and do his work. None of his teachers apparently could, judging by the notes that cascaded daily from his backpack.

"Dear Mrs. Goodman," read a recent note from his language arts teacher, "Your son appears to have a chronic need to use the facilities during the class period. His insistence that he 'must go or else' is either an indication of some sort of physiological disorder or the sign of an accomplished liar. Kindly instruct him to empty his bladder before class. If the problem persists, I expect a note from a urologist."

"Dear Mrs. Goodman," read another note, discovered last week under Jeffrey's unwashed gym suit (no telling how long it had been there), "Your son's incessant belching in homeroom—whether the result of indigestion or misplaced theatrical ambition—has become a real nuisance. It is impossible for the other children to hear the announcements over the PA system. Please speak to him about proper classroom etiquette and/or the importance of a healthy breakfast to settle his stomach."

Only yesterday there had been a particularly dire note from the principal: "Dear Mrs. Goodman," the missive read, "Your son has once again thrown an eraser out of the second-floor window. This time, it hit Mr. Fialkow, our vice principal, grazing the side of his head. A direct hit would certainly have caused a concussion—or worse. We cannot emphasize enough the seriousness of this infraction and the need to make sure that no such possibly fatal incidents occur again."

The stress engendered by such notes was considerable, and Carla found herself in a continual round of meetings with the nurse, the guidance counselor, and the vice principal (now liable to be less understanding as the recipient of a potentially fatal blow).

Jessie, however, was one of the few adults with a surefire strategy for managing Jeffrey. It all seemed to hinge on her potato latkes. Jessie's method went like this: "Jeffrey, if you finish your math homework, you get a latke. No math homework, no latke." Jeffrey would finish his math homework and get a latke. "Okay, the math is done." Jessie would nod approvingly. "Now, to study the vocabulary. Study the first ten words, you get a latke." The ten words studied, Jessie tested him; if he answered correctly, the latke was forthcoming; if not, it was back to more studying. This went on until all the homework was completed. The method was labor-intensive, and Carla worried that without the coveted reward to concentrate his mind, Jeffrey would accomplish very little—a fact supported by his performance at school, where there were no latkes to be had.

Carla told Jessie to make sure that Jeffrey was in bed by ten (with no Game Boy under the covers) and to take a message should there be a call from the elusive bar mitzvah entertainment motivator—the name now given to the once-lowly deejay, and much harder to get hold of under this more august title.

Jessie assured her that everything would be done, and they

were almost out the door when she called after them in a concerned voice: "I do hope the ostler remembered to saddle the horses!"

Mark had originally speculated that his mother-in-law's remarks might be a side effect of her blood-pressure medicine, and had advised her cardiologist to change her prescription. But Jessie had been on the new medicine for two weeks now, with no apparent improvement. The odd remarks kept coming, to the point that Carla had placed a large dictionary on the table in the front hall for consultation when her mother said something particularly cryptic.

"I think we'd better try a neurologist," said Mark as they got in the car. "Not that it'll make any difference. Except for treating seizures and migraines, neurologists can't do anything but give bad news."

"Maybe it's a seizure," said Carla hopefully.

"Trust me, it's not a seizure."

"So you think she's just losing it?" Carla said sadly. It was a thought that had occurred to her and she had tried to put out of her mind. Now she was struck by the depressing symmetry of the situation: Just as her daughter was entering the age of reason, her mother was leaving it. Time spent volunteering at the geriatric center had given her a vivid sense of where this process might lead.

"I wouldn't jump to conclusions," said Mark, seeing his wife's distress. "It may simply be a passing phase. And it hasn't kept her from doing what she's always done. That was a nice sweater she just knitted for Stephanie, for example, and she's still one hell of a good cook."

"There *was* the venison stew," Carla reminded him.

"But it was tasty, whatever it was," said Mark. "She hasn't lost her touch. Give it time. See how she is in a few weeks."

They all got in the car, but before backing out of the driveway, Mark paused and turned to Carla. "By the way," he asked, "what's an ostler?"

Chapter Six

The caterer WAS LOCATED IN WHAT LOOKED LIKE AN ABAN-doned warehouse in the farthest reaches of northeast Philadelphia. They were greeted by one of the owners, a middle-aged man named Moishe, who bounded toward them wearing a yarmulke on top of a toupee—something that struck Mark as particularly redundant.

The inside of the building was cluttered with aluminum pans, serving bowls, and cardboard boxes, but an area had been cleared in one corner where a small table had been carefully set with three place settings. There was a magenta cloth on the table, matching magenta napkins, and plates with magenta trim, as well as glasses and cutlery. This apparently was where the Goodmans were to sample the bat mitzvah meal.

"I set the table according to the color scheme that our bat mitzvah girls tend to favor," said Moishe, motioning to the table and addressing Stephanie, "but of course we have the books for you to look through to choose what you like if this isn't to your taste." He gestured to a library of black leather volumes on shelves across the room.

"The young lady should sit here." Moishe gestured to the center of the table. "And I'll take her order for a beverage." He bowed his head in pleasing subservience to Stephanie. "Your choice of Diet Coke or iced tea."

"Diet Coke," said Stephanie demurely.

"And the folks should sit on either side," motioned Moishe, more perfunctorily, failing to take their beverage order.

"We're going to give you a sampling of some of our most popular items," he explained. "But you also have a list here." He handed them a calligraphied sheet that seemed to go on forever. "These are other options that you can choose from. Here you see the meat menu and here the dairy. Note that some are starred to indicate a cost over and above the standard package fee. Some, with the dagger, are seasonal, and some, which require additional time to prepare, are in italics"—his hand swept across the menu quickly, indicating a veritable jungle of symbols and typescript. "Generally," he said, as he saw Mark and Carla looking confused, "the items we'll be serving you tonight are the ones most people choose, and they fall within the standard package price."

He turned to Stephanie to give a personalized translation: "I'm simply showing what we have, because we want the bat mitzvah girl to be happy, and sometimes she wants to choose something out of the ordinary. But as I say, most choose from among the items you'll get to sample today—and I'll be frank with you about which ones are the all-out favorites with the teens." He turned to Carla and Mark in an aside: "I'll send on the hors d'oeuvres menu another time. The hors d'oeuvres tend to get a bit complicated, and I like to leave it to Mom and Dad to make those selections at a later date." (Experience had shown that it was best not to overload the customer, especially with the child present, since messy scenes were likely to result.)

"So without further ado, let's have Eduardo, our chef, bring out your first course." Moishe retreated to a mysterious area behind the cluttered office that one assumed to be the kitchen. Almost immediately, a large Hispanic man, wearing a chef's hat and a mildly irritated expression, emerged holding a tray with three bowls of salad. "This is Eduardo, the best kosher chef in the Northeast." Moishe gestured toward the chef. "And here's your salad course," he announced, "a very good starter, since if they want to go up and schmooze or do the hora, it won't get cold. We're doing a meat meal for you, since that tends to be the favorite with the kids. Our nondairy ice cream is awesome," he turned to Stephanie, "and the cheese on the cheesesteaks—you'd think you were at Pat's in South Philly, not that I know myself, but I've been told.

"Anyway, the salad has croutons, tomatoes, cucumber, walnuts, a little arugula for those who like the fancy lettuce, with a nice vinaigrette. A big favorite." Mark and Carla sampled the salad and observed that it was good. Stephanie, who didn't eat salad, waited patiently.

"Okay, that's the salad," said Moishe, "Now for the soup. It's good to get everyone settled down with the soup. We have a nice matzo-ball soup—lightest matzo balls in the Delaware Valley—no offense to Grandma."

The soup was brought out by the surly chef. Stephanie, who liked matzo-ball soup, agreed that it was good.

"The kids can have the matzo-ball soup too," said Moishe. "Usually we give them mozzarella sticks as a first course—tastes just like real mozzarella—but we can substitute the matzo-ball soup if you want; we do it a lot." Stephanie said she wanted the matzo-ball soup instead of the mozzarella sticks.

"Done," said Moishe.

"Next, we have a palate cleanser, a nice sorbet." Eduardo brought out three dishes of sorbet: two yellow, one red. "Raspberry or lemon, your choice."

"Lemon," pronounced Stephanie.

"Lemon it is.

"Then we have the main dish for the grown-ups. We're going to bring you three choices here: the pistachio-crusted sea bass, the chicken with tomato and pesto glaze, and the filet mignon with shiitake mushrooms and red wine. I'll tell you frankly here that the sea bass and the filet are generally the favorites. Nothing wrong with the chicken, mind you." Carla and Mark sampled the three dishes and agreed to go with the sea bass and the filet.

"Now we'll bring out the kids' choices," said Moishe. "Here we have a cheesesteak—and you tell me if you can tell the difference from the real thing. We also have the hotdog and the hamburger, the ten-foot hoagie, the chicken nuggets, and the pasta with meat sauce—all big winners. Generally, we serve three of these, so there's plenty to satisfy if a kid doesn't like something."

Stephanie was biting into the cheesesteak with the air of a serious connoisseur. "It's pretty good," she admitted. Mark took a bite to assure himself that Stephanie had not been snowed by an impressive sales job, and had to admit that it was indeed pretty good. Stephanie also chose the nuggets and the pasta, which, according to Moishe, were what most kids chose.

"And now for the final and most important course," said Moishe, looking knowingly at Stephanie. "The dessert. Can we make it taste like ice cream?—that is the question. Not one of the Four Questions, I'll grant you, but an important one." Eduardo brought out a tray with the faux ice cream and a variety of toppings, which Stephanie carefully prepared into a sundae.

"It tastes real," she said, to which Moishe exclaimed, "What did I tell you? For the adults, we serve a nice plate with fresh fruit and a chocolate torte." He obviously did not intend to bring this out, having accomplished the task of selling the child on the ice cream.

"I'm sure it's wonderful," said Carla, relieved to see Stephanie behaving with such docility. How, she wondered, might she perfect Moishe's mixture of flattery and bullying so as to ingratiate herself with her daughter?

"Fine," said Mark, glad to have the thing over with. "We'll take it."

"And the table setting?" asked Moishe. "Would the young lady like to look through our sample books for other options?"

"I like this one," said Stephanie, to Carla's surprise. Her daughter had never made a decision this quickly before in her life.

"A wise choice, if I may say so," said Moishe. "It's our favorite setting by far. Your daughter, I can see, has a good eye."

"That she does," said Carla, trying to share in the goodwill that Moishe had generated. Stephanie, however, would have none of it—this was a love-fest between her and Moishe alone—and she shot an annoyed glance at her mother. Still, there was no fighting, and they shook Moishe's hand at the door with a certain amount of relief.

"Now that was easy, wasn't it?" said Carla as they drove home, Stephanie having fallen asleep in the backseat.

Mark grunted. Moishe's brand of salesmanship rubbed him the wrong way, and he still wasn't thrilled by the idea of serving food that imitated other food. But he had to admit that it had all tasted pretty good and that the whole thing had transpired more painlessly than expected. The cost, of course, was another story. He had put down a substantial down payment, and the final bill for the meal promised to be very painful indeed.

Chapter Seven

I broke UP WITH KEVIN," ANNOUNCED MARGOT AS SHE AND Carla settled into a booth at the back of Sal and Joe's, a family-owned Italian restaurant in Maple Shade, just outside of Cherry Hill. It was the custom of the sisters to have lunch at least once a week to "catch up," mostly with Margot's fast-paced love life. Sal and Joe's was a favorite meeting-place, since they were both partial to the mussels marinara.

In the current instance, it had actually been two weeks since they had last had lunch. This was because Margot had been away in L.A. taking depositions for a big case involving half the Philadelphia mob. ("Construction and union graft are passé with organized crime these days," Margot explained. "They all want to be in movies.")

Carla had hoped to begin their lunch talking about their mother's condition, but her sister's announcement effectively pre-empted this. Margot's latest romantic misadventure would have to be thoroughly worked over before they could move on to other things.

"Which one was Kevin?" asked Carla. She had difficulty keeping Margot's boyfriends straight. It was not only that there were so many but the relationships were so short-lived. In some cases, calling them relationships was a stretch. Was two weeks to-gether—even if it meant taking a private jet to Paris or relaxing on the shores of Lake Como—a relationship? Carla wasn't sure.

"Kevin's the guy in L.A. in 'development.' I don't know what development is," noted Margot, "but it seems to involve having lunch with lots of rich, famous people to talk about projects that never get off the ground. How he's managed to make so much money when he's never produced anything is a mystery to me. I suppose I could figure it out if I had more time with him. But that, as I say, doesn't seem to be in the cards."

"How long did you go out?" Carla wondered how this liaison had passed her by unnoticed.

"Three months. But of course we didn't see each other much, since he was in L.A. and I was here—which helped." Carla might have said that it hindered, but she supposed that this was a matter of perspective. Most of Margot's relationships fizzled out much sooner. In Kevin's case, the longevity seemed to be a function of tantalizing emails that had piqued Margot's interest until they were replaced by the fact of his person. Probably his work in "de-velopment" took the same course, with the money coming in at some intermediate stage.

"He was fine in theory," Margot sighed. This was not an unfa-miliar complaint with regard to Margot's boyfriends. They looked good on paper and often looked good in clothes (and even without them), but did not hold up to sustained human contact.

Margot paused at this point to give the waitress her order—and to note the handsome young man, resembling the young Al Pa-cino, who was staring appreciatively at her near the pizza oven. He was obviously an employee, neither Sal nor Joe, but possibly a rel-ative of one of them.

Handsome young men and prosperous older ones tended to stare at Margot. As Uncle Sid, even in decline a great admirer of female pulchritude, put it: Margot was "a hot tomato." People prone to less metaphorical description said she looked like the actress Rachel Weisz—only better. (Penelopé Cruz and Salma Hayek were other actresses whom Margot was said to look better than.)

"So what was the problem with Kevin?" asked Carla, with mild curiosity. There was a certain sameness to these conversations. Although the reasons for Margot's failed relationships were multitudinous, the basic pattern tended to be the same. The last one had been a real-estate magnate with houses in Aspen and the South of France who, it turned out, had been functionally illiterate and gotten through college on Cliff's Notes. Before that was the British fashion photographer, straight out of a Judith Krantz novel, very handsome and exceptionally good in bed, who turned out to have a video archive of the women he slept with. Margot had escaped taking her place in that library by the skin of her teeth, quite literally—she had seen the reflection of the camera eye in the bathroom mirror as she was brushing them before one of their trysts.

"So what was wrong with this Kevin?" Carla repeated, hoping that they could conclude the conversation quickly and move on.

"Bad personal hygiene," sighed Margot. "You'd think someone who drove a Maserati would change his underwear."

"You'd think," agreed Carla. "But driving a Maserati can exempt you from a lot of things."

Margot acknowledged this to be true. When would she learn? Her record in love was abysmal; each new foray led to disappointment, though fortunately not to heartache. Margot's heart was rather resilient—at least she liked to give that impression.

Much of the problem, as both sisters had long ago concluded, had to do with Margot's appearance. While Carla was pleasant-looking (the words *cute* and *pretty* came to mind), Margot was something else entirely (*striking* and *stunning* were the operative terms). If Carla had inherited her mother's sweet nature and domestic sense, Margot had inherited her looks.

"You should have seen your mother at your age," Milt Kaplan used to expound to his daughters, as he sat back after one of

Jessie's excellent meals. "She was a knockout with the disposition of an angel. Boys would come from all the way across town to carry her books when she walked to school, and she used to take a few extra along so nobody would feel left out."

"So what are you saying, Dad? I should bring extra books to school with me?" Margot would ask, sensing that the story was somehow directed at her.

"I'm not saying anything." Milt would put up his hands. "I'm just describing. Is it a crime for me to talk nicely about your mother?"

Despite his protests, Milt was indeed intending an object lesson for his daughter. What he failed to understand was that the kind of looks that Margot had inherited from her mother—the shapely figure; thick, curly hair; long, wide mouth; narrow, densely lashed eyes; and high forehead that had made Jessie Kaplan the toast of Vineland—had different effects in the world as it currently existed. In Jessie's day, a beautiful woman was an ornament to grace the arm of some lucky alpha male. In the postfeminist era in which Margot came of age, beauty had become a more slippery signifier. It could brand as much as it could elevate, and often did both at the same time. Thus a dull girl with good looks was immediately judged to be a bimbo, while a sharper one with the same looks would be seen as a bitch, with the capacity to humiliate any man who crossed her path.

Margot happened to fall into the latter category. She had been characterized as "scary smart" ever since junior high school, when she was often first to finish the timed math tests. Boys, dazzled though they were by her thick lashes and sweetheart mouth, were petrified that she would make them look like fools.

In the end, only fools and men with monumental egos or bank accounts dared to approach her. According to Mark, here lay the root of her problem: She scared off the nerds, who ultimately had the best characters and made the best husbands. "Look at me," he liked to tell her, "I'm a nerd with a capital N. But you wouldn't give someone like me the time of day." He seemed pleased by this notion. As much as he loved his sister-in-law, the idea of being married to her raised the hair on the back of his neck.

"I've decided to carefully assess all future dating prospects," Margot announced to Carla now, throwing an empty mussel shell rather violently into the bowl as if it were Kevin, complete with Maserati and dirty underwear. "As a first order of business, I'm going to compile a checklist of what I want in a man, and I won't bother with anyone who doesn't measure up."

Carla found herself objecting to this approach: "I like the idea of your being more discriminating, but you can't be so scientific about it. You're not buying a car or a pair of shoes; you're looking for a soul mate."

"Since when do they have to be mutually exclusive?"

"Are you saying that a pair of shoes can be a soul mate?"

"No—though I've gotten a lot of solace from a nice pair of Manolo Blahniks. I'm saying that I don't see why I shouldn't be at least as careful finding a husband as I'd be buying a luxury item. When I purchase a car, I read *Consumer Reports,* take a test drive, and look under the hood—or at least I get Calvin to look under it for me." (Calvin was the mechanic at the service station near Rittenhouse Square where Margot lived, and who existed in her thrall. When men did not dub her an A-1 bitch, they tended to operate in slavish servitude to her—or as Mark put it: "to play Igor to her Dr. Frankenstein.") "I think I ought to do at least as much research and evaluation if it's someone I plan to spend the rest of my life with. Besides, I'm a very high-end item, and I wouldn't want to sell myself short."

"But people aren't like cars," protested Carla. "There can be problems with the engine and they can stall out occasionally but still be worth holding on to. And with your attitude, you may end up with nobody."

Carla was now beginning to sound like their late father. Milt Kaplan had often warned Margot that if she continued to be so snooty she would never get married. (Jessie, by contrast, had never voiced concern on this score. "Let her take her time and look around," she used to tell her husband, who sometimes wondered if his wife would have liked to have looked around a bit more herself.)

"And so what if I don't get married?" Margot replied testily to her sister's advice. "I have an interesting job and a nice salary. It's not as though I need the diversion or the security. And for love and companionship, I always have Mom, not to mention you, Mark, and the children."

Carla was always disarmed when Margot made this point. Her sister was, she knew, a devoted daughter and deeply attached to the Goodman family, for whom she was forever buying unnecessary gifts: an Italian silk smoking jacket for Mark ("for my evenings relaxing over a cigar at the club," noted Mark facetiously), a Smith Brothers T-shirt the size of a postage stamp for Stephanie (its price inversely related to its size), a top-of-the-line skateboard for Jeffrey (who needed a skateboard like a hole in the head and which Carla feared it was likely to produce). Margot was also a regular provider of coveted Flyers tickets for Mark and Jeffrey (sky box, gourmet cheesesteaks included), and was known, on Sunday afternoons, to whisk Jessie, Stephanie, and Carla off for afternoon tea at Philadelphia's Four Seasons Hotel (a repast which cost as much as dinner for ten at Sal and Joe's). She also had the habit of picking up designer "pieces" for Carla and Jessie (a Chanel suit, a Gucci bag, a Hermès scarf). Carla wore these items on the infrequent occasions when she wanted to impress the glitzier elements of Cherry Hill. Jessie hung them in her closet and didn't wear them at all.

Margot's acts of generosity toward her sister's family did not go unappreciated. Stephanie and Jeffrey viewed her as their beloved, nutty aunt, and even Mark, liable to suspect the worst in people, acknowledged that Margot had a good soul, though you wouldn't know it looking at her.

Carla, for her part, viewed her sister's devotion with a pang. She suspected it involved large amounts of what in psych class they called "displacement." Though there were times when she envied Margot's high-powered career and was fed up with her own work-day routine, she still believed that a good marriage was fundamental to a happy life. She sensed deep currents of loneliness in her sister and fervently hoped that she would soon find that most valuable of life assets: a soul mate.

"So how's Mom?" Margot brought forth at last, throwing the final mussel shell into the bowl. "I spoke to her last night and she sounded more cheerful than I've heard her in a long time."

"She *is* more cheerful," Carla agreed. Jessie's mood had not been what she wanted to discuss, but she had to admit that Margot was right. Both sisters had been concerned when their mother had acted draggy and depressed for a prolonged period following their father's death two years ago. Carla had finally insisted that Jessie give up her Vineland apartment and move in with her own family in Cherry Hill. It had now been three months since the move, and there was no doubt that Jessie's spirits had improved.

"She's definitely happier," Carla continued carefully, "but she's happy in a strange sort of way. Her behavior"—she struggled for the right word, and took refuge in Stephanie's vocabulary—"is weird. I've been meaning to talk to you about it. Mark thinks she should see a neurologist—or maybe a psychiatrist. Frankly, it's hard to know what to do."

"What do you mean?"

Carla saw she had finally captured her sister's attention.

"It's her speech: odd words and phrases inserted into her everyday conversation."

"Odd in what sense?" Margot assumed her lawyerly, inquisitional tone.

"'Archaisms,' I suppose you'd call them. They seem to date back to maybe the sixteenth or seventeenth century."

Margot considered this for a moment. "Perhaps she's been

watching some of the old movies on the Turner Classic Movie channel," she finally suggested. "*Robin Hood* with Errol Flynn or *Henry VIII* with Charles Laughton. I loved those movies when we used to watch them on Million Dollar Movie, remember? The vocabulary from the films could be affecting her."

"It's possible," said Carla doubtfully, "but she doesn't really watch that much television. And if she were absorbing the vocabulary, that would be odd in itself, wouldn't it? Since when do people start talking like old movies?"

"Well, she *is* getting on in years—and she's lonely," said Margot with a trace of wistfulness. "I wouldn't mind having a movie in my head where Prince Charming comes along and sweeps me off my feet."

"He will," said Carla reassuringly. "Just be patient."

"Well, maybe you should be patient with Mom, too," counseled Margot, who, when not dealing with her own life, possessed a good deal of common sense. "Let's talk about how she's doing next week. I have a case coming up, but I'll work in a lunch with my big sister next Wednesday if you can make it into the city."

"It's a date," said Carla.

"I wish!" sighed Margot. "If I could have you cloned in male form, then maybe I could have a relationship that lasts."

"You just need to look in the right places and be more open-minded." Margot glanced at the admiring Al Pacino near the pizza oven, and Carla hurried to qualify: "And I don't mean in that direction; he looks like he's about nineteen."

"Older woman, younger man is in," observed Margot—then, seeing her sister's annoyed expression, "Okay, okay, I'll try to look for a bona fide nerd, preferably with a medical degree. But I'm late for court now, and the judge is already mad at me for not letting him look down my blouse." She put a twenty-dollar bill on the table, shot the young man near the pizza oven a parting glance, and strolled out of the restaurant in her Manolo Blahniks.

Chapter Eight

The following FRIDAY AFTERNOON, CARLA STOLE A FEW hours to do some errands. She made a brief stop to pick up Mocha Twists and frozen chicken satay at Trader Joe's (staples in the family diet), to look for some 30A bras for Stephanie at Marshalls, and to buy some replacement glass tumblers at Williams-Sonoma (every few weeks, the family's collection of water glasses diminished through mishaps generally related to Jeffrey).

With these missions accomplished, she continued down the highway to the area's mega-bookstore to check out the books in the psychology section. It was her hope that the experts would say that throwing erasers out of windows was to be expected from high-spirited pre-adolescent boys, and that strange archaisms were not uncommon coming out of the mouths of septuagenarian widows.

As Carla approached the bookstore, she realized that an event was in progress. The place was packed with half the female population of Cherry Hill. Who could possibly draw such a crowd? Carla's first thought was that the attraction must be a former overweight celebrity who had written a book on how she lost two hundred pounds through strenuous diet and exercise (with a little help from stomach stapling) or a chef from one of Philadelphia's most expensive restaurants hawking a collection of low-calorie gourmet recipes (the low-calorie gourmet meal being to the credulous suburbanite what alchemy had been to the credulous medieval scientist).

But the sign near the front of the store soon made it clear that the featured attraction was neither a former celebrity fattie nor a calorie-conscious gourmet chef. The personage in question was Dr. Leonard Samuels, well-known Cherry Hill psychiatrist and author of the new self-help book *How I Stopped Worrying and Learned to Love My Mother-in-Law*.

Carla had certainly heard of Dr. Samuels. Her friend Jill Rosenberg had consulted him prior to her son Josh's bar mitzvah: "He made it so that I almost had a good time," said Jill by way of testimony to Samuels's miraculous abilities, "and I've never had a good time in my life."

Samuels was also a frequent guest on the local public radio show *Voices in the Family*, and was much quoted in the area's much-maligned but scrupulously read local newspaper, the *Camden Courier Post*, on issues ranging from school violence to geriatric sex.

In short, Samuels had a reputation in Cherry Hill, and now, with his new book, he was on his way to an even bigger one. Why, thought Carla fleetingly, couldn't Mark do a little of this sort of self-promotion? He too was a doctor, superlatively trained and with a pleasant way with people when he wanted to make the effort. He too was providing a valuable service—albeit one involving a lower end of the anatomy, though no less important for that.

But Carla had no time to dwell on possible pubic relations opportunities for her husband right now. There was too much going on around her. As she entered the store, she saw that Samuels's books had been arranged on a large display table in an intricate pyramid at which women, eager to obtain a copy, were violently grabbing, so that harried salespeople were obliged to continually reassemble the pyramid on an ever-diminishing scale.

"I love the title," one matron was overheard to say. "It's taken from that Woody Allen movie."

The title was actually an allusion to the 1964 classic Stanley Kubrick film, *Dr. Strangelove, or How I Stopped Worrying and Learned to Love the Bomb.* But the origin of the title hardly mattered to the assembled throng. They liked it because, quite simply, they really wanted to stop worrying and learn to love their mothers-in-law.

As Carla inched her way forward through the crowd, she could hear various testimonials to Dr. Samuels's genius wafting around her.

"He cured me of my psoriasis," said one. "He told me that I didn't have to go to my brother's Passover seder if I didn't want to. I said, 'David, I love you, but I'm sick to death of sitting through you reading every goddamn prayer in the Haggadah and singing all those verses of "Chad Gadya" when you know I have to get up at six A.M. for work the next day.' Once I'd said it, my skin cleared up in a week."

"He gave me my Jonathan back," said another woman reverently. "He said, 'Instead of trying to make him feel guilty, tell him to go live with his father, if that's what he wants. I took his advice. Jonathan stayed with Nathan for a week and that was the end of it. I never heard a peep out of him again about liking his father better. Now he goes to visit the bum on holidays and for a week in the summer and he's glad to come home. He knows who loves him."

"I was at my wit's end with Ian over the bar mitzvah thank-you notes," said another woman, who was holding several copies of Samuels's book with the obvious intention of giving them as gifts to needy friends. She was speaking to another woman, who appeared to be hanging on her words. "He refused to write them," the first woman explained to her companion. "God knows, we did everything. First, we grounded him; then, we took away cable; then network TV; then Nintendo and PlayStation II; then his CD player and the Internet; then dessert." These deprivations were recited as though they were the plagues visited upon the Egyptians in the Old Testament, and the woman who was listening opened her eyes wider and wider as the punishments were enumerated. "Still, he wouldn't finish them," explained the woman. "What else was there?" She looked queryingly at her companion, who shook her head in mystification. "So I consulted Dr. Samuels, and you know what he said?" The other woman opened her eyes even wider, as if she couldn't stand the suspense. "He said, 'To hell with the thank-you notes! Give him a list of the telephone numbers and have him call everyone and say a few words. They'll love it and he won't have to put pen to paper.' You know what? We followed his advice and it worked!"

Carla had begun to grow genuinely interested in Dr. Samuels. The testimonials were impressive and the size of the crowd, many of them clutching multiple copies of his book, was more so.

At this point she had inched close to the center of the store, where Samuels was positioned behind a small table in preparation for the signing. He was a large man of about sixty-five, with the kind of craggy face and squat, powerful body common to certain Jewish men who had grown up poor and prided themselves on being as tough as the Italian kids on the block (and having the broken noses to prove it). Samuels now stood up from the table and put his hand in the air to establish his intention to speak. Possessing a natural sense of authority, which was at least three quarters of his success, he immediately got results: The loud chatter died down to a hum of excited whispers.

"Let me be frank with you folks," said Samuels, speaking in the friendly, no-nonsense manner that was his trademark. "There's nothing here that you couldn't find out for yourself." He held up a copy of his book, which had a picture on the cover of an attractive, smiling woman who had obviously taken his advice and learned to love her mother-in-law. "That doesn't mean, of course, that you don't have to read it."

There was appreciative laughter.

"When you have kids and parents, husbands—and wives"—he gestured toward the few lone men huddled toward the back of the store—"let's face it, things get complicated. You forget what's important. You fixate, you escalate, you make a big *mishegoss* out of what should be a nothing. What I give here"—he tapped the book casually with his bearlike hand—"are commonsense solutions. There's no magic involved and probably, if you weren't so busy doing whatever it is you do, you could figure it all out yourself. But the fact is, you can't. I've made it my living and you haven't.

"So there you have it. Buy the book. Learn something. But remember one thing—The book is general. That's why they call it self-help: You read it and you help yourself. Not everyone can do that. Some people don't go in for reading books, and some people need more personalized attention. If you fall into that category, call me up and make an appointment. I'll be frank with you: You may have to wait a month to see me—I'm booked solid—but it'll be worth the wait.

"Now, I say this knowing there are those among you who have a problem with seeing a psychiatrist. Seeing a psychiatrist, you think, means you're crazy—like your cousin, the one who had the Ponzi scheme and the drinking problem, and ran off to Vegas with the stripper."

There was another wave of appreciative laughter.

"You're thinking, *He* needed a shrink, but I don't. But let me tell you—your crazy cousin needed a shrink, but so do you. Everyone needs one sooner or later. The reason? Life is hard, and we can use all the help we can get. After all, you hire someone to clean your house; why not someone to clean up here?" He tapped his head. "One thing I guarantee: If you come to see me, you'll come out of the office feeling better than when you came in.

"So that's it, folks. Buy the book; make an appointment if you need to. Remember, you only have one life. There's no point going through it feeling miserable."

The throng erupted in appreciative exclamations of "I love you, Dr. Samuels!" and "God bless you, you saved my life!" Samuels gave a nod of acknowledgment, then put up his hand in the same gesture he had used when he began speaking, though now it was suggestive of a blessing. Then, he sat down to begin the hard work of signing copies.

Carla picked up one of Samuels's books and took her place on line. When she got home, she thought, she would call for an appointment.

Chapter Nine

*N*o!" *said* STEPHANIE, GLANCING DISMISSIVELY AT THE dress her mother was holding up for her inspection. They were standing in the junior department of Bloomingdale's in the King of Prussia Mall. The hour was growing late.

For weeks now, mother and daughter had traipsed through the department stores and boutiques of South Jersey and Philadelphia, searching for that elusive garment: the bat mitzvah dress. Only last week there had been an exhausting outing to Franklin Mills, a carnivalesque sprawl of department store outlets, as large as a small city, where drastically reduced designer merchandise was thrown into large, unsifted heaps. Mother and daughter had spent hours digging in bins and pushing through racks without striking pay dirt.

There had already been two previous forays to the King of Prussia Mall, numerous jaunts to the nearby Cherry Hill Mall, and even pilgrimages to celebrated malls in northern New Jersey. To Carla, each mall appeared to contain more or less the same stores and the same merchandise, but Stephanie and her friends, attuned to the fine points of mall ecology, could discern subtle differences among them in the way a trained wine connoisseur could discern the differing qualities of a flight of chablis.

The King of Prussia Mall was the elite megamall of the region. Not to find a dress there was to arrive, more or less, at the fashion terminus, with nowhere left to go.

"Honey, you didn't really look," Carla protested now, holding the dress above the rack like a bullfighter trying to entice a bull, in this case a recalcitrant twelve-year-old. It seemed to be exactly what her daughter was looking for: black, cut on the bias, scooped neck, no ruffles.

"Puffed sleeves," Stephanie noted succinctly.

Carla's heart sank. They had seen countless dresses over the past few weeks, some quite lovely, but each with a fatal flaw that disqualified it—in this case, puffed sleeves.

With the bat mitzvah only a few months away, one might have expected Stephanie Goodman to be home, studying her Torah and haftorah portions so as to perform them flawlessly for the family and friends who would be gathered at great price to witness her induction into the religion of her forebears.

But to expect this would be naïve. Only a handful of relatives, most of them deaf, had enough knowledge of Hebrew to critique Stephanie's performance of the scripture, while everyone, down to her six-year-old cousin from East Brunswick, could pass judgment on the dress.

Still, there had to be a point when you said *enough already!*

"Stephanie," said Carla, trying to take a casual, enticing tone, "why don't you try the dress on? I have a feeling that the sleeves will flatten out when you wear it."

Stephanie shot her mother an angry glance. "No!" she said, her voice growing shrill, "I won't wear puffed sleeves. I'm not a Disney character."

There was no arguing with this. Stephanie was at an awkward age when her body seemed to have been assembled by a dyslexic creator. Her feet were too big, her shoulders too narrow, her face too childish for the makeup she insisted on applying with a trowel every morning. The entire effect, though appealing in an ungainly sort of way (at least to a mother), was in no sense Disney-esque.

Carla sighed and hung the rejected garment back on the rack. They would simply have to try again tomorrow. The trick now was to get out of the store without a scene.

"I'll never find it!" Stephanie's voice had become a plaintive whine as they walked past the makeup counters where young women proffered spritzes of perfume like barkers at a carnival. "I'll never find one half as nice as Lisa's!" Lisa's, discovered in the backroom of Loehmann's (akin to finding gold in the backyard), stood as the benchmark for the bat mitzvah dress among seventh-grade girls at the Cherry Hill middle school.

"You will, honey, you will," said Carla reassuringly.

Yet to be honest about it, she had her doubts. They had inspected every dress in the numerous shopping emporiums of the Delaware Valley and would now have to retrace their steps in the hope of new inventory. This prospect made Carla want to sit down in the middle of the King of Prussia Mall and weep.

After hearing Dr. Samuels at the bookstore, she had proceeded to make an appointment. As he had warned, his schedule was heavily booked, and the first opening was four weeks from the day she called. Fortunately, that date was rapidly approaching, and she was relieved to think that on Thursday evening she would finally be reaping the benefits of Samuels's much-touted sagacity. Perhaps he would have some ideas about how to handle her daughter's exacting taste in a bat mitzvah dress—or, better yet, some tips on where they might find it.

Chapter Ten

*W*hen *Carla* AND STEPHANIE RETURNED HOME FROM the mall, Jessie was preparing dinner and humming.

"What's that song?" asked Carla, struck by the strange intricacy of the melody.

"'Now I See Thy Looks Were Feigned,'" said Jessie cheerfully. "It's a rondeau."

The odd allusions had not abated.

Carla decided to ignore Jessie's answer but made a mental note to look up *rondeau* in the dictionary later. The Webster's in the hall had gotten a lot of use lately, though occasionally it failed to serve and Carla had to resort to the library to consult the more capacious Oxford English Dictionary.

At this point, Mark came in the door, looking disheveled. "I'm bushed," he announced, throwing himself down onto a chair. A clamor that had been gradually escalating in the other room as Stephanie and Jeffrey wrestled over a CD that neither one really wanted was suddenly accompanied by shrill screams. "Would someone tell those goddamn kids to shut up?" he snapped crankily.

Jessie brought Mark two Tylenol with a scotch and then went into the other room to speak to the children. In no time, the racket had died down. Jeffrey and Stephanie came into the kitchen looking puzzled, and Stephanie motioned with her eyes for her mother to follow her into the living room.

"What's wrong with Grandma?" asked Stephanie when they had retreated together. "She's acting really weird."

"What did she say?"

"She came in while Jeffrey and I were fighting and told us"— Stephanie paused, obviously intent on recalling the exact phrase— "not to sully 'the family's cousin'—something like that."

"The family escutcheon?"

"Yeah, that's it."

Yes, Carla thought, it *was* weird. Where had the words come from that her mother was using with such alarming frequency? Margot's theory about her picking them up from old movies did not hold water. There were too many and the contexts too varied. Perhaps, Carla thought, she'd been listening to the vocabulary tapes they had bought for Jeffrey at the Teacher's Store. He was supposed to listen while sleeping and have the words creep into his brain through osmosis. The technique had not worked on him, but perhaps Jessie had borrowed the tapes and her brain was more conducive. But since when were *rondeau* and *escutcheon* fifth-grade vocabulary words?

"Dinner's ready," Jessie called from the kitchen. "Make haste."

"Make haste?" said Stephanie. "Weird!"

Once everyone was seated, Jessie began putting pieces of a strange-looking food onto their plates.

"What's this?" asked Jeffrey, inserting a large forkful into his mouth without waiting for an answer.

"Shepherd's pie," replied Jessie, "my most acclaimed recipe."

"I don't remember you ever making shepherd's pie," said Carla suspiciously. She had had the dish in a London pub during her junior summer abroad—but not, to her knowledge, before or since.

"It's pretty good," said Jeffrey, shoveling the shepherd's pie into his mouth with gusto and washing it down with large gulps of chocolate milk. "Is there any venison in it?" Jeffrey had liked the alleged venison stew that Jessie had made the month before. At the question, Stephanie put down her fork and waited anxiously for her grandmother's reply.

"I don't use venison in my shepherd's pie," said Jessie huffily. "Dame Quigly did. Couldn't abide it."

"Dame Quigly?" Mark looked up curiously. "Odd name. Is that a friend from the JCC senior group?"

At this point, however, the phone rang, interrupting the flow of conversation. It was Jeffrey's guidance counselor, calling to discuss his behavior issues. Carla went into the other room for privacy and then called Mark in to relay the conversation.

"She says his behavior suggests Attention Deficit with Hyperactivity," sighed Carla. "She recommends we consider putting him on Ritalin. I really don't like having him take medicine on a regular basis at his age."

Mark began thumbing through the *PDR* looking for the side-effects of Ritalin. "I can't say it's something I know much about," he said. "We probably need to consult Finkel." (Finkel was their pediatrician.)

"But Finkel only knows about colic," said Carla doubtfully, "and not much about that." Her confidence in Finkel had been undermined when he appeared on *60 Minutes* and told Mike Wallace that he didn't really know what colic was, even though he was presumed to be a national expert on the subject—an example of intellectual humility, fine for a classical philosopher, but not exactly what one wanted from a pediatrician.

"Try a psychiatrist, then," suggested Mark. "It's really more up their alley."

So here was something else to consult Dr. Samuels about, thought Carla. She was going to have a lot to discuss at her Thursday evening appointment.

Chapter Eleven

Carla had BEEN MEANING TO SPEAK TO HER MOTHER about her behavior for the past several weeks, but each time she considered broaching the subject, something came up to prevent her. Deep down, she knew she was stalling, hoping that Jessie would return to her rational self and no talk would be necessary.

But the behavior had gotten worse. The odd references had become more plentiful and more frequent, and Carla felt she could delay no longer. If she intended to consult Dr. Samuels on the subject tomorrow evening, she needed to talk to her mother today to get a better handle on what was going on.

It wasn't until after dinner, when the plates had been rinsed and the dishwasher loaded, that she finally had a chance to be alone with Jessie. The kids had gone upstairs, presumably to do their homework, though really to converse with fifty of their closest friends on Instant Messenger. Like the size of portions in restaurants, the number of friends kids had seemed to have increased geometrically over the past generation. In Carla's day, it was maybe three or four; now it was more like forty or fifty. Stephanie dealt with these numbers by sending out mass e-mails addressed, "Hi Everybody." Unfortunately, the responses tended to come in one by one and had to be handled individually, a task that took up most of the evening.

Mark had gone off to his pottery class. He had signed up for the Introduction to Pottery Workshop at the Y, at Carla's urging, and it had become a source of refuge from the trials of medicine. "Clay is messy," he acknowledged, "but it doesn't have the noxious odor of fecal matter. And the vase doesn't sue you if it turns out wrong."

This left Carla alone with her mother.

"Are you feeling okay, Mom?" She embarked on the topic now, sitting down next to her on the sofa and speaking in a serious tone.

Jessie was watching *Entertainment Tonight*, as she always did after dinner. She glanced up at Carla over her glasses, then back to the screen, where Julia Roberts was smiling toothily at the *Entertainment Tonight* reporter. "Never felt better," she said brightly. "Pretty girl, that Julia Roberts. Rather on the large side, I'd say, but they've been growing them bigger for the past centuries."

Carla took a breath, then continued: "You've been saying some peculiar things lately, Mom. I wonder if you might be, well, a bit confused."

Jessie looked up sharply at this. "I should think I am," she said. "It's hardly surprising."

Carla hadn't expected such a frank admission. "I suppose so, given your age, but still, you were always so clear-headed."

"Well, I hope I still am," said Jessie irritably. "I should like to see how well you'd do if it all suddenly came back."

"Came back?"

"For goodness' sake, Carla, can't we talk about this later? Look, there's Winona Ryder; they say her name was Horowitz. Poor girl! The stress of the public stage. It takes its toll, you know. Will used to complain of it all the time. Though at least then you could ride a few miles out of town and escape the hue and cry. It's why he kept the Stratford house, though why it couldn't have been a nice place near Poppa in Venice was beyond me. Why would he want to plop down right where that woman could get her claws into him? But he was always soft that way. Couldn't bring himself to cut her off—which is what caused us the trouble."

Carla grabbed the remote and snapped off the television. "Mother! What are you talking about: 'Will,' 'Stratford,' 'the public stage'! Have you gone totally out of your mind?"

"Calm down, dear. I'm sorry to be rattling on like that, but lately, it's hard to keep things straight."

"What's hard to keep straight?" asked Carla, beginning to feel frightened.

"Oh, then and now." Jessie shrugged.

"Then?"

"Venice, London," Jessie said dreamily.

"Mother, you were born in Vineland, New Jersey. You went to Vineland High School. You married Daddy and worked in the bakery. You are currently living with your daughter and son-in-law in Cherry Hill, New Jersey."

"Honestly, Carla, you don't think I know that?"

"Then what's this about Venice and London?"

"Oh, that was before. It has nothing to do with you, dear." Jessie waved her hand in what Carla thought was a rather condescending gesture. "It's been coming back in dribs and drabs for the last month or so, and lately, it's become more—how shall I say?—present . . ." Jessie trailed off; then, turning away, switched the television back on as Britney Spears appeared in a skimpy outfit of denim and fringe. "Perhaps next time, I'll come back as something like that," she mused.

Carla moved closer to her mother on the sofa and placed her hands on her shoulders. "Mom, would you try for a moment to be rational? I must say it's very disturbing listening to you."

Jessie turned down the volume on the remote and addressed her daughter in a serious tone: "Well, dear, I can certainly understand how you feel. I thought that Shirley MacLaine was off her rocker too, and I still think she made the half of it up—it doesn't ring right. But sometimes life surprises you. What was it Will used to say: 'There's more going on, Horatio, than you dreamed up in that philosophy of yours'? Can't recall who Horatio was, though."

"Isn't that from *Hamlet*?"

"Who knows? I could never keep the plays straight; he wrote so many."

"Mother, are you saying, are you implying—some sort of delusional relationship—with William Shakespeare?"

Jessie sighed. "I'll grant you, it wasn't the expected thing, especially for that time. An Englishman, and a gentile on top of it. He said he had Jewish blood on his mother's side, but then, they always say that if they think it will help. He came to Venice to see that friend of his, Kit Marlowe, who everyone thought was dead but was really hanging out with the cross-dressers on the Rialto. That's how I met him."

"Mother! I want you to stop this at once. Since when do you know anything about William Shakespeare?"

"It's true. I was never a literary person."

"So where did you get this—information—you're spouting?"

"Where did I get it? From him, where else? He was smitten the first that he saw me, as he liked to say. I was taking a platter of kugel over to the rebbe's house across the campo and he stopped me and said that my eyes had bewitched him."

"Mother—William Shakespeare's been dead four hundred years."

"Don't I know that? What do you think—I was born yesterday?"

"So what is all this about Venice and London, and knowing Shakespeare?"

"I'm just saying that that Shirley MacLaine wasn't wrong, though I still think she embroidered. It's come back to me lately as clear as the bakery in Vineland. Clearer. Will was a more colorful character than your father. Not that Milt didn't have his points.

He could bake a good rye bread, but he couldn't write a poem to save his life, and the thought of him in breeches—well!"

"Mother, I want you to see a doctor. They probably have medication for this kind of thing."

"I don't want medication. It's nice to remember. If you don't want me to talk about it, I'll be more careful. I can't promise that something won't slip out now and then, but I'll make an effort. Now, if you'll excuse me, I'm feeling a little tired. I think I'll go to bed."

Chapter Twelve

*S*o you're SAYING THAT MOM THINKS SHE'S WILLIAM SHAKE-
speare?" said Margot distractedly, twirling a piece of lettuce
on her fork and glancing around the restaurant, a fashionable
bistro on Rittenhouse Square near Margot's apartment.

The restaurant had changed ownership recently and, with it,
décor. Carla, who had eaten here when it had featured leather arm-
chairs and heavy drapes, thought at first she was in the wrong
place when she saw the spindly wrought-iron tables and Japanese
lanterns. But then, all the restaurants on Rittenhouse Square were
continually changing ownership and décor, rather in the way their
patrons were continually changing boyfriends and wardrobes.

As usual, Margot had begun to draw attention. The waiter had
already sent over a bottle of wine, courtesy of two businessmen at
the next table, and a man in an ascot at the bar had been eyeing her
since they came in.

"Margot!" Carla addressed her sister sharply in the tone she
used when Stephanie got out of hand: "Mom doesn't think she's
William Shakespeare; she thinks she had a *relationship* with
William Shakespeare. Stop looking around please and listen!"

Margot responded sheepishly. "Sorry," she said, banishing the ascot from her consciousness and giving Carla her full attention. "So tell me again what's going on."

"Okay—remember how I mentioned she'd been acting strangely lately? Well, now it's a full-blown delusion, very elaborate and detailed. She actually thinks she had an affair with William Shakespeare in another life—'Will,' she calls him, if you can believe it. She thinks she was the so-called Dark Lady of his sonnets."

"That's pretty amazing," said Margot. "I wonder where she picked up that story."

"I haven't a clue. But, believe me, this is no small-time fantasy. She has loads of background material. More than I ever learned in my Shakespeare course at BU. Maybe she's been reading on the sly—which seems unlikely, since you know she was never one for books. Or maybe she has all this stored memory based on movies—like you suggested last time—or things she heard in the past. You know how they say that sometimes people who have strokes or mental trauma can suddenly speak languages they never learned, just because they heard them spoken once or twice? It could be something like that."

"Could be," said Margot, chewing her lip.

"But I can't imagine what triggered it," continued Carla. "She didn't hit her head or anything, and there's no evidence of a stroke—Mark ruled that out. Dad's death, of course, was painful— you remember how blue she was for a while—but I wouldn't call it traumatic. Anyway, it's been over two years since he died."

"If it's Dad's death that's behind it, it *is* strange," mused Margot. "Not that they didn't have a good life together. But given that she married Dad on the rebound . . ."

"What are you talking about?"

"She told me about it once when I was going out with that Harvard guy who was supposedly related to the Kennedys. He turned out to be sleeping with three girls in my dorm—which at least verified his pedigree. I got kind of sad when I found out, though, as you can imagine, it was mostly my pride that was hurt. But Mom seemed to take it worse than I did. She said she'd been in love with someone once—a Saul something-or-other—and he two-timed her with one of her friends. That's what made her decide to accept Dad so quickly—not, she said, that she ever regretted it. But obviously that other relationship made an impression. It must have happened at least thirty years before the time she mentioned it to me."

"So mom has an authentic secret history as well as an imaginary one," mused Carla.

"Yes—and maybe the latter is some odd manifestation of the former. You know: repressed desire, secret longing, that sort of thing."

"Come on," said Carla. "I'm the psychology major. Mom's a doll, but complicated she's not. Repressed desire—give me a break!"

"I don't know," considered Margot, "I think you're just used to seeing her in a certain way. I'll tell you what: Let me probe the situation a bit. I'll speak to her and see if she gives me the same story. If there's consistency to it, that at least tells us something about the tenacity of the delusion. It might help us get at the precipitating cause."

Carla nodded. She found her sister's detached and logical approach to the situation reassuring. Not for nothing was Margot *Philadelphia* magazine's choice for the best criminal lawyer in the Delaware Valley, with a list of mobsters a mile long waiting for her to defend them.

"Then we can decide whether to do anything," continued Margot.

"I've read there are antihallucinatory drugs."

"But from what you say, she's not hallucinating exactly; she's—what does she call it?—remembering."

Carla shrugged. "She's remembering hallucinations. Or maybe hallucinating memories. I don't see that it matters."

"The question is whether or not it's doing her harm."

"It can't be doing her good to live in a dream world."

"I'm only saying that we have to weigh what's best for her. You know how depressed she was before."

Carla considered this. There was no denying that her mother's spirits were much improved and that she appeared happy in her delusions. But that was part of what was so disturbing. It was as though Jessie had found an alternative world that suited her better than reality.

"You can't imagine how upsetting it is to have Mom talking this way." Carla sidestepped the issue of her mother's mood. "You know how levelheaded she's always been."

Margot nodded sympathetically. "I could take her in for a while, if you want. A change of scene might do her good."

"No," said Carla quickly, "she needs the routine of the house. Besides, you're at work during the day, which would leave her alone too much of the time." (The idea of Jessie puttering around Margot's Rittenhouse Square apartment, with its white-on-white minimalist décor and empty refrigerator, seemed like the worst possible idea.) "I can certainly handle having her. It's just that with Mark so unhappy with his practice and the teachers saying that Jeffrey should go on Ritalin, it comes at a bad time. And there's the bat mitzvah to worry about, and the fact that Stephanie can't find a dress. It's all I need to have Mom channeling Shakespeare's girlfriend."

"Well, one thing I can do," Margot responded with relief. "I can help Stephanie find a dress. That can't be too hard. . . ."

Chapter Thirteen

Why didn't YOU TELL ME ABOUT THE NEW DATE FOR Back-to-School night?" Carla asked, standing in the door of her daughter's room. Stephanie was sprawled out on her bed, studying her French vocabulary, listening to her haftorah tape, and using the curling iron on her hair.

Stephanie's room was in a chaotic state. Carla had recently read a magazine article that counseled against criticizing children for minor infractions like messy rooms. The advice had seemed logical enough at the time, but when faced with a week's worth of clothing on the floor, an entire cosmetic counter on the bureau, and a veritable trash heap of crumpled tissues on the bed, she found that logic went out the window.

Lately, she had tried to adopt a see-no-evil approach and taken to squinting when entering her daughter's room. This was an art she was beginning to perfect, and she noticed that her peripheral vision had now weakened to the point that she could look at Stephanie and see her as if etched in relief against a blank background.

"Didn't you have a sheet about the new Back-to-School Night that you were supposed to give me?"

The original date for Back-to-School Night had been changed

when the middle-school principal tripped on a skateboard left un-attended in front of C Hall and had to spend two weeks in traction. When Carla heard about the accident, her first thought was of Jef-frey (her tendency was to think of Jeffrey when any school-related mishap occurred). In this case, however, her suspicions were ill-founded, since Jeffrey was in elementary school and, despite an impressive level of hyperactivity, could hardly have made it across town during fourth period to leave his skateboard in front of the middle-school C Hall.

Part of Carla's irritation about Back-to-School Night came from feeling she should have known about the new date. It was one of the disadvantages of being a stay-at-home mother that any failure to keep abreast of the myriad of details attached to the chil-dren's lives seemed like an unconscionable breach of responsibil-ity. A twinge of guilt took hold as she peeked out from the corner of her eye at a pile of papers near the foot of her daughter's bed. One was inscribed in bold print with the message MARK YOUR CAL-ENDARS: NEW DATE FOR BACK-TO-SCHOOL NIGHT.

"Isn't that the sheet?" asked Carla, motioning accusingly to-ward the paper.

"What?" said Stephanie. It was hard to say whether her atten-tion was more engaged by the sound of the cantor's voice on the tape or the need to hold the curling iron in one hand while balanc-ing the French book in the other.

"Would you turn that thing off?" said Carla in exasperation.

"You don't have to yell!" Stephanie used the phrase "you don't have to yell" as a catch-all in any situation in which she felt herself the object of criticism. Carla generally failed to deflect this strate-gic move and would become caught up, before she knew it, in a pointless quarrel about tone of voice.

"I said"—Carla kept her voice as steady as she could—"that I didn't know tonight was Back-to-School Night. If I hadn't run into Mrs. Gupta in the supermarket on the way home from seeing Aunt Margot, I would never have known."

"Sorrreee," said Stephanie in an unapologetic tone. "I thought you did." She picked up the sheet at the foot of her bed and held it out. "Here."

"It doesn't do me much good now."

"I said I was sorry."

"Well, I don't know how we're going to handle this," said Carla with annoyance. "Your father is at an important medical meeting, and I have an appointment with Dr. Samuels. It takes months to get an appointment with him, so I can't cancel."

"Have Grandma go," suggested Stephanie with a shrug. "She's nice and the teachers would like her." (The implication was that Carla was not nice and the teachers would not like her. Stephanie was adept at this sort of oblique insult.)

"I don't think that your grandmother is really in any shape for it right now," said Carla. "You know how strangely she's been behaving lately."

"Oh, my teachers wouldn't mind," observed Stephanie. "Most of them are so out of it, they wouldn't even notice. Besides, the weird words would go over big with my English teacher, Mr. Pearson. He likes weird old words. He's the one who makes us memorize all that Shakespeare."

Carla nodded in recollection. There had been something of a fracas early in the term regarding this teacher's requirement for memorization. At first, Stephanie had reacted violently in opposition: "He's like back in the Dark Ages. No one expects you to memorize poetry anymore; it's a waste of time. I could be learning capitals for Mr. Perrone." (Mr. Perrone taught cultural geography and was forever assigning them capitals of countries that kept changing.) "Can't Daddy write a note saying that I have some kind of dyslexia with memorizing stuff?" (Mark, as a physician, had been prevailed upon in the past to write notes to get Stephanie out of gym class for such dubious complaints as an ingrown toenail, sprained pinky, or heat rash.)

In this instance, however, Mark dug in his heels and took the side of the teacher. He happened to have had a positive experience in the sixth grade memorizing "The Cremation of Sam McGee" and could still remember raising his voice and shaking his fist during the key scene of McGee's incineration. "Best educational experience of my life," he pronounced. "Wish I'd done more of it."

As it turned out, Stephanie's opposition to memorizing poetry evaporated when the first assignment was from *Romeo and Juliet*, a play that, despite the passage of over four hundred years, still speaks eloquently to the hormone-driven sentimentality of early adolescence. It didn't hurt that Stephanie was given the Juliet portion of the balcony scene to memorize, and that Kyle Chapin, seventh-grade heartthrob, was assigned the part of Romeo.

Stephanie had commandeered Jessie to help her with this assignment. Since moving in, Jessie was usually game to drill her granddaughter on vocabulary words and math formulas, and so it seemed only a short step to ask her to read the part of Romeo in the assigned scene.

In that first session, grasping the book tightly in her hands, Jessie had listened with rapt attention as Stephanie launched forth in Juliet's immortal words:

O Romeo, Romeo! Wherefore art thou Romeo?
Deny thy father and refuse thy name;
Or, if thou wilt not, be but sworn my love,
And I'll no longer be a Capulet.

This was Jessie's cue, but, enthralled by Stephanie's recitation, she had lost her place. Stephanie patiently pointed out to her grandmother where they were in the text.

"'Aside,'" said Jessie.

"You don't say 'aside,'" Stephanie stopped her to explain. "It means that you speak the next lines directly to the audience. Juliet isn't supposed to hear them."

Jessie nodded in apparent comprehension and turned to address the wardrobe across the room: "'Shall I hear more or shall I speak . . .'" She paused here, as this was the end of the line, and then abruptly added the words that began the next line: "'At this?'"

Stephanie intervened again: "You don't have to pause at the end of the line if there isn't any punctuation," she explained carefully. "Just read it like ordinary speech." (Jessie's mistake was one committed by half of Stephanie's class.)

"Okay," said Jessie, who appeared to grasp this more quickly than most of her granddaughter's peers. She turned toward the wardrobe again: "'Shall I hear more, or shall I speak at this?'"

Stephanie nodded and now embarked on the meat of Juliet's speech—that portion that packed a romantic wallop guaranteed to spark love in Kyle Chapin (or whatever romantic feeling a seventh-grade boy is capable of). Stephanie placed her hand on her heart as she recited the famous lines:

'Tis but thy name that is my enemy.
Thou are thyself, though not a Montague.
What's Montague? It is nor hand, nor foot,
Nor arm, nor face.

(Here, Stephanie gestured to each of the bodily parts enumerated in what she took to be an original piece of dramatic business.)

O, be some other name!
What's in a name? That which we call a rose
By any other word would smell as sweet.
So Romeo would, were he not Romeo called,
Retain that dear perfection which he owes
Without that title. Romeo, doff thy name;
And for thy name, which is no part of thee,
Take all myself.

"Beautiful," murmured Jessie, and took up Romeo's next line with apparent ease: "'I take thee at thy word. Call me but love, and I'll be new baptized.'"

Here, however, she paused, as if the line had sparked an unforeseen rumination. Then, she read the line again:

"'Call me but love, and I'll be new baptized.'"

"Gram, you said that already. Go on to the next line: 'Henceforth—'" she prompted.

But Jessie seemed confused and Stephanie finished off the line herself—"'Henceforth I never will be Romeo'"—then closed the book. It was the end of the assigned passage, and she sensed she had strained her grandmother's attention beyond its limits—a fact she understood, since her own attention was often so strained. She thanked Jessie for her help and trotted from the room, full of anticipation of iambic flirting with Kyle Chapin, and of using the new styling mousse to create tendrils that Juliet would no doubt have worn for the occasion.

Since that initial practice session, Jessie had been called upon again and again to help Stephanie memorize portions of Shakespeare. Carla had noted, listening as she often did at the door, that her mother quickly grew at ease with Shakespeare's language, which was rather surprising for a woman of seventy-two who hadn't gone beyond the tenth grade. Obviously, Jessie had an affinity for this sort of material that had never been tapped.

It now occurred to Carla that these sessions might have been responsible for precipitating her mother's Shakespeare delusion—though it was hard to see how they could have sparked something so detailed and elaborate.

"So he's a good teacher, this Mr. Pearson?" Carla returned to the subject at hand: Back-to-School Night and Stephanie's English teacher.

"I don't know," said Stephanie, drawing back at this effort to enlist her on the side of an adult value judgment. "He's cool, I guess."

"He's young?" asked Carla

"I suppose." Stephanie now appeared doubtful. "Not that young. Not as young as me—but not as old as you."

"Thanks for clarifying that," said Carla dryly.

"But he's not married," added Stephanie. "Pam asked him. He'd be good for Aunt Margot—he's probably about her age—but she'd never go out with him."

"Why not?"

"Since when would she go out with a seventh-grade English teacher?"

"You have a point there. But you think he'd be good for her?"

"Sure," said Stephanie. "He's so into poetry—it means he can feel things. And he's kind of cute, even if he's not Abercrombie."

"Well, you've sold me," said Carla, feeling a wave of affection for her daughter. She took a breath and stepped into the room, hearing something plastic crunch under her foot but ignoring it. She reached out and hugged Stephanie, who seemed surprised at the gesture, but did not resist. In point of fact, Stephanie found her mother as unpredictable in her responses as her mother found her: She was never sure whether Carla might yell at her or praise her for something. Her friends appeared to have the same problem with their mothers, which they put down to what they'd deduced from various TV specials to be the symptoms of peri-menopause.

"I think we should send Grandma to Back-to-School Night and tell her to check out your English teacher for Aunt Margot," said Carla, after they'd hugged.

"Sure," said Stephanie, losing interest in the subject and focusing her attention on the curling iron.

Carla began to back out of the room, automatically picking up the crumpled tissues and the empty bottle of Snapple as she went.

"Don't touch anything!" warned Stephanie, holding the curling iron aloft in the manner of a drawn sword.

"But it's a mess in here!" Carla had lost control of her squint and made the mistake of surveying the room. "It's a pigsty!" she pronounced now as this fact came forcibly home to her. "I can't understand how a girl your age can stand living this way!"

"That's because you're not a girl my age!"

"It's disgusting, young lady, disgusting. I want you to clean it up!"

"You don't have to yell!"

And so it went, until Carla realized that it was six-thirty and if she was going to drop Jessie off at the school and make it to her seven P.M. appointment with Dr. Samuels, she would have to save the rest of the fight for another time.

Chapter Fourteen

So, sweetheart," SAID DR. SAMUELS, PEERING IN AVUNCULAR fashion at Carla over his bifocals and leaning back in the plush recliner behind his desk. "Tell me what's bothering you."

As he had made clear at the bookstore a month earlier, Dr. Samuels was not your conventional psychiatrist. He had no use for the medical mumbo-jumbo that many psychiatrists employ to give their work an aura of importance. He did not pretend to arcane knowledge or boast long years of esoteric training. Instead, he presented what he did in straightforward and pragmatic terms. "Life is mostly common sense," he liked to say, "though sometimes you need a little help with the sense."

Leonard Samuels had started his practice thirty-five years ago in Cherry Hill. He had come to this suburb of Philadelphia when it had only recently been settled by Jews eager to live outside the confines of the big city. Denied access to the venerable South Jersey towns of Moorestown and Haddonfield, this population had taken root in the intervening space, creating a sprawling suburb with a wide array of services tailored to their tastes and needs. As the residents liked to say, "We have no cherries and no hills, but we do have the best discount shopping in the Delaware Valley, a few good diners, and more synagogues than you can shake a stick at."

Struggling with the pressures of upward mobility and assimilation, they also had a predictable cornucopia of neuroses. Leonard Samuels, therefore, had his work cut out for him.

Samuels liked to say that he had originally vacillated between a career in medicine and a career in the rabbinate. He had found the perfect compromise, he explained, in the practice of psychiatry, where he could solve problems and pontificate but did not have to answer to a higher authority.

He based his practice on the assumption that he could help solve his patients' problems because he had similar ones himself. He too had grown up poor and been nagged by an ambitious mother to work hard at school. He too had resented the pressure and the constant criticism (the familiar refrain in response to the 98 percent on the test: "So where's the other two points?"). But in retrospect, as he reminded his patients, who were in the throes of nagging their kids to death, his mother had been right and the pain he'd suffered had been all for the good. "Look at how well I turned out," he would say, gesturing proudly to the wood-paneled office. "Sometimes it's your duty to make your children miserable."

Because Samuels believed his patients could profit from his own experience, he made no secret of his personal life. On the contrary, flying in the face of psychiatric convention, he flaunted it. One wall of his office was covered with photos of his children and grandchildren, with a section devoted entirely to pictures from their bar and bat mitzvahs. Another wall was decorated with his wife's neo-Expressionist paintings. ("Had she started earlier, who knows?" he often mused. "She might have been another Picasso or Chagall.") A third wall contained prized baseball memorabilia. Having grown up in Brooklyn, he had been an avid Dodgers fan as a child, and his subsequent devotion to the Mets was so strong that he was known to tell Yankees fans to go elsewhere. (Now living outside of Philadelphia, he made special allowance for the rubes who rooted for the Phillies.)

To have an established weekly appointment with Dr. Samuels

was highly prized among the cognoscenti of Cherry Hill. Just as area residents believed that an engagement ring should never be less than two carats ("It's an investment!"), they likewise believed in maintaining a standing appointment with Dr. Samuels ("You never can tell when you might go off the deep end"). Even if the bar mitzvah was over and the problem with the daughter-in-law resolved, who knew when a crisis might hit or a child or husband might need to be set straight about something?

It occurred to Carla, seated in the armchair facing Dr. Samuels, that perhaps she didn't have the right credentials to be his patient. She didn't even own a mink coat.

"None of it seems that important," she said hesitantly in response to his question about what was bothering her. "I'm probably making too big a deal of it."

"If it bothers you, it's important," Samuels said encouragingly. "Just jump right in and get your feet wet!" Part of Samuels's success was that he viewed a visit to him as a kind of recreational opportunity. "How often do you get to talk about yourself for an hour?" he liked to remind his patients. "Even your mother won't listen to you for an hour—so take advantage and enjoy."

"I guess I'm feeling overwhelmed," began Carla, emboldened by Samuels's encouraging tone. As she spoke, he motioned with his hand, as though directing a car to back up into a vacant space, and she proceeded more rapidly: "Jeffrey, my ten-year-old, has been showing signs of ADHD, and I'm not sure I want to put him on the medicine. It seems like a drastic step. And Stephanie—that's my twelve-year-old—has a bat mitzvah coming up and is acting very oppositional. Not that she's not generally oppositional, but lately it's been more so. And Mark—that's my husband—is having difficulties at work. He's a physician, and the state of medicine being what it is—"

Samuels put up his hand, indicating that he'd heard enough (i.e., the car had made it into the space). It was his operative method to listen for a minute or two and give advice. Most of his patients appreciated this: "Usually, they make you do all the work," explained one devotee. "Samuels doesn't waste your time. He gets the gist and tells you what to do."

"Okay," Samuels said now, "I think I've got the picture. You've got some stress. Stress is normal. The question is: Are you handling it well? And how much of the stress should really involve you? Let's take a look: First, your son—I'd say, have him come see me. I'll tell you if he needs to go on the medicine. If he does, it's not the end of the world. It'll make life a lot easier for you and he'll be happier.

"Second, your daughter—she's oppositional. Nothing new for a twelve-year-old; it comes with the territory. But you need to lay down certain rules. If she deviates, ground her. It's amazing what grounding can do to get them into shape at that age.

"Third, your husband—that's really a matter between himself and his profession. He'll work it out. He's a physician; you won't starve. But I'll also let you in on a secret: A little self-promotion won't hurt. Look at me." He pointed to his book prominently displayed on a side table, and to an array of articles with his byline that had been arranged on a bulletin board near the window.

Carla nodded. Dr. Samuels, she could see, had a way of sorting things out. She had sensed the value of self-promotion when she first saw Samuels at his bookstore appearance. Now it came home to her that her husband could do some of the same sort of thing—with her help. The idea of grounding Stephanie for bad behavior and of bringing Jeffrey in for a consultation also seemed like reasonable strategies. She felt better already.

"Is that all?" asked Samuels cheerfully, slapping his hands down on the desk as if to imply that this was small potatoes compared to what he normally saw—a reassuring response in itself.

"Well, there's the issue of the bat mitzvah dress," added Carla tentatively. She had wondered whether such a trivial point should be raised in a psychiatric session, but decided to plunge ahead.

"Not a trivial matter at all," said Samuels, as though reading her mind. "My suggestion is that you drop the young lady off at the mall once a week and let her look. As the affair gets closer, she'll find something—otherwise, she can wear what's in her closet. Let her know that for motivation. Just make clear that it's not your responsibility to find the dress; it's hers. And no need to travel too far. You tell her: Find it in the Cherry Hill or the King of Prussia Mall or go without."

Carla nodded again. She wondered why she hadn't thought of this herself. ("That's the beauty of him," her friend Jill Rosenberg had told her. "He'll tell you everything you already know, but somehow you need to pay two hundred dollars an hour to really believe it.")

"How's your mood?" said Dr. Samuels, leaning forward to inspect Carla more closely over his bifocals. "You look okay to me." ("He can spot depression a mile away," Jill had said admiringly. "He had me on antidepressants almost before I came in the door.")

"I'm not generally depressed. It's just that lately, with the bat mitzvah and so forth, it sometimes seems like too much."

"I'll tell you something," said Samuels, gesturing to the wall of bar mitzvah pictures in front of him. "I've been through it. I've seen my daughter go through it. This is a stressful time for any parent. A wonderful occasion, yes—I wouldn't have it taken away—but not an easy one. Even Mother Teresa would be stressed—not that she had to host a bar mitzvah, but you catch my drift. You seem to be handling things fairly well. Just detach a little bit—recognize that everything will turn out, maybe not the way you want but good enough.

"Okay, let's review," said Samuels now, glancing down at his notes and proceeding briskly as he prepared to bring the session to a close: "Bring the boy in and we'll have him taken care of. Don't worry so much about your husband, except maybe to give a little push for some creative PR. And believe me, your daughter will find a bat mitzvah dress if she realizes that otherwise she has to wear some *shmatta* in her closet."

This was the wrap-up that Dr. Samuels liked to give at the end of each session. "Never underestimate the need for repetition," he often explained at the monthly workshops he held for therapists who wanted to follow in his footsteps: "Say it, then say it again. Even the bright ones have a hard time remembering."

"Thank you," said Carla, genuinely relieved to see her problems swept into a neat pile. "There is one more thing, though," she faltered, wondering how to best relay the bizarre nature of this last issue. "It involves my mother."

"Ah!" said Samuels, settling back. Obviously, the mother was the final piece in the puzzle. "Mothers generally pose a problem around the time of the bar mitzvah," he observed.

"Well, it's not really that," said Carla carefully. "My mother was a bit depressed after Dad died, but her spirits improved when she moved in with us. She's been a real help around the house and very easy to get along with—no trouble at all."

"That's a change of pace," noted Samuels. In point of fact, he had never heard of such a thing before.

"Yes, she doesn't butt in to our lives at all," noted Carla. "But lately, she's been behaving strangely. I suppose you could say she's delusional. She actually thinks"—Carla paused to give her audience a moment to prepare for this—"she thinks she existed in another life as the girlfriend of William Shakespeare."

Samuels cocked his head. "That *is* a new one," he acknowledged.

"It's particularly odd, since she presents the situation in a very matter-of-fact way," continued Carla, her confidence growing as she felt she had interested Samuels in a novel situation. "She seems to believe that this was a past life that she is remembering. She says she knows that it's unrelated to the life she's living now."

"Highly compartmentalized fantasizing," murmured Samuels, stroking his chin. "Interesting."

"Yes, and she seems surprisingly happy to remember this past life. It doesn't distress her in any way. She's full of anecdotes and references—in fact, it's amazing what she's dredged up that I never dreamed she knew about that period."

"And it disturbs you to see her so caught up in something that doesn't involve you?" asked Samuels, peering over his bifocals and (Carla realized uneasily) echoing the thought Margot had caused her to entertain that afternoon.

"Well, yes, I feel upset. It's as though she wants to create another life that has no connection to the life she's living."

"And why should she be so gung ho about the life she's living?" (Jill had warned that Samuels could sometimes turn on you and side with the opposition—as when he had refused to condemn Josh's unsupervised trip to the mall and had focused instead on what he called Jill's "narcissistic overprotectiveness"). "Is there anything so exciting going on in her life right now?" repeated Samuels, peering sternly at Carla over his bifocals.

"No," said Carla, reflectively, "but she has us—her children and grandchildren. We love her and want her to be part of our lives. And it's upsetting to think that she's lost contact with reality. Who knows where it might lead?"

Samuels seemed to consider this for a moment. "Well, I'd say you have two separate issues going on here," he finally concluded. "One is that your mother may be delusional—certainly a point of concern, especially if it impedes her daily life. The other is your wanting her to make your life the centerpiece of her own. There, the problem lies with you. She has a right to be the center of her own life—and maybe this thing with Shakespeare is a way of allowing her to do that. I'd recommend having her go out more. Find a way for her to meet new people."

"You're saying my mother needs a social life?"

"And why not? Being a grandmother isn't a full-time job. Why do you think Sylvia and I go down to Florida every January?"

"But her references are so bizarre," protested Carla. "Her story about Shakespeare is so detailed. It's—embarrassing to hear her go on about it."

"What harm is it doing? If it's not hurting her, ignore it. You might ask that she curtail some of the talk in public, out of courtesy to family and friends, but let her indulge in private with you. It probably serves a cathartic purpose. The creative impulse, you know, is wonderful thing." He motioned to his wife's paintings on the wall. "It continually takes new and unexpected forms."

"So now you're saying that my mother's stories are some sort of artistic expression?"

"I wouldn't presume to say anything," said Samuels, sitting back in his chair and putting his hands up. (It was his philosophy never to push too hard. "I throw out some ideas," he liked to explain to his therapy workshop students, "but I don't bully. These people can tell bullying a mile away—most of them are experts at it—so they don't respond well. I give my opinion, let them think it over, and usually, after they go home and have a good meal, they come around to agreeing.") "I wouldn't even discount the fact that she might be telling the truth," he added mischievously. "Maybe she *is* the reincarnation of Shakespeare's girlfriend."

"Dr. Samuels!" Carla exclaimed, surprised at what she took to be his flip tone.

"If you like, you can bring her in," he continued, unfazed by her exclamation. "We can book back-to-back with your son. I'd enjoy the opportunity. How often, after all, do I get to meet Shakespeare's *geliebta*?"

"Dr. Samuels!" Carla exclaimed again.

But he responded seriously now: "In my profession, you don't rule anything out. There are, you know, 'more things in heaven and earth, Horatio, than are dreamed of in your philosophy.'"

Chapter Fifteen

Jessie stood IN THE FOYER OF THE MIDDLE SCHOOL, GAZING down at the piece of paper Carla had handed to her as she left the house. It was Stephanie's course schedule, and Carla had instructed her to go to each of the classes on the list. "Pay particular attention to Stephanie's English teacher," Carla said. "Stephanie actually likes him and thinks he might be a good match for Margot. We want you to check him out."

Jessie was pleased to be entrusted with such an important mission but confused as to how to carry it out. The school seemed a vast labyrinth of aluminum and concrete, its corridors stretching out in all directions. Apart from the smell of dirty socks, it was nothing like the schools she had known in her youth: dowdy, three-story brick structures with central staircases and classrooms that lined up consecutively in logical order. All the classrooms on the sheet seemed to have been written in code. What had become of numbers like 1, 2, and 3? Obviously, they had gone the way of the lindy hop and the typewriter—not to mention the bagatelle and the quill pen.

Jessie had been standing in a bewildered state in the middle of the entryway until a pimply youth with a badge identifying himself as a member of the student council finally came over, glanced at her schedule, and pushed her in the direction of one of the maze-like corridors. A disparate array of parents—some in jogging suits, some in saris, and some in mink coats—were milling about, peering into classrooms and checking their sheets of paper assiduously.

"Do you know where A-15C-1 is?" asked a woman with long fingernails and a humongous diamond ring who was holding her daughter's schedule at arm's length as though it were an accessory that didn't match her outfit.

"I'm afraid not," said Jessie. "I'm looking for A-13D-4."

"Here it is," said a beefy man in a Rutgers sweatshirt, who seemed relieved to find someone going to the same place. "I'm Tyler's dad," he said, putting out his hand.

"I'm Stephanie's grandmother," said Jessie.

They entered the room, where a heavyset woman in a jumper and the air of a drill sergeant motioned them to sit down. Jessie and Tyler's dad joined a group of parents huddled inside the room. They all looked anxious but also relieved that they were no longer in middle school.

"Seventh-grade earth science. Mrs. Pulansky," said the woman in a no-nonsense tone. Mrs. Pulansky did not define earth science, which Jessie imagined to involve digging outside the school, but instead spent the time explaining her grading system, which she also said she would post on her Web site. She then put a number of cryptic sentences on the blackboard that she identified as her Web page, her e-mail address, and an earth science chat group where she said that the children could discuss the subject matter (left mysteriously undefined).

When the bell rang, indicating that they should move on to the next class, Tyler's dad edged up to Jessie and glanced at her schedule.

"I see we're taking all the same classes," he said happily. He had been ostracized in middle school for being overweight and, ever since, had made a point of establishing solidarity wherever he could. At work, he was said to be a great guy, no one guessing that his warmth and good cheer were developed to counteract the self-loathing generated in the seventh grade.

"I went to this school, so I know my way around," said Tyler's dad.

"How nice," said Jessie.

"Not really. I was miserable, but it helps me to think that I got through it without a major suicidal or homicidal episode. I tell Tyler all the time, this is the low point; it'll only get better from here."

Jessie followed Tyler's dad down the hall to the next classroom, which turned out to be something called cultural geography. The teacher, a very decrepit-looking man who had perhaps spent too much time with maps and atlases, explained to them the importance of the current unit on latitude and longitude, all the while twirling the globe on his desk as though trying to place them in a trance. Tyler's dad said that he thought he had had the man for seventh-grade geography (it wasn't cultural geography then)—though it might have been someone who looked like him.

Math followed, where a very small woman with flyaway hair explained a system involving various problems and projects by which their children could gain extra credit. The assumption seemed to be that everyone would fail the tests and need to have their grades buoyed. Some of the parents were furiously scribbling notes on the fine points of this system while others were staring out the window.

Next was health, where a very young woman with bleached blond hair, a short skirt, and high vinyl boots explained how the children would become thoroughly versed in sexual reproduction. "They've had bits and pieces in elementary school and in fifth and sixth grade, but now it's the whole shebang," said the teacher, straightening the seam of her skirt and pushing a strand of hair seductively behind her ear.

Finally came language arts, and Jessie followed Tyler's dad into a classroom more inviting than the others. It was covered almost entirely with a colorful array of material. Facsimile pages from the first folio of Shakespeare's plays were prominently displayed near the blackboard, and other Shakespeare-related memorabilia—pictures of Christopher Marlowe, Queen Elizabeth I, and Ben Jonson, as well as posters from film versions of the plays—scattered the walls. The impression, as Jessie saw it, was artfully designed to catch the fleeting attention of the restless seventh grader. She settled into a chair toward the front, where she could view the instructor at close range. He had been riffling through papers in a file cabinet near the window, his back to the class, so that when he turned around, the surprise of his appearance caused her to let out a gasp.

"Are you all right?" The teacher looked solicitously in her direction.

She nodded weakly, continuing to stare. He was about thirty-five, of middle height, dressed in jeans and a sweater, his hair slightly disheveled, as though the idea of combing it had not interested him long enough to be fully accomplished. But it was his face that captured her. It was, she noted at once, *his* face. The head was well-shaped with clearly defined features; the eyes had a gentle penetrating quality that one might call intellectual but were also playful, even mischievous; the hair was fine and beginning to recede, making the forehead appear even more prominent. It was not quite the face on the frontispiece of the first folio—she glanced over to where a copy of that document was taped to the wall next to the blackboard—they had never gotten him quite right there, she thought.

"My name's Hal Pearson," said the young man, smiling at the group, and appearing, or so Jessie thought, to give her a particularly warm glance. "I'm your kids' English teacher. You can e-mail me if you have practical questions about grading and curriculum—no need to waste our time with that here. Instead, I thought we'd spend the next half hour doing the sort of thing we do in this class. I've already discussed four of Shakespeare's sonnets with the parents before you. They were full of ideas—just like their kids. You're my last class, so I thought I'd end with sonnet number one-thirty, one of my favorites." He handed a pile of papers to the parent at the corner desk to be passed out to the others, though for some reason he handed Jessie her sheet individually.

"As you may know," said Hal, "Shakespeare's sonnets are wonderful, highly personal documents. It's not too clear when they were written; most estimates date them from around 1593 to 1600."

"Fifteen ninety-seven," said Jessie under her breath.

"Give or take a year or two." Hal nodded in Jessie's direction. "We see language and imagery from the plays of that period, which would put Shakespeare in his midthirties at the time—quite young, which is odd, given several allusions that would seem to suggest an older man."

"Made himself out a man of the world," muttered Jessie.

Hal paused and looked curiously in her direction, then continued: "The sonnets are written to two people, the first group of a hundred twenty-six to a young man, probably a nobleman, with whom Shakespeare was infatuated."

Jessie let out a slight snort, and Hal nodded with apparent understanding: "I realize that this idea may strike some of you as unseemly, and of course we don't know to what extent the sonnets express a consummated relationship. Nonetheless, the idea of love transcending the particularity of gender seems very central to the great creative spirit that we associate with the Bard."

Jessie made a face but said nothing.

"Most of the remaining twenty-seven sonnets seem to be written to a woman," Hal continued. "We refer to her as the Dark Lady, because it appears she had dark hair and eyes. While the young man is associated with a more refined and even spiritual passion, the Dark Lady is associated with something more sensual and earthly."

"Spite," muttered Jessie with particular vehemence.

Hal seemed momentarily startled by her comment but then

continued briskly, motioning to the Xeroxed sheet. "This sonnet is typical of the sonnets written to the Dark Lady," he explained, "and is more straightforward than most. So I thought it might be a good one to share tonight. Let me read the sonnet to you and then get your response."

He cleared his throat and read aloud in a strong, sonorous voice:

My mistress' eyes are nothing like the sun;
Coral is far more red than her lips' red;
If snow be white, why then her breasts are dun;
If hairs be wires, black wires grow on her head.
I have seen roses damask'd, red and white,
But no such roses see I in her cheeks;
And in some perfumes is there more delight
Than in the breath that from my mistress reeks.
I love to hear her speak, yet well I know
That music hath a far more pleasing sound.
I grant I never saw a goddess go;
My mistress, when she walks, treads on the ground.
And yet, by heaven, I think my love as rare
As any she belied with false compare.

"So," he said, looking expectantly around the room at the parents, who had settled into surprising attentiveness. Some had laughed during the reading, which seemed to have pleased him enormously. "What do you think? How would you feel if the sonnet were written to you?" His eyes panned the women in the room.

"I'd be insulted," said a carefully made-up woman whose hair was streaked a color not found in nature. She straightened slightly as she spoke, as if she had decided to take the poem as a personal affront. "He says she has bad hair and bad breath. It seems very rude to put that in a love poem."

Hal nodded. "Good point," he said. "Anyone else?"

The man behind the woman who had just spoken shifted in his seat, then finally burst out, "That's what's wrong with you women!" he exclaimed. "You have no sense of humor. He's having a little fun, what's the harm?"

Hal nodded encouragingly again.

"He admires her inner beauty," said another woman with long gray hair and a peasant blouse. "He doesn't care that she doesn't look like a fashion model."

"Yes," said a large woman in a pantsuit. "But it's also buying into society's standards. He's saying he loves her, but he's also pointing out where she falls short. Men do that all the time. I love you, but why don't you lose twenty pounds? That sort of thing."

Several women in the room nodded.

"I think"—it was Tyler's dad, speaking for perhaps the only time ever in a middle-school classroom—"Shakespeare wants to say that the lady isn't cookie-cutter and so he can't use the standard expressions that poets use to describe their loves. Her eyes aren't as bright as fire; her lips aren't as red as—?"

"Coral," said the large woman in the pantsuit helpfully.

"Right, coral. That's what we've been taught to say. He doesn't buy into it."

Hal, who had been nodding vigorously during all these comments, now exclaimed in a tone of unfettered enthusiasm: "This is great! This is fantastic! In just a few minutes, you've managed to open up the sonnet and show the full range of what's going on in this poem."

Jessie raised her hand.

"Yes," said Hal, nodding encouragingly in her direction.

Jessie spoke rapidly and with obvious emotion: "I knew what he was up to. Very sly. Write a nice poem, but get a few digs in. And that one's not the worst of them. There are a lot more that are worse: how his false eyes do dote, how she's telling him lies, being loose with the men, that sort of thing. But always it's, 'Don't you see how much I love you?' 'Don't you see it's because I'm jealous?'"

What does he care if he writes slander that will last maybe a thousand years?"

"Okay," said Hal carefully, "there's something in that, too." He was obviously used to the incoherence of his students and unwilling to dismiss what he didn't understand. He therefore nodded to Jessie before turning to address the group as a whole: "I sense that you all bring your life experiences to bear in the way you interpret the sonnet, which is exactly the point. It's a very rich piece of work and open to a variety of readings. It reflects how complicated and contradictory Shakespeare's feelings for the lady probably were, as opposed to the purer emotion he felt for the young man."

"What are you talking about?" interrupted Jessie sharply.

"Pardon?" said Hal, stopping short.

"Don't give me that about the young man. A pure concoction. The young man wasn't the point."

"He wasn't?"

"Of course not! It was spite, pure and simple."

"Spite toward the young man?" Hal asked, puzzled.

"Stop with the young man already. No, it's all about making the lady jealous."

Hal cocked his head as though he had missed something, then continued in a patient voice. "Okay," he said slowly. "But I don't know if we have much support for that reading. Given that there are no more than twenty-seven sonnets addressed to the lady and a hundred and twenty-six to the young man, it would seem that the man occupied the more central place in the poet's affections."

"What are you talking about?" said Jessie again. "He wrote a lot more than that to the lady."

"He did?"

"Of course!"

The class seemed to be following this exchange with interest. They had never heard anyone quarrel about poetry before.

"Are you—a literary critic?" Hal asked.

"Lord no," said Jessie. "But I should know what he wrote."

"You should?" he seemed puzzled for a moment, then, as though a light went on: "An amateur enthusiast!"

The bell rang at this point and the rest of the parents left the room. Jessie remained in her seat, smiling at Hal. He smiled back. Anyone who took an interest in Shakespeare, however eccentric, was a source of pleasure to him.

"You look the same, you know," said Jessie, tilting her head to one side and nodding in obvious pleasure, "and I see you've chosen to give up the mustache." She glanced over at the picture from the frontispiece. "A wise move, if I may say so."

"You think I look like—William Shakespeare?" said Hal, also glancing at the picture and trying to mask his satisfaction. It was a thought that had occurred to him before, though no one else had ever mentioned it.

"Oh, that picture's not really like him," said Jessie dismissively. "They got the shape of the face all wrong and made the eyes too droopy. No, you're the image of him—down to that." She pointed to a small mole on his forehead.

Hal flinched, looking surprised and a bit frightened. "You are—?" He seemed suddenly to notice that Jessie was not the right age to be a parent of one of his students.

"Jessica Kaplan, Stephanie Goodman's grandmother," she explained, continuing to hold her head to one side and smile. "Her parents couldn't make it tonight. They sent me instead."

"Stephanie has wonderful insights into poetry," said Hal, pleased to be reminded of one of his best students, but shifting uneasily under Jessie's gaze. "I suppose she gets that from you."

"Oh, no, I was never one for poetry. Some things rubbed off; they were bound to—but it wasn't really in my nature to think like that." She paused and her voice became dreamy. "You said your name was Hal Pearson. Hal was one of his favorite characters and a nickname for his son, Hamnet—he couldn't very well call him Ham, could he? You see how these things come back."

"Excuse me?" said Hal.

"Never mind." Jessie waved her hand, but continued staring at Hal and smiling. "Margot must be about your age. Margot's my daughter. Not Carla, Stephanie's mother; she's already married to a nice doctor. This is my other one. She looks just like I did; at least, they say so."

Hal seemed more and more bewildered.

"Well," said Jessie, sighing and assuming a brisker tone, "I have to go now. I promised not to keep Carla waiting."

She pulled herself up from the desk but without taking her eyes from Hal's face. "You'll come to Shabbos dinner some night soon," she said, as if stating an established fact. "We can talk more then. I'll check with the doctor for some dates when he can get home on time. His schedule is hectic, and sometimes he stops at the tavern, but I'm sure we can work something out." She reached out to pat Hal's arm in a gesture of affection and support. "Don't worry, it'll be worth your while. You can meet Margot, and I'll make the chopped liver you like."

Hal looked confused and seemed about to formulate a question, but Jessie had already turned to go. As she walked to the door, she glanced at the sonnet that she was still holding in her hand and muttered irritably under her breath: "Only twenty-seven to the Dark Lady—ridiculous!"

Chapter Sixteen

When Carla PULLED UP IN FRONT OF THE SCHOOL AFTER her appointment with Dr. Samuels, she could see that her mother was engaged in conversation with a large man in a Rutgers sweatshirt. They were both holding sheets of paper and appeared to be talking animatedly. As she opened the door, she could hear Jessie saying in the same pleasant, instructional tone she used to show Stephanie how to baste a chicken: "The last two lines are really all you need. They tell you what the poem's about. I used to go straight to them to get the point."

The man nodded. "Thanks for the tip. Never had much experience with poetry. 'Casey at the Bat' was about as far as I ever got."

"It's another language." Jessie nodded sympathetically. "It's a matter of being exposed."

"Our kids are lucky that way," said the man.

Jessie nodded again. "Back then, there were fewer opportunities. Most were no better than cannon fodder."

"Sure," said the man, figuring that Jessie was talking about her own youth. "World War Two, Korea—"

"And the War of the Roses."

"Yup," said the man, a bit confusedly. "Fortunately, I didn't have to go to war, but that didn't help me much. Teachers managed to make Shakespeare seem like a bad case of the flu. It helps to have one with a little enthusiasm like this Mr. Pearson—brings the stuff to life."

"Yes," said Jessie, "it's a nice touch to have him come back as an English teacher. And seventh grade. He used to say their minds were useless by the time they turned sixteen."

The man nodded, but seemed relieved as Carla motioned to her mother to get in the car.

"So how was Back-to-School Night?" she asked, noting that Jessie's face was flushed. "I see you've managed to make friends."

"Yes, everyone was nice, though I can't say that Stephanie's teachers are very inspiring. With the exception of Mr. Pearson. It was wonderful seeing him again after all this time. Gave me quite a shock at first. But once I got used to it, it made sense."

Carla swallowed. "What made sense?"

"Will coming back like that. As a teacher—he always had a streak of that in him, always trying to get me to read. Then, of course, there's the practical side of it. He can talk up the plays, point out the good lines, get the word out."

"Did you—discuss all this with him?" asked Carla slowly.

"Not in so many words. It was clear he didn't have a clue. He's too young. It only comes back later, once the curtain is about to fall."

Carla was silent. It suddenly occurred to her that her mother's fantasies might be a way of helping her face death. "But you did speak to Mr. Pearson," she finally continued. "What did you talk about?"

"Oh, the sonnets mostly. I set him straight about a few things. He had them all wrong, gave far too much credit to that sniveling Pembroke who wore his breeches too tight and was always hanging around trying to get things dedicated to him—as if Will cared a jot about him. I'm not saying that there weren't some episodes in that line—he and Kit Marlowe talked a lot about 'the varieties of love' and so forth—but everyone knew that it was me he was trying to make jealous. Then, when I wouldn't listen, he wrote the Venice play and broke my heart." Jessie paused. "He was the love of my life, you know. No offense to your father—it was another life. Of course, there was someone who might have given them both a run for their money. . . ." She paused again, as if realizing she were veering off on another line of thought, then continued in a more matter-of-fact tone: "Anyway, I didn't tell Mr. Pearson any of that. I didn't want to keep you waiting. Besides, we'll have more time later."

"Later?"

"I invited him to come for Shabbos dinner one night. He seemed very pleased by the idea. I dropped a hint about Margot, so that may have had something to do with it. And I promised to make my chopped liver. He loves my chopped liver—he may not remember, but he does."

Chapter Seventeen

"*There's no* REASON WHY YOU CAN'T DO MORE WITH YOUR practice," Carla explained to her husband one evening soon after her visit to Dr. Samuels. "I'm not talking about anything too pushy or obvious. You just need to be more savvy about the business aspects and get the word out that you know your field and care about your patients."

Carla had been thinking this over in light of Dr. Samuels's success. Psychiatry was a languishing field—in worse straits even than gastroenterology—but Samuels had refused to languish. She felt Mark could take a lesson from him.

"I heard that Drexel University has co-op students who will work for a term or two at reasonable pay," she suggested. The idea had come to her after Margot had noted that a Drexel student, an English major doing an internship in the DA's office, was finding inconsistencies in her cases that the regular staff would never have noticed. "These kids watch the crime shows on TV, so they ask all kinds of questions they don't teach in law school. Like when they had the lab analyze dirt under Mr. Giannini's fingernails for mud from the Schuylkill River—not the sort of thing he'd acquire at the family barbecue, his alleged alibi when the body was being disposed of. Now, that's straight out of *CSI*. Let me tell you, I wish I had one of these media-savvy kids working for me." It had occurred to Carla that a student well versed in the slicker medical dramas might be helpful to Mark as well.

"You could hire someone to analyze the weaknesses in the practice," she suggested to him now, "evaluate office efficiency and cash flow, for example, or put some promotional materials together. Ever since Katie Couric had her colonoscopy on TV, intestines have been big news. You've got loads of ideas on colon care that would be worth publicizing. I'm convinced that if you want to make the practice work, you need to take the initiative in this."

Mark, though lacking the enthusiasm Carla would have ideally wished, said he was game to try anything; things couldn't get any worse. And so, she went ahead and called the Drexel co-op office. The harried placement officer, used to employers with a very vague sense of what they needed, reached into a grab-bag of miscellaneous students and sent over three, each from a different major, to interview for the job.

The first student, a film and video major with aspirations to be the next Andy Warhol, did not seem like a good candidate. Although he claimed to want to make a documentary film on the medical field, his black fingernails and multiply pierced eyebrows, not to mention his observation that "blood always makes for good visuals," caused Carla to suspect that the documentary he would make might not be suitable for *Action News*.

The second candidate, a finance major, did not fit the bill either. He seemed horror-struck when Carla explained how the medical profession had become beholden to the insurance companies. "So you're saying your husband went to school for, like, fifty years and now they won't let him make a living? It's sick. I'm sorry, but trying to squeeze out a few more pennies here and there isn't what I consider challenging work. My advice to Dr. Goodman is to go work for the insurance companies; that's where the money is." As for this student's own aspirations—he was headed for Wall Street, where capitalism could proceed unimpeded.

The third candidate, fortunately, was more promising. A stylishly attired black woman named Yvette, majoring in communications, she seemed to have some very good ideas about what might be done to put Mark and his practice on the area's GI map.

"You need to be more proactive," said Yvette authoritatively. "I mean, no one's going to care about getting colon cancer unless you scare them about it. And your husband needs a serious makeover. He's got a nice-enough personality and he's not bad-looking," she observed with clinical objectivity, "but I'd totally rehaul his look. Change the suit—where did he get it, Men's Wearhouse?" [He had.] "Get a more colorful tie, maybe a bow tie—we'll have to see if that works for him. And the haircut, please!—he looks like someone from one of those eighties shows. The point is to make him a spokesperson for his field, which means he has to look credible but hip." She waved her hand in the air. "So that's the cosmetic aspect," she concluded. "Then there's outreach. We need to put together a list of the health editors at the local papers and TV stations. I'll write a press release and have my boyfriend, Jeron, who's in media arts, make a video that shows Dr. Goodman talking about some hot issue in the field. We can brainstorm about what that is. But first he has to change the hair. I won't take the job if he doesn't."

Carla felt that Yvette knew what she was talking about. The next day, she took Mark to the trendy Louis Christian Wayne Robert Salon and Spa on Route 70 for a haircut that at first embarrassed him to death but that he quickly became rather vain about. Yvette, now satisfied with the hair (they could improve it with mousse for the video, she said), came onboard and proceeded to begin work on "outreach."

Meanwhile, Carla had finally informed Mark and the children about the full extent of Jessie's fantasy life. She had hesitated to do so out of concern that her family would find her mother's condition off-putting or frightening. It was one thing to have a grandma with memory lapses and confusion, another to have one who believed she was the reincarnation of Shakespeare's Dark Lady.

But the Goodman family reacted with surprising equanimity. They seemed to feel that Elizabethan delusions were no big deal and, if anything, a nice change of pace.

Stephanie, for one, had already gleaned something of the matter in the course of her study sessions with her grandmother. After the initial reading of *Romeo and Juliet*, Jessie's abilities with the text had picked up to an astonishing degree. She was now correcting Stephanie on errors of pronunciation and launching forth with explanations about archaic words and phrases. "When the character says 'Anon,'" Jessie elucidated, for example, "it means something like 'Be there in a jiffy' or 'On the double.'" Stephanie also noted that her grandmother sometimes used phrases that echoed the language of the plays—as in "Prithee, Stephanie dear, I do like your hair today!" or "By my troth, that's a nice necklace!" Stephanie found these remarks weird, though no weirder than when her best friend, Elaine, dyed her hair orange—and with the definite advantage of making Jessie an excellent resource for English homework.

Jeffrey responded to the news of his grandmother's delusions even more enthusiastically. Given that his sense of the line between fact and fiction was extremely weak, he thought it was "really neat" that Grandma believed she had lived back then. As he saw it, they had swords and armor in Shakespeare's time, and maybe she could bring back some souvenirs.

Mark, driven to a crazed state of his own while calculating his new malpractice insurance, noted that Jessie's condition had its benefits. "I'd sure as hell like to go back in time to when the medical profession got some respect," he grumbled to Carla. "Maybe your mother can ask her boyfriend to write a play about the tragedy of modern medicine."

Chapter Eighteen

Who else IS COMING TO DINNER?" MARGOT LOOKED SUSPIciously at the extra place setting as she walked into the Goodman dining room one Friday evening several weeks later. "Carla!" Margot spoke her sister's name accusingly.

Margot knew that Carla was determined to find her a "decent" man—decent being someone other than the (usually married) captains of industry or (multiply divorced) Eurotrash that Margot tended to go out with. Margot felt it her duty to be outraged by her sister's matchmaking, though, secretly, she would have been deeply disappointed if Carla ever stopped making the effort.

"I didn't invite this one," said Carla now. "And it's not about you for a change," she half-lied. "It's someone Mom met who she seems to think is interesting. We're hoping that maybe he can shed light on her condition."

"A psychiatrist?" asked Margot.

"Not exactly."

"Who then?"

At this moment, the doorbell rang and Jessie, looking flushed and excited, poked her head out of the kitchen and waved an oven mitt toward the door. "Would somebody get that? It must be Will—I mean Mr. Pearson."

Carla went to the door and opened it. Hal Pearson, dressed in a rather shabby suit but with his hair fully combed, was standing in the doorway, holding a bouquet of flowers. "Is this the Kaplan-Goodman residence?" he asked. "Home of the fascinating Jessica Kaplan and her brilliant granddaughter, Stephanie Goodman?"

Carla had to admit that her mother was right: Hal Pearson had some charm. And he wasn't bad-looking, either. She stepped aside so that he was directly facing Margot, who was standing behind her.

Margot looked at Hal. He had a gentle, pleasant face of the kind that she normally wouldn't look at twice. Still, she did look.

Hal, for his part, stood stock-still. The sight of Margot took his breath away.

"I'm Carla Goodman." Carla proceeded briskly with the introductions. "And this is my sister, Margot Kaplan. Margot, this is Hal Pearson, Stephanie's English teacher."

Mark now appeared in the doorway behind Hal. Generally, he didn't get home from work until seven or eight P.M., but he had promised Jessie he would leave the office early to be on time for her dinner. He looked surprisingly cheerful given the probable headaches of the day and the fact that the work left behind would have to be completed tomorrow. It had now been almost a month since Yvette had begun to assist him in promoting the practice. Perhaps, Carla thought, seeing Mark in such good spirits, something had come of her efforts.

She gave him a questioning look and he mouthed *tell you later* while stepping forward to shake Hal's hand energetically.

"So you're Jessie's latest find," he said almost boisterously. "She's been raving about you since Back-to-School Night."

"She met him at Back-to-School Night?" whispered Margot to her sister. "Next she'll be bringing home stray dogs."

"Margot!" Carla hissed. "Be nice!"

"Why doesn't everyone sit down in the living room and have a drink," suggested Mark, embracing the role of host with enthusiasm. Carla hadn't seen him in this mode for several years—and she was reminded that he had been a fairly gregarious and fun-loving person before the trials of medicine began to wear him down.

"We have wine and beer—or I can mix you something," he offered.

"Beer would be fine," said Hal.

"Gin and tonic with a twist of lime," said Margot archly.

"There's some eggplant dip and crackers in the living room," said Carla, leading the way. She turned to Hal. "You eat eggplant, I hope? Nightshade vegetable, you know." Carla's knowledge of food allergies and aversions had increased dramatically since working at the Golden Pond Geriatric Center. Not that her own family were slackers in this area. Just last night, Jessie had prepared a spaghetti dinner in which the pasta had to be carefully partitioned from the meat sauce owing to Stephanie's problem with tomatoes (except, for some reason, when it appeared on pizza).

"I eat everything," responded Hal, glancing at Margot, as though hoping to gain points for this. He had gotten over being stunned by her appearance, though his eyes continued to be drawn in her direction. "I'm from northeast Philly, Feltonville—we're not picky about what we eat out there. It's a matter of grabbing what's on the table before someone else gets it."

"You can say that again!" exclaimed Mark. "I hail from the Great Northeast, too. Oxford Circle. Hey, did you used to hang out at the Country Club Diner on Cottman Avenue? I think I remember seeing you there."

"Sure. I was addicted to their cheesecake."

"Me too! My dad worked at the Wanamaker's on Cottman and the Boulevard, furniture department."

"Probably went a hundred times," said Hal, equally pleased by these connections. "I remember when my folks bought me my desk there. They said they didn't want me doing my homework on the kitchen table like they did. My dad supervised the old Sears warehouse on Roosevelt Boulevard that closed down about ten years ago. He said Sears was fine for appliances, but for a desk, we had to go to Wanamaker's."

Both men laughed. "I used to walk by that warehouse all the time," said Mark gleefully. "Where'd you go to high school?"

"Masterman," said Hal, referring to one of the city's elite public schools.

"Desk paid off, then. I went to Central!" It was another public school that required a test for admission.

"Two talented and gifted young men," noted Carla. "Anyway, I'm glad you eat everything, Hal," she continued, changing the subject. "Jessie's been working on a special meal for you all day. You seem to have made quite an impression on her."

"And vice versa," said Hal. "Your mother"—he looked at Carla and then let his gaze linger a moment on Margot—"seems to know a lot about Shakespeare."

"It's a surprise to all of us," said Margot rather dryly. "My mother has the heart of an angel and enormous common sense—at least she used to—but she hasn't got a literary bone in her body. I don't think I've seen her read a book in her life, except maybe a cookbook."

"Perhaps you've underestimated her," said Hal gently. "Or perhaps she's been doing more reading lately. It's amazing what great literature can do to expand the mind."

"She *has* been helping Stephanie with her Shakespeare assignments," noted Mark. Despite his underlying affection for Margot, he enjoyed putting her in the wrong—especially since it was a position she was so unused to occupying.

"So you're of the literature-as-psychedelic-drug school of pedagogy," said Margot, ignoring Mark's comment and continuing to address herself to Hal.

"I suppose I am," responded Hal, taking up the idea with a certain relish. "Dostoyevsky, for example, seems to me to be a mind-altering drug. I remember that I actually crawled under my bed to read him in college. It was cramped and dusty, but that seemed the right setting."

"Hmm," said Margot, obviously not prepared to be charmed by this anecdote. She too had been an English major in college, but of the pragmatic sort that reduced the literary work to an intellectual formula. She had gone on to transfer this skill to the analysis of legal evidence with great success.

"So you think Mom started reading literature and her eyes were opened?" she said, continuing her interrogation. Something about the understated certainty that Hal brought to the discussion irritated her.

"I wouldn't presume to say what's going on with your mother." Hal shrugged. "I can only report that she seemed to have a lot to say on the subject of Shakespeare. It wasn't terribly coherent, I grant you, but that only proves that she was wrestling with new ideas and trying to work things out for herself. I have to admit that I find that early stage of discovery—when things don't quite make sense—the most exciting."

"A lover of incoherence!" declared Margot. "I'm afraid you wouldn't get very far in the legal profession."

"I don't know," said Hal, smiling. "Incoherence seems to me a valuable legal strategy, to be employed when all other forms of argument fail."

"Touché!" exclaimed Mark.

"Perhaps we should let Mom speak for herself," interrupted Carla, sensing that her sister was getting agitated and wanting to bring things back to the original subject. "You see," she proceeded, addressing Hal earnestly, "our mother has recently had some odd ideas about Shakespeare and, well, it might be best if she tells you how she—uh—stumbled on them."

Before she could say more, Jessie came out of the kitchen to greet Hal. "I'm glad you could make it," she said, touching his arm and smiling. "I can't tell you what it means to have you here."

"I'm honored to be invited," said Hal, smiling back.

There was a moment of silence as everyone registered an emotional charge to the encounter and didn't know what to make of it.

"Well, dinner is ready," Jessie announced finally, breaking the silence. "Tell the children to come down."

Mark shouted a few times up the stairs. The kids were engaged in their usual evening activities. Jeffrey was watching a rerun of *Seinfeld* (he could recite every episode practically verbatim, and had recently informed Mark's cousin Dolores that her name rhymed with a certain part of the female anatomy). Stephanie was on the computer, doing her homework and instant-messaging her friends. These two activities had become so symbiotically entangled that no parent that Carla knew had figured out the means of disentangling them. Efforts to get Stephanie off the computer inevitably resulted in her screaming that she was doing her homework, even as the little box with her screen name—"hotgirl22"— continually popped up on the book-report-in-progress.

Stephanie had initially been mortified at the prospect of having her English teacher to dinner and announced that she would remain sequestered in her room for the duration of his visit. Jessie, however, could be shrewd when she wanted. She had simply shrugged her shoulders at her granddaughter's Garbo-like pronouncement and said that she would tell Mr. Pearson that Stephanie wasn't feeling well—though he would no doubt be disappointed, since he had spoken so highly of her at Back-to-School Night.

"He did?" Stephanie had responded, eager to know more. "What did he say?"

"Only that you were one of his best students—and with such an ear for poetry! But I'm sure he'll understand if I say you're under the weather."

"But he might not believe I'm sick and think I was trying to avoid him or something," Stephanie protested—forgetting that this was precisely what she'd intended. "I guess I can come down for a while."

Now that the time for her appearance had arrived, however, she seemed unsure of how to greet her teacher in the alien environment of her home. Fortunately, Hal intuitively took up the line that Jessie had employed.

"How's my brilliant student?" he queried enthusiastically as Stephanie slunk into the room. "I've got to tell you that the essay you turned in today, 'Why Macbeth Is So Insecure,' is a real eye-opener. I never thought to compare Macbeth to an unpopular kid, or Lady Macbeth to the stereotypical bully. I don't think I'll ever read the play again without taking into account middle-school group dynamics." He turned to the others with an expression of genuine pleasure. "It's what makes teaching so rewarding—not so much helping the students as having the students help me see things I never saw before. I'm always surprised at what I can learn from fresh minds like this." He nodded toward Stephanie, who blushed violently with pleasure.

Jeffrey, meanwhile, oblivious to the company, had run ahead down the stairs, sat down at the table, and poured himself a glass of milk. He was now mixing in the Hershey's syrup, rattling the spoon loudly against the glass.

"Jeffrey, would you please mix your chocolate milk more quietly," said Carla in an angry whisper. "It's very vulgar to stir so loudly."

"It doesn't get mixed well if I don't stir hard," complained Jeffrey. "The chocolate stays on the bottom."

"Well, perhaps you should mix it in the kitchen next time," suggested Carla in an absurd effort to get the last word, "at least when we have guests."

Jessie now motioned the rest of the group to the table, making a good deal of fuss arranging the seating. In the end, Hal was placed at her right hand, next to Carla and opposite Margot. It was a felicitous arrangement for Hal, who could look at Margot without any appearance of strain—though with the result that, in the course of the meal, he would sometimes forget to put food in his mouth or, when he did (at Jessie's urging), forget to chew it.

Chapter Nineteen

Once everyone WAS SEATED, JESSIE TOOK HER PLACE AT the head of the table but did not sit down. She had placed two candlesticks near her setting. She took a scarf out of her pocket, draped it over her head, and lit the candles. Then she somberly sang the blessing. Everyone was surprised. The Goodmans celebrated the Sabbath on a rather erratic basis and found the seriousness with which Jessie performed the ritual now to be out of character. The whole thing was embarrassing—although even Mark had to admit that it was also strangely beautiful.

"I've never seen you so into it," said Margot as her mother took the scarf off her head and sat down. "Even when Grandpa was alive you hardly took it seriously."

"I wasn't thinking so much about it then," said Jessie. "Lately, I've been more tuned in, what with Stephanie's bat mitzvah coming up—and other things." She nodded toward Hal. "I wanted Mr. Pearson to have a traditional Shabbos dinner."

"Actually, I'm not Jewish," said Hal with amusement, "though family lore has it that my great-grandmother was. It would explain my taste for lox, brisket, and chopped liver. But that might only be a function of growing up in northeast Philly, where most of my friends were either Jewish or Italian—I'm also partial to manicotti and pasta fazool. But my best friend, Gabe Stern, was an Orthodox Jew, so I've certainly had my share of Shabbos dinners. Gabe now works as a research scientist at the NIH, and I just got an invitation to his son's bar mitzvah. I remember Gabe chanting from the Torah at thirteen, and I'm looking forward to hearing his boy do it now."

"You're looking forward to the food, too," noted Mark, who liked to call himself a culinary Jew.

"I confess that I am," agreed Hal.

"I know, I know." Jessie waved her hand with a touch of irritation. "You were always crazy for my cooking."

Carla and Margot looked at each other. "Maybe you should explain to Mr. Pearson what you mean," said Carla.

The request for an explanation had to wait, however, as Jessie was concentrating on scooping the chopped liver from the large serving bowl and putting it onto the individual plates.

"I hope you still like my chopped liver," she said as she gave Hal an extra-large portion.

"I like chopped liver, so I'm sure I will." He smiled, trying to make sense of this comment. Had Stephanie perhaps brought the chopped liver in on Ethnic Foods Day?

Jeffrey had already begun eating. "Grandma's chopped liver is awesome," he pronounced between mouthfuls.

"Jeffrey likes everything Grandma makes," explained Stephanie with some scorn. "He even liked her venison stew."

"My Aunt Ruchel made an excellent chopped liver back then," said Jessie. "But everyone said mine was better. Even Kit Marlowe liked it. And he was finicky."

Hal raised an eyebrow.

"Ah, I forgot the garnish!" She rushed back into the kitchen.

Everyone was silent for a moment until Stephanie kicked Jeffrey for putting his elbow on her fork, and a fracas ensued that forced Carla to switch places with him.

"So," said Hal, turning to Mark when things had settled down. "I hear you're a doctor. A noble profession."

"Not so noble anymore," said Mark sadly. "The HMOs have sucked the nobility out of us. They're a blight on the profession."

"I don't know about that," said Margot, inspired to take the other side, as she often did, for the sheer sport. "Doctors got away with murder before they came along. Personally, I like to know what I'm paying for and whether I'm getting my money's worth."

"You're being a fool," said Mark, growing red in the face. "Medicine can't be reduced to a ledger book. What the hell am I supposed to do with the poor schlub who comes in with hepatitis C and his company's HMO doesn't happen to have a prescription plan? Pay for the Interferon myself? And what about the young woman who takes a cruise to the islands and turns up with some bacterial infection that her insurance doesn't happen to have on its list of treatable maladies? Ship her off to a leper colony?"

"There are bound to be glitches," said Margot, as though Mark were simply trying to complicate the issue. "They'll get ironed out in time."

"Meanwhile, let's hope you don't contract a rare parasite," said Mark, glaring at his sister-in-law, as though the thought of her, at that moment, with such a thing was not altogether displeasing.

"I suppose there needs to be a mutual process of correction," noted Hal diplomatically, "both sides recognizing room for error and abuse. But I do sense that what we're gaining by reining in the doctors, we're losing through the greed of the HMOs. And the biggest problem is putting a price tag on those incalculable aspects of human life."

"Well stated!" exclaimed Mark. "Human beings are not just a collection of parts. You can't just go in for a tune-up."

"I think you're being hypocritical," said Margot, warming to the argument. "As a specialist you're already treating the body like it's on an assembly line. But when someone else wants to do it, you complain."

"Progress requires some specialization," acknowledged Mark, "but it doesn't mean that we have to ignore the whole for the parts."

"I agree there," said Hal, as though this were something to which he'd given some thought. "Our modern bureaucracy—that social assembly line—doesn't know how to link part and whole, form and content, or understand the complex links between private and public life. That's where the poetic sensibility comes into play. It reminds us of these connections and carries the imprint of the soul."

"Very eloquent," said Margot. "Sounds like one of the English papers that I wrote in college at two in the morning."

"I'm sure you got an A," said Hal. "You seem to be very sharp."

"But lacking in soul. It's always been my weak point."

"Remediable," said Hal. "Nothing that a dose of Shakespeare wouldn't cure."

"So Shakespeare is your all-purpose remedy? A kind of moral castor oil."

"Better tasting than that."

"Maybe you need to have your patients read some Shakespeare when they come to your office," Margot suggested to Mark. " 'To be or not to be? Whether 'tis better to have a tube placed up the rectum and live a long life, or to forgo that indignity and shuffle off the mortal coil.' "

"Funny," said Hal.

"Not such a bad idea," ruminated Mark. "They could read Shakespeare while sitting on the can. The prep's the worst part. It would help take their mind off things."

Hal nodded. "And Shakespeare has quite a lot of material dealing with that end of the human anatomy. Very big on flatulence—I use that to hook the thirteen-year-old boys in my classes."

"I'm sure you have those seventh-graders on the edge of their seats," observed Margot.

"Margot!" whispered Carla, not wanting her to cast aspersions against Hal in front of Stephanie. Stephanie, however, was not listening, but glaring at Jeffrey across the table for hogging the breadsticks.

Jessie now came in from the kitchen with the garnish: parsley and cherry tomatoes that she laid on the side of each plate of chopped liver with great care.

"Lovely," said Hal, looking appreciatively at his plate.

"Nice presentation," agreed Mark, whose mood, uncharacteristically good to begin with, seemed to be improving steadily in the presence of an articulate ally. Normally, he was left to battle with Margot on his own, and since arguing was her profession, he inevitably lost.

"Mom," said Carla, feeling it was time to move past the amenities and broach the subject they had been skirting all evening, "you were going to explain to Mr. Pearson about your, uh, knowledge of Shakespeare. I think this might be a good time."

Chapter Twenty

Jessie settled BACK IN HER CHAIR. "LET'S SEE," SHE SAID, "where to begin?" She looked around the table and, having satisfied herself that everyone was enjoying the chopped liver, continued: "So I met him during that trip he took to Venice. Not Venice, Florida"—she looked over at Carla and Margot—"your father and I spent a few weeks there after we were married—very nice but not the same thing. I'm talking Venice, Italy. It was 1594 or five."

"You mean 1954," Hal corrected politely.

"No, 1594," said Jessie. "As I explained to Carla, it was another life. I know it's hard to believe. When Wanda Pinsky thought she was Ava Gardner, do you think I believed her? Not for a minute. For one thing, Ava Gardner was still alive, and for another, I knew that Wanda was crazy for Frank Sinatra, and what with that husband of hers, it was no wonder she let her imagination run away with her. My case is different. I remember—places, people, details even from the plays—and I was never one for literature. I told him so when he wrote me all those sonnets." She paused and continued wistfully: "I remember the disappointment, the heartbreak, the *tsuris*. As Will said: 'The course of true love didn't go so smooth.'"

"*A Midsummer Night's Dream*," said Hal.

"Yes, the one with a lot of meshuggener people running around in a forest with fairies casting spells and mixing everything up."

Mark and Carla had been rolling their eyes during this exchange and Margot had placed her head in her hands. The children seemed to be largely oblivious; Jeffrey was eating a second portion of chopped liver, and Stephanie was applying lipstick with the help of a pocket mirror. Hal, however, was paying close attention and now spoke with surprising seriousness.

"So you believe that in an earlier life you existed as the lover of William Shakespeare—the mysterious Dark Lady of the sonnets?"

Jessie nodded. "Not so mysterious. But I was the Dark Lady. I looked just like Margot—and he wasn't used to that sort of thing."

Hal turned and looked at Margot, who rolled her eyes again, but couldn't help blushing.

"The English women were very horsy and fair-skinned, and of course there weren't many Jews; they were all chased out a hundred years or so before. Italy wasn't much better. But Venice was a port, you see, so they needed the business. Poppa was a good businessman. They respected him. All that about his being such a devil in the play was made up. Will wanted to get back at me, that's all."

Hal had taken a file card from his breast pocket and begun jotting this down.

"What in the Lord's name are you doing?" whispered Margot.

"I'm taking some notes."

She looked at him disapprovingly. "I hope you're not planning to write a book and turn our mother into a laughingstock."

"Not at all. I simply find her ideas worth recording. She has a well-defined grasp of time and place, and an impressive sense of how Shakespeare fit into her world. We do know that the playwright Christopher Marlowe may have gone to Venice when it was thought he was killed in a duel—the death staged for political reasons. And there has been speculation that Shakespeare may have visited him there. We know that some of his plays were set in Italy, including of course *The Merchant of Venice*, probably written soon after the sonnets. It revolves around the Jewish character of Shylock, who lends the Christian merchant Antonio money to finance his young friend's courtship."

"Up to that point," said Jessie, nodding as Hal provided this background, "there was some truth. We had no problem with that much of it. Poppa did lend the young man money—though he hardly charged any interest and didn't even expect to get the money back. It had happened before, and he chalked it up. To think that Will took such advantage!"

Hal elucidated for the company: "In the play, Shylock lends money to the Christian merchant under the agreement that if the merchant doesn't pay it back by the determined date, then he will take a pound of the merchant's flesh as compensation."

"Neat!" exclaimed Jeffrey. "A pound of flesh—from where?"

"Excellent question, young man. That question would become a point of some contention later in the play. For when Antonio loses his ships at sea and cannot pay back the debt on time, as promised, Shylock attempts to execute the agreement. That's when you have the famous scene in the courtroom in which the girl, Portia, for whom the loan was taken out in the first place, disguises herself as a lawyer and turns the tables on Shylock. She finds a loophole—that you can't take a pound of flesh without also drawing blood, and that blood is not part of the agreement. As a result, Shylock is forced to give up all his money to the merchant and, as an added punishment, has to convert to Christianity on top of it all."

"No fair!" protested Jeffrey.

Jessie patted Jeffrey's hand approvingly. "Absolutely right, sweetheart, but of course the whole plot was to make us look bad. That, and the other part with the daughter."

"Yes," continued Hal, taking her cue to continue the story. "Shylock in the play has a daughter who runs off with a Christian, one of Antonio's friends. Her name"—he paused—"was Jessica."

Everyone stopped eating for a moment and looked at Jessie.

"At least he could have changed my name," she said irritably. "I understand he was angry because I'd broken off with him, but to put the name out there like that—it was a low blow. He was always saying that his poetry would live for a thousand years. So there you have it, Jessica abandons her father—sells the ring. There *was* a ring that Poppa gave to Momma that passed to me—I'd never have sold it for the world, no less for a monkey."

"In the play, Jessica sells her mother's ring for a monkey."

Jessie continued, incensed: "He was a genius, I grant you—how else do you take such spite and turn it into something that lasts? But it's spite all the same." She had begun to grow teary-eyed.

"I'm sorry," said Hal.

"Thank you," she sniffed, drying her eyes with her napkin. "You can't know it, of course, that you're him come back, but I'm sure you've had feelings now and then—they're like shadows that pass inside your brain. They only start to get stronger later."

Hal looked at Jessie quizzically. Jeffrey, who was taken with the idea of having once been someone else, looked toward his grandmother and exclaimed stridently: "Who was I, Grandma? Say I was James Bond, please!"

"James Bond is a fictional character," corrected Stephanie superciliously. "He never existed."

"There were books about him," objected Jeffrey. "They based the movies on books."

"Yes," said Stephanie, with strained patience. "Just because they were based on books, doesn't mean that the characters were real. The characters in the books were made up."

Hal intervened. "Well-expressed clarification, Stephanie. But Jeffrey's view is also understandable. Nowadays, we tend to associate movies with made-up stories and books with historical fact. But it's true, Jeffrey, that some books are based on real life and some are made up. And Ian Fleming made up the Bond character."

"I knew that," said Jeffrey defensively. "But I can come back as Ian Fleming."

"That's true," agreed Hal. "Fleming lived a very exciting life."

Jeffrey stuck out his tongue at Stephanie to indicate he had won, while she simply took out her lip gloss and began reapplying it.

Jessie, diverted from her recitation, had gone into the kitchen to bring in the next course, leaving the rest of them to talk freely.

"You're acting as though you believe what my mother is saying," Carla spoke accusingly to Hal. Things were not going quite the way she had planned. Hal appeared to be encouraging Jessie, as if she had tapped into some delusion of his own about *being* William Shakespeare.

"It's not a question of believing," responded Hal gently. "The fact is that her story casts interesting light on the composition of the sonnets and of *The Merchant of Venice*, a play always viewed as problematic. Whether I believe in reincarnation or not isn't the issue. What matters are the ideas. As a scholar and critic of Shakespeare, they interest me enormously."

"But that's ridiculous," said Margot. "If you take what she says seriously, you're encouraging her in her craziness."

"I don't think she's going to be persuaded one way or the other by anyone," said Hal, "so I don't think it's fair to blame me for encouraging her. I'm just what you could call a good listener. It's what critics do. They listen. They don't discount anything. They try to learn from the text."

"But our mother is not a text," objected Carla. "She's a human being."

"Everything is a text," said Hal. "And I don't mean to be dehumanizing in saying that. We read whatever we see. As soon as I walk in the door, I read your living room for what it tells me about your taste and your interests. Same with a person. I don't have access to your inner thoughts and feelings, but I can see the outside and hear what you say. Based on that, I draw conclusions about who you are."

"And the conclusion to be drawn from my mother," said Margot, "is that she's nuts."

"I won't disagree that her ideas are highly eccentric and, according to our notions of logic, irrational. But I'm not prepared to dismiss everything she says out of hand. Especially since her words have a curious coherence based on what I know of Shakespeare during that period."

"So what do you intend to do?" asked Carla. "Are you going to have the Shakespeare Association do tests on her?"

"I don't know what I'll do," said Hal, "but I can't deny that I find her remarks intriguing. I've always had a special interest in *The Merchant of Venice*—in the way it incorporates so much contradiction and so many shifts in tone. It may be that having seen or read the play at some past time in her life she now finds herself able to see it more clearly than the rest of us. The notion of a former life is the scaffold she has erected to hang her interpretation."

"That makes sense," said Carla, nodding—she was relieved to see that he was at least trying to explain her mother's statements logically.

"Or it may be that she met someone in the course of her life who had great insight into the play and the period and relayed this to her. And that now, for some reason, it's come back to consciousness."

"That makes sense too," said Carla.

"Or maybe she saw the recent Michael Rubbo documentary on Christopher Marlowe—I think it was on public television a year or so ago—that dealt with the idea that Marlowe staged his own death and escaped to Venice, where he actually wrote the plays that were then attributed to Shakespeare as a kind of cover for him. Maybe she unconsciously incorporated elements of that documentary into an elaborate fantasy."

"I'll buy that," said Carla, feeling increasingly relieved.

"Or maybe she really was Shakespeare's girlfriend," said Jeffrey, finishing off the chopped liver on his sister's plate and belching loudly.

"And that's a possibility too," said Hal.

Chapter Twenty-one

So?" said CARLA TO MARK AFTER EVERYONE HAD LEFT AND the kids had presumably gone to sleep (though Jeffrey was in fact playing the superviolent Nintendo game he had borrowed from a friend, and Stephanie was picking out her outfit for the next day, a time-consuming task that generally involved trying on a dozen tops and leaving them inside-out on the floor).

"I think the evening went well," said Mark. "I liked Stephanie's teacher a lot."

"That's not what I meant," said Carla irritably. "What happened at work that put you in such a good mood?"

"Oh, that," said Mark with mock indifference. He had obviously been dying to tell her all evening. He now sat down on the stool in front of her vanity table, began taking off his shoes, and embarked on the story with relish.

"Well, you know how skeptical I was about your wanting me to promote the practice and so forth? I'm no PR maven, and doctors, after all, are a dime a dozen. But I have to amend my view and admit you were right. First of all, Yvette's been a godsend. The girl's a marketing genius, and I don't just mean the haircut, which I must say was a wise packaging move." He patted his head proudly.

"I can't tell you the number of compliments I've gotten from my female patients—and the nurses are much more helpful; the word in the hospital is that I'm very sexy." He moved his eyebrows in a seductive manner à la Groucho Marx.

"I suppose I better watch out," Carla laughed. "But then, I always thought you were very sexy."

"But you're exceptional," said Mark. "We're talking man—or rather *woman*-on-the-street sexy. Yvette is an expert on that. But more to the point, she really knows how to reach the media. She interviewed me and read some background articles, then drafted a press kit that only required minor tinkering. Then, she got her boyfriend, a very creative, savvy guy, to make a video in which I remind all fifty-year-olds to make a colonoscopy appointment. Yvette and I came up with a really great closing line: 'Those polyps may be growing as we speak; do it now!'"

"Snappy," agreed Carla.

"So we sent out the print material and the video about two weeks ago," Mark continued, "and today, someone called from the *Courier Post*. They said they thought the piece on warning signs for colon cancer was important and want me to write a column for the paper, maybe a monthly or bimonthly piece on digestive health—from soup to nuts: nutrition to bowel function. Yvette says I could give her the main points, she'll draft the columns, and I can polish them. It would look good on her résumé when she applies to Columbia Journalism School next year."

"That's great!" exclaimed Carla. "Think of the visibility you'll get with a column in the *Courier Post*!"

"And that's not all," said Mark ebulliently. "After the *Courier Post* guy called, Yvette picked up the phone and called the special features editor at *Action News*. She told them I'd be writing the column and would they maybe like a segment some week encapsulating my main points? They said sure. They'd been impressed by my video: I had good on-air presence—which I suppose meant the haircut—and with a print byline, I'd have credibility as an expert. Yvette says that's called synergy. So I'm set to go on a week from today. The topic is spastic colon, one of my specialties."

"This is fantastic!" Carla exclaimed again. "Next thing you know you can write a book on *How I Stopped Worrying and Learned to Love My Colon*—and they'll want you on *Oprah*!"

"I don't know about that," said Mark modestly, "but I do think that being in the paper and on TV is bound to help the practice. Who knows, but if things work out I might finally be able to hire a partner."

"That would be great," agreed Carla. "You'd have less night call, and maybe you could find someone who'd be right for Margot—and kill two birds with one stone."

"Carla!" said Mark with amusement. "Stop trying to set up your sister; she can take care of herself."

"You know she can't, so don't say that," protested Carla.

"You have a point there," agreed Mark.

"I just want her to find a man as sexy, smart, and caring as you."

"Well, I thought that Hal Pearson was a nice fellow. I liked him a lot."

"Hal Pearson? Don't be silly. Margot hated him!"

"She did?" said Mark, surprised. "I didn't realize that."

Chapter Twenty-two

*A*s *Dr. Samuels* HAD SUGGESTED, CARLA BOOKED BACK-to-back appointments for Jeffrey and Jessie as soon as his schedule permitted. She had greatly anticipated the visit, though now that the day had finally arrived, she felt nervous. She was worried that Jeffrey would squirm in his chair and fail to answer questions, and that Jessie would ramble on incoherently about Shakespeare. She knew she was being foolish. Wanting her son and her mother to behave sanely for the psychiatrist was like wanting to clean the house before the cleaning woman arrived.

When Carla told her mother she had made an appointment for her to see a psychiatrist, Jessie did not protest. If her daughter felt a psychiatrist was worth seeing, then she would see him. Although she remained firmly entrenched in her story, she was perfectly willing to recount it to anyone who was interested. Indeed, it seemed to Carla that her mother relished telling the story, and gained in spirits and confidence the more she did so.

Jeffrey, on the other hand, was not so accommodating. He objected to going to a "shrink," as he put it—a term he had learned from his friend Sean who went to one "so my parents won't feel so guilty about getting divorced" and who said it was "really boring." He was also concerned that the appointment, scheduled directly after school, would prevent him from going home for a snack. Jeffrey's appetite was enormous, and snacks were to him second in importance only to meals. Fortunately, Jessie put his mind at rest on this score when she promised that she would bring a surprise snack when they picked him up—the idea of a surprise allowing his imagination to range freely over a vast array of culinary delicacies.

On the afternoon of the appointment, Carla and Jessie pulled up in front of the elementary school to pick up Jeffrey. He was standing near the flagpole being chastised by the vice principal (still sporting a large gauze bandage on the left side of his head) for throwing his backpack, in the manner of a shot put, at the third-graders.

As soon as Jeffrey entered the car, he demanded his snack, and Jessie passed him a large paper bag that contained a bologna sandwich, a dill pickle, and an assortment of *ruggelach*. These were some of Jeffrey's favorite foods (then again, most everything was) and assuaged him for the time being.

Once they arrived at the office, however, he began to grow restless, especially since they were obliged to wait to see the doctor.

As with much else from which Samuels deviated, he did not hold to the conventional fifty-minute psychiatric session. "It's ridiculous," he declared to his workshop students. "The problems aren't the same; the time shouldn't be the same. It's common sense." Samuels was, as already noted, a great proponent of common sense.

Superficially, Samuels's approach might appear to resemble the clinical technique employed by the famed French psychoanalyst Jacques Lacan. Lacan was known to alter the length of his sessions in order to throw patients into a state of psychic confusion and thereby achieve greater access to their unconscious. But any resemblance to the Lacanian method was, in Samuels's case, purely accidental. "I don't have any fancy ideas about the length of my sessions," he protested, when the idea was raised by one of his more theoretically inclined workshop students, "and God forbid I would take advice from the French about anything, except maybe a good cassoulet." (One of Samuels's hobbies was gourmet cooking.) "I see people for as long or as short as they need—end of story."

Since Samuels's patients often had their appointments delayed while he concentrated on a particularly knotty case, he had tried to make arrangements to relieve the tedium of waiting. To this end, he provided an extensive assortment of reading matter in his outer office. Besides his own book, of which several copies were scattered about, there were multiple other options, since he recognized that his clientele, despite a certain superficial homogeneity, had diverse tastes.

One shelf of the bookcase contained an impressive collection of sports books, including a glossy tome, not very thick but much thumbed through by male patients, entitled *Great Jewish Athletes.* Another shelf contained art books, specializing in some of the more unconventional modern artists favored by Sylvia Samuels, who considered herself an authority in this area. A third shelf contained an extensive collection of cookbooks, chosen by himself. Sylvia, as Samuels often explained, was devoted to her canvases and brushes but had no interest in the culinary arts, and so he did all the cooking. This revelation made his older female patients wonder what kind of wife this Sylvia was, talent or no talent, to make her husband cook her meals. With these patients, Samuels traded recipes and cooking tips—but the women would always pause at some point in the discussion, shake their heads, and mumble under their breaths: "Such a good man, and a doctor no less, saddled with the cooking; it's a *shanda*"—before launching into the fine points of making *schav.*

Samuels also kept a nice stock of comic books and *Mad* magazines for his younger clientele and those, as he put it, who were young at heart. *Mad*, he liked to say, had been his psychic lifeline as a boy, teaching him the fine art of ridiculing authority. He often expounded on how he feared for modern youth, who seemed to prefer mindless gross-out humor to character-building, nose-thumbing parody.

During the first fifteen minutes in the waiting room, Jeffrey was extremely restless, jumping up again and again to pull comic books from the shelves and complaining loudly that he was thirsty and wanted a glass of chocolate milk. But after a certain interval had elapsed, he began to settle down. By the time a woman in a powder blue jogging outfit, large diamond stud earrings, and a vast quantity of smeared mascara exited Samuels's office, clutching a wad of tissues, Jeffrey had been quietly reading a *Mad* magazine for almost half an hour.

It had been decided that Carla would sit in on Jeffrey's session, Jessie being content to remain in the waiting room, looking through the cookbooks. She had found one that particularly interested her entitled *A Font of Fressing: Traditional Jewish Cookery*, and was engrossed in a recipe for *knaidlach*.

When Jeffrey and Carla entered the office, Samuels was seated magisterially behind his desk. He motioned for Jeffrey to take the seat opposite and for Carla to retire to the small folding chair in the back of the room.

"So," said Samuels, surveying Jeffrey over his bifocals, "I hear that you're an energetic young man." The statement was strangely belied by Jeffrey's present state. He sat quietly slumped in the chair and was not, as was usual in such circumstances, swinging his leg back and forth or playing with his yo-yo. "You seem rather subdued today, if I may say so," continued Samuels. "May I ask if you are under the weather? Perhaps you had a demanding gym class this afternoon or are coming down with a bug?"

"No," said Jeffrey, "I'm fine."

"I don't understand it," intervened Carla. "Normally, he'd be climbing the walls. This isn't his usual style at all." She felt vaguely apologetic, given that she had billed Jeffrey as hyperactive and now appeared to have misrepresented him.

"Perhaps he's nervous," suggested Samuels. "Are you nervous, young man?"

Jeffrey said he wasn't nervous.

"Well, let's get started, shall we?" said Samuels, rubbing his hands together. "Would you mind if I ask you some questions?"

"Sure," shrugged Jeffrey.

"I'd like to hear about your diet—what, if you don't mind telling me, do you like to eat?"

Jeffrey brightened perceptibly. This was a subject dear to his heart. "I like almost everything," he proclaimed proudly, "but I really like Grandma's chopped liver and her pot roast. Also, her venison stew," he added as an afterthought.

"I see," said Samuels, "an adventurous eater. Very good. But what's your usual fare? For breakfast, for example, give me the rundown."

"For breakfast," said Jeffrey, embarking on the subject with relish, "I'll have Grandma's challah french toast and two Pop Tarts. And sometimes a bagel with lox spread and some Bob Evans sausage."

"A hearty breakfast. Very ecumenical," noted Samuels. "And for lunch?"

"For lunch," continued Jeffrey, pleased that someone was finally asking him to expound on something he liked and knew well, "I'll have a bag lunch that Grandma makes—maybe a bologna sandwich, a few chocolate-chip cookies, and an apple. I usually leave the apple, but sometimes, if I'm hungry, I eat it. I also have a slice of pizza and some chicken nuggets from the school cafeteria." He looked across at Dr. Samuels proudly. He had taken care to be accurate about the apple, since he felt he owed it to Samuels for having asked him to talk on such an interesting subject.

"Snack?" queried Samuels, writing something on a pad with a flourish.

Jeffrey cocked his head as if reviewing a very large panoply of items.

"Never mind," said Samuels before he could begin. "I think I get the idea. And what do you have to drink?"

"Jeffrey likes chocolate milk," interjected Carla from the back of the room. "I let him have it, since I think it's important to have as much calcium as possible at his age, and he won't drink the milk plain."

Samuels put up his hand, as though he were directing traffic and Carla was about to make an illegal turn. "Please, Mom, we want Jeffrey to tell us."

"Chocolate milk," said Jeffrey, pleased that his words carried so much weight.

"And how much chocolate milk do you drink?" asked Samuels.

Jeffrey furrowed his brow as he worked out the calculation. "I'd say—ten glasses a day—maybe eight or nine. It depends. I usually have three of those little cartons at lunch that they sell in the cafeteria, but sometimes they run out," he clarified.

"So you have chocolate milk whenever you can?" queried Samuels. "When you come home from school, for example?"

"Yeah," said Jeffrey. "I usually have two or three glasses when I come home. Grandma says it's too much, but I do anyway."

"Smart woman, your grandma," said Samuels.

"I wish I had some now," said Jeffrey.

"I bet you do," said Samuels. "But notice how quiet you've been without it."

"I suppose," said Jeffrey, unimpressed by this insight. "But I still wish I had some."

"Well, I'm going to tell you something, young man," said Samuels, peering over his bifocals and assuming a more severe tone. "I'm going to ask you to not have any more chocolate for a while. Milk, yes, it's a necessity for a growing boy—but you're to cut out the chocolate milk."

"What!" cried Jeffrey in an outraged tone. So this was what came of telling a doctor about your diet. "I gotta have chocolate milk. I'll die without it!"

"No," said Samuels, "I assure you that you will not die without it. In fact, you will be much better without it."

"I don't want to be much better! Please," whined Jeffrey, "let me have it. I promise to be good."

"It's not a question of your promising anything. The chocolate is having an adverse effect on your system. It's not within your ability to control its effects."

"You mean like the monster in *Alien* that takes control of the bodies it gets into?"

"Exactly."

"Neat," said Jeffrey. "But I still want to drink it."

"Of course you do," said Samuels. "We all want to do things that aren't good for us. But we use our will power and don't do them."

"I don't want to use my will power," moaned Jeffrey. "I love chocolate milk."

Samuels was silent for a moment, looking ruminatively at the boy over his bifocals. Finally, he spoke with great seriousness. "Did you see the movie *Spider-Man*?"

Jeffrey nodded sulkily. "Sure," he said.

"Do you remember what happens at the end of the movie?"

"Yeah. He tells the girl that he can't be her boyfriend cause he has to be Spider-Man."

"Exactly," said Samuels. "He gives up the girl in order to do what he has to do. You have to give up the chocolate to do what you have to do."

"It's not fair," said Jeffrey. "It's easier to give up the girl."

Samuels nodded. "That means you have to be tougher than Spider-Man."

Jeffrey considered this. "Tougher than Spider-Man?"

"Yes, you have to do something harder. Are you up to the responsibility? Are you capable of such heroic action?"

"I guess," said Jeffrey, obviously taken with the notion of being tougher than Spider-Man.

"I think you are," said Samuels. "And I think you'll find that you're a lot happier without the chocolate milk. You'll be able to concentrate better in class and have more friends, because they'll think you're smarter."

"They will?"

"Absolutely, I guarantee it," said Samuels. "You'll be a better version of yourself. Sort of a super-Jeffrey. You'll like yourself better."

"Cool," said Jeffrey.

"Now go into the other room and wait while I talk to your mother."

"Are you saying that the whole problem was the chocolate milk?" groaned Carla, once Jeffrey had left. She buried her face in her hands. "How could I have let this happen?"

"Don't worry about it," said Samuels, dismissively. "It happens all the time. It's not the end of the world. These things sort of creep up on us. That's why we go for help. You did absolutely the right thing, so don't have a moment's guilt about it."

"I should have put it together," sighed Carla. "I should have been more aware. My mother told me he was drinking too much chocolate milk, but I said she was being old-fashioned."

"It's not your fault," Samuels repeated reassuringly, "though I will say your mother is to be commended for her insight."

"When I think he might have gone on Ritalin," wailed Carla, suddenly realizing this.

"That wouldn't have been the end of the world either. But it's better that we solved the problem this way. I may be wrong here, of course, we'll have to see how he is in a few days, but my instinct tells me: Cut out the chocolate milk, and your boy will concentrate just fine. Make sure he drinks a few glasses of plain skimmed, but keep him off chocolate for a while. Now send in your mother. You can run Jeffrey home, so he can get started on his homework, and come back. I estimate I'll want a bit more time with her."

Chapter Twenty-three

*W*hen *Carla* RETURNED AFTER DROPPING JEFFREY AT home, Jessie was still sequestered with Dr. Samuels. They remained so for almost two hours, which, considering that Samuels had dealt with Jeffrey in a little over half an hour, struck Carla as a source of concern. What could they possibly be talking about for so long? Perhaps Samuels was ascertaining the precise degree to which her mother was psychotic. As the minutes ticked by, she became increasingly agitated. Finally, the door opened and Jessie emerged with Dr. Samuels bending toward her, deeply engrossed in conversation.

"I think the *knaidlach* recipe is too complicated," she heard Jessie saying. "Mine is much simpler and, I guarantee, delicious. They're as light as a feather. Will used to say that his friend Ben Jonson should take a lesson from my *knaidlach*. You see, he thought Jonson's plays were too heavy-handed."

"Sounds like quite a recommendation for your *knaidlach*," said Samuels cheerfully, holding a sheet of paper that obviously contained Jessie's recipe. "I've wanted to make them for ages, but that recipe in the *Font of Fressing* cookbook scared me off. I'll give it a try and get back to you."

"Don't forget to use sea salt," warned Jessie. "You can get it at Whole Foods."

"You betcha," said Samuels. "I'll follow it to the letter."

Carla, who had been watching this exchange in a state of wonderment, now intervened—there was no telling how long they might go on the subject of the *knaidlach*. "Mom, why don't you look at a few more recipes while I talk to Dr. Samuels," she said, trying to keep from registering irritation. It had occurred to her that she was spending two hundred dollars an hour for her mother to talk recipes. She then recalled Samuels's brilliant diagnosis of Jeffrey and relented. Samuels must know what he's doing.

"You mother's a charming woman," he said, once they had seated themselves in his office. "She must have been a great beauty once."

"She was," said Carla impatiently. "But that's hardly the point. She's suffering from extreme delusions."

"Well," said Samuels, "I suppose in a technical sense she is delusory. . . ."

"In a technical sense? What other sense is there?"

"My dear, there are all sorts of other senses. We don't want to go about labeling. Labeling is very destructive."

"For the love of God," said Carla, "the woman is talking about hanging out with William Shakespeare. I'd say we need to label her something. *Nuts* might be about right."

"I hardly think it's necessary to think like that. Your mother is a delightful woman. She had me on the edge of my chair, I can tell you."

"What are you saying? You're not going to do something? Put her on medication? Give her shock treatments? Something?"

"I think it would be a mistake to do anything at this point. She seems to be functioning rather well. She seems happy. She's a pleasure to talk to. It's my opinion that you'd do best to leave her alone. Let this thing work itself out. I have a feeling that it will take its course."

"You think the delusions will pass?"

"I think she'll move on. And I don't say that morbidly, though she is seventy-two years old and when you get to that age—and I'm hardly much younger myself, mind you—you think realistically about the end. But she appears to be in excellent health, so that's not what I mean. I imagine she'll find something else to occupy her imagination."

"So you recommend we do nothing?"

"In a word, yes."

"And when she talks about it?"

"Let her talk."

"And what should we say? How should we respond?"

"Respond naturally. Maybe ask some questions. Mostly listen. You'd be surprised—you may learn something."

Chapter Twenty-four

Carla had RECENTLY COME UP WITH THE IDEA OF ASKING Mr. O'Hare, a resident of the Golden Pond Geriatric Center, to help choose the hors d'oeuvres for the bat mitzvah.

The caterer had recommended that Stephanie be excluded from this process, and Carla felt it best to exclude Mark as well. Both her husband and her daughter were likely to have trouble absorbing the wide range of choices available, and to become confused and quarrelsome, especially when they began jockeying the hors d'oeuvres they liked best against the cost of said items.

Mr. O'Hare, by contrast, seemed just the person to consult on the subject. Although he could not eat solid food himself, he had strong opinions about food and a decisive manner that might serve well in sifting through the myriad of options.

Carla had first become acquainted with Mr. O'Hare when her father had been admitted to the Golden Pond Geriatric Center during his final illness. O'Hare had developed something of a bond with Milt Kaplan as a result of his unabashed admiration for Jessie. O'Hare himself had been married twice, "to goddamn shrews" as he put it, so that Jessie's temperament combined with her physical attributes (still discernible, especially to a sharp-eyed octogenarian) made her a continual source of wonder to O'Hare.

Milt Kaplan had not been displeased by this. Even at death's door, he had warmed to the reminder of his incredible good fortune in a wife.

Carla had started volunteering at the center after her father's death and had kept up her contact with O'Hare. In particular, she had assumed the responsibility of helping him eat his dinner (served at the convenient if macabrely early hour of four P.M.). Eating dinner for O'Hare was a complicated task, given that he was not only physically incapacitated but unusually stubborn and cantankerous.

"We have veal for dinner today, Mr. O'Hare," Carla would announce in a typical encounter, taking a spoonful of pureed veal and bringing it up to his mouth.

"You don't expect me to eat that crap," O'Hare protested. "Get it away from me, goddammit."

"Mr. O'Hare," Carla responded calmly, keeping the spoon where it was, "you know you need to eat something to keep up your strength."

"I don't have any strength to keep up, and I don't need to eat that crap," O'Hare snapped. "I don't see you eating it either, honey."

"You're right," agreed Carla. "That's because I can chew the regular veal that you see Mrs. Stein is eating over there. But seeing as you have difficulty chewing, we simply put the veal into a blender and you've got yourself more or less the same thing."

"Like hell it's the same thing," growled O'Hare, glancing at Mrs. Stein with a mixture of envy and disdain. "If it doesn't look the same, it's not the same!" he added with strict, empirical logic. Then, as was common with these obstreperous types, he opened his mouth and allowed himself to be fed the pureed veal without further discussion. Only after Carla had wiped his mouth did he embark on a new subject.

"How's your mother?" he asked, his tone softening a bit. "A beautiful woman, your mother, though a lot of good that does me."

"Yes," said Carla, determined to ignore the fuller implication of this remark, "she was devoted to my father."

"Devoted, I don't know," said O'Hare irritably. "That's the phrase they use, but it doesn't mean much. You get used to people, that's all. Take Gloria—I didn't like her, but I was used to her. Now, what am I supposed to do with myself?"

"Well," said Carla—it seemed to her part of her job to answer this sort of question—"you could get involved with some of the workshops."

"Please," said O'Hare scornfully, "I can't even feed myself and you want me to make pot holders."

"Maybe you could take part in one of the group discussions," she suggested.

"Discussions about what?" O'Hare snarled.

"There are lots of topics. They post them on the bulletin board every morning. Things like politics, money management, pollution. I saw Mr. Pinsky add one this morning on the role of the United Nations—an important subject."

"Who wants to discuss the United Nations?" O'Hare snorted. "Besides, Pinsky doesn't want to discuss; he just wants to quarrel."

It was in the wake of conversations like these that Carla had hit upon the bat mitzvah hors d'oeuvres as a project that might engage the fastidious O'Hare. Here was something neither physically taxing nor ostensibly controversial. She broached the subject gently: Would he consider assisting her in making this important selection? It would be a great help to her if he would.

Surprisingly, O'Hare appeared to be amenable. Indeed, his mood began to improve as soon as she showed him the massive list of options that she wanted him to review. He studied the list carefully, then began to pose questions.

"What is a chopped liver canapé?" he asked Carla.

"Chopped liver on a cracker with a garnish of maybe caviar or pimiento," explained Carla.

"Aha!" He slowly made a small mark with a pencil on the side of the menu. "And mini-gefilte fish with red and white horseradish dip?"

"That's a form of blended fish, chopped and molded into a kind of ball," explained Carla. "It's actually very tasty. Come to think of it, you could probably eat it, since it's ground up and easy to digest. I'll have Mom make some and bring it in. The red horseradish is milder than the white. Most men go for the white; the women like the red."

"You people are very adventurous in the food department," noted O'Hare. He had come to view the whole thing as akin to an exotic vacation taken without the necessity of leaving his bed.

Carla agreed that Jewish people did enjoy food and were always willing to try something new.

"I can see that this bat mitzvah thing is a really big deal," O'Hare observed. "Nice to put the child center stage like that; builds character. And the party sounds like a goddamn blast. We forget that the kids grow up and so forth," he motioned feebly with his good hand in the direction of himself.

"Yes," admitted Carla, "but it can get out of hand. Spending so much money and attention on a child isn't necessarily the healthiest thing in the world."

"And why not?" demanded O'Hare, his temper flaring. Having spent so much time with the hors d'oeuvres, he had come to take a vested interest in the bat mitzvah as a whole, almost as though he were hosting it himself. "What the hell do you want to wait around saving your bucks for? Better to spend it on the kids. Wish I'd had one of these goddamn bat mitzvah things for mine."

"Well, you're being a great help to me now," said Carla gently, trying to deflect what she felt might be the rising tide of O'Hare's wrath. "By the way, Mr. Pinsky said he wanted to drop by later this afternoon. I told him I'd wheel him in, if you didn't object. I thought you might like to have some company."

"Not Pinsky," said O'Hare, growing more irate. "All he wants to do is fight about politics. What's the point, I say? Life goes on no matter what we think." But then he paused and seemed to reconsider. "Pinsky's a Jew, isn't he?"

"Yes, I suppose he is," noted Carla, nonplussed by this rather bald query.

"Well, maybe he can explain some of this goddamn food to me."

Carla agreed that Pinsky probably could be of help on this score, and so O'Hare agreed to have him in as a consultant. When Carla left for the day, O'Hare and Pinsky were quarreling, not about UN intervention in the Middle East, but about the meaning of a "mock-sushi station" and an item marked "mashed-potato sundae bar."

"Do you think they put chocolate sauce on the potatoes?" asked Pinsky.

"What are you talking about?" said O'Hare. Having been involved with the hors d'oeuvres longer, he was better able to grasp the metaphorical aspects of the terminology. "It's a way of putting it, that's all. It means they have different toppings on the potatoes—gravy, cheese, mushrooms, that sort of thing."

"And the mock-sushi station?" asked Pinsky, who had begun to defer to O'Hare's understanding, despite having actually hosted three bat mitzvahs himself—though admittedly long ago (his daughters were now in their forties), his late wife having handled all the details.

"Mock-sushi," said O'Hare with a strained patience, "because you people can't eat shellfish and most people are afraid of raw fish anyway."

"Mini quiche?"

"Bite-size cheese pies."

"Chicken satay en brochette?"

"Pieces of chicken on skewers with that peanut sauce for dipping."

O'Hare certainly knew his bar mitzvah appetizers, Pinsky had to admit.

Several days later, the two men had assembled a list of selections that included a roast beef carving area, a mock-sushi station, and a mashed-potato sundae bar, along with such circulating hot hors d'oeuvres as baby lamp chops, spinach in phyllo, and that perennial favorite, "pigs in a blanket"—though, in this case, they were mock-pigs. First, second, and third choices were marked in consideration of Carla's budget.

"We don't know what you plan to spend," said Pinsky, "so we worked it out so you could go all out or opt for something more modest. O'Hare's for letting out all the stops, but, personally, I think there's no sense blowing it all on the bat mitzvah. In ten years, you'll have a wedding to pay for, and then you'll really have to spend the money. I had three girls, and they had ritzy tastes. Almost put me in the poorhouse."

That night, Carla reviewed the final list, which had been carefully transcribed by Pinsky in the capacity of scribe. She was pleased to see that she agreed pretty much with all the choices (though her tendency, in line with Pinsky's advice, was to go with the less pricey items).

Chapter Twenty-five

*A*s *Carla* SEALED THE ENVELOPE CONTAINING THE FINAL selections that would be sent off to Moishe the next day, a blessed calm pervaded the living room. Jessie was in her bedroom watching *Entertainment Tonight*, Stephanie had gone to a friend's house to work on a relief map for cultural geography, and Jeffrey was doing his homework upstairs (the elimination of the chocolate milk making it possible for him to sit down and get it done). Mark was quietly ensconced in the opposite armchair, reading a book entitled *How to Protect Yourself from the Malpractice War* and taking notes in the event that the material might serve for a future column.

Then the doorbell rang.

"Oh my God!" said Carla, "I completely forgot that the bar mitzvah entertainment motivator was coming over tonight."

"Why do we need an entertainment motivator?" asked Mark irritably. "Can't we just hire a deejay and leave it at that? How complicated could it be to play a few records?"

"CDs," corrected Carla. "From what I hear, it's not so simple. Jill Rosenberg said it's important to have someone who knows what the kids like and can make the party work."

"We already have a band," objected Mark, who took a certain

pride in having discovered that group after hearing them on the radio while driving home from work several months earlier. The band had been featured on the public radio station WHYY for its "authentic klezmer music," and Mark had been impressed by how classy they sounded.

Carla hadn't known quite what to make of the idea of a klezmer band. She was used to bar mitzvahs in which the band was of the modified Benny Goodman variety, where women in low-cut gowns and men in combovers sang old standards, then snapped their fingers as they segued into something more hip (i.e., songs from the 1980s). But she was reluctant to countermand Mark on the subject. He had taken very little interest in planning the bat mitzvah up until now, and it didn't seem wise to thwart his enthusiasm.

Discussing the issue with her friend Jill, however, had put things in perspective. "Classy is all well and good," said Jill, shaking her head at Carla when she was told about Mark's decision, "but classy can be the kiss of death at a bar mitzvah. You're going to have to hire an entertainment motivator with some *shpilkus* to counteract that klezmer," she noted, as if she had devised a chemical antidote to the possible toxicity of the band.

Jill had regaled Carla with stories of bar mitzvahs in which everyone sat glumly at their tables, refusing to dance. "Nowadays, people won't get up without some motivation," she explained. "They're used to sitting in front of the TV. You need to set a fire under them. That's the business of the entertainment motivator. He forces people to have a good time."

Carla opened the front door now, curious to see what an entertainment motivator looked like. A man of indeterminate age in a form-fitting shirt and leather pants bounded into the room. He was carrying a large suitcase and exuded an enormous amount of energy. Soupy Sales, the popular 1960s TV/radio personality, had perhaps had something of the same energetic style.

"I'm Griffin," said the man, pumping Carla and Mark's hands.

He handed them a card with *Griffin* written on it in gothic script and a picture of a gold dragon next to the name. "I'm due at the Rothsteins' at nine, so I'll make this short and sweet." He snapped open the suitcase. "Let me show you some of the exciting stuff we have for you. We tailor the affair to your specifications, of course." He gave a swift glance at the room, as if trying to assess their net worth, and with a quick motion extracted a tape from the suitcase and looked around for a VCR. Apparently, most families had VCRs within striking distance of the front door, and he seemed surprised when Carla explained that theirs was upstairs.

Everyone traipsed upstairs, where Griffin popped the tape into the VCR. A scene of violent festivity immediately appeared on the screen. Two young women in short-shorts, striped vests, and high boots, who looked like extras in a Bob Fosse musical, were dancing wildly in front of a vast throng. Standing behind them on a platform with a microphone, Griffin was directing "Grandma" to "shake her booty" as the camera panned to the image of a woman in her eighties and a young man in a bandanna, skin-tight pants, and a cut-off T-shirt, who had taken her by the hand. "Let's go, Grandma Sadie!" said Griffin into the microphone, while the vast throng could be heard egging her on as she shimmied opposite the young man in the T-shirt.

"I'm showing you here one of our more popular packages," explained Griffin soberly (the outlandish images transpiring on the screen might have been a funeral procession given his tone of voice). "We have three entertainment facilitators, as you can see— two female, one male, not including yours truly. We try for very high energy and getting everyone involved. That's the key to a successful bar mitzvah. You don't want Cousin Edgar, the sour-puss, to stand off to the side and look miserable. That can throw the whole party off." Griffin spoke as though he had conducted an extensive study of the successful bar mitzvah and these were his scientific findings.

The tape now panned to one of the female entertainment facilitators as she grabbed a middle-aged man with a dazed expression and launched into a provocative bump and grind. "Come on, Dad, show us your stuff!" cried Griffin on the tape to the apparently mortified father of the bar mitzvah boy, as the crowd clapped rhythmically in time to the gyrations of the female entertainment facilitator. The camera panned to the other female entertainment facilitator, who was doing something of the same thing with a pimply youth in braces who was standing stock-still and staring straight ahead into her cleavage. "Okay, Sammy, show Dad how it's done," instructed Griffin. The bar mitzvah boy remained immobilized as the young woman in short-shorts bumped up against him.

"Don't you have something a bit more toned down?" asked Mark, taken aback by the images on the screen.

"I'm showing you the package that my more low-key customers go for," said Griffin in a miffed tone. "This is my classiest—and I should add, most economical—package. Many families tend to like things a bit more flashy: five entertainment facilitators, cowboy theme, strobe lights, that sort of thing. But I could tell when I met you that you weren't the flashy types, which is why I showed you this package."

"It still seems a bit—much," said Mark, imagining himself the object of the bump and grind.

"Well, we could go with our two-facilitator package," said Griffin doubtfully. Obviously, this was slumming, but his tone implied that he was prepared to give the customer what he wanted—up to a point. "I don't have a tape of that, I'm afraid, but you can imagine that it would be less of everything."

"Less of everything sounds great," said Carla hastily. She could tell that Mark was on the verge of reneging on the whole thing, which would throw the bat mitzvah into disarray. Stephanie, who had gone to at least ten bar mitzvahs by now and was, in the manner of a teenager, determined to have everything the same as her friends, expected a deejay, and it would be close to impossible to book anyone halfway decent at this late date.

Carla was sensitive to the need to meet Stephanie's expectations regarding the deejay, since she was still suffering the aftereffects of a fight they had had the week before. A pitched battle had occurred when Stephanie insisted that she wanted her party to have a day-at-the-spa theme. Her friend Lisa's bat mitzvah had had this theme, which featured "stations" for massages, facials, manicures, and so forth.

Carla had been outraged by the idea. "The theme of your bat mitzvah is your initiation into the faith of your ancestors," she had lectured severely. "Any other theme would be both vulgar and sacrilegious."

Stephanie, riled more by her mother's tone of voice than by her refusal to support the spa theme, accused Carla of being stupid, mean, and living under a rock (presumably those who did not live under rocks embraced bat mitzvah spa themes as the way of the world).

Thankfully, Jessie had stepped in at a crucial moment and calmed the storm. She had mentioned, in a casual sort of way, that curling irons and nail polish might embarrass some of the male guests. Stephanie's grandfather, she recalled, had been petrified by the beauty parlor, and it would be a shame to scare the boys, especially at this fragile, impressionable age. Stephanie had taken these comments to heart and dropped all lobbying for the spa theme—though she had continued to bear a grudge against her mother for days afterward. Remembering this, Carla now felt averse to weathering more of her daughter's wrath if the deejay fell through.

"We'll go with the two-person package," asserted Carla. "I'm sure it will be fine."

"If that's what you want," said Griffin grudgingly. "I assume you'll follow the standard order of events."

"Standard order?" asked Carla. She could tell that Griffin was beginning to view them as a remedial case, woefully ignorant of bar mitzvah etiquette. He glanced at his watch, perhaps wondering if he was wasting his time.

"The standard order," he explained, with a note of exasperation, ticking the items off with crisp alacrity, "is the hora first to get them up and about; then the *motzi*, the blessing, with Grandpa and maybe Dad; then the presentation of the family, with music picked out to match each personality; then the first dance—"Sunrise, Sunset" if it's father-daughter, which in your case it is; then some old standards to get the fogies on their feet, and then the contemporary stuff—Britney, Justin, Christina—so the kids can have a good time." He seemed to have recited this fearsome litany without taking a breath, and continued now, filling in the fine points. "We put the theme pieces in there, of course: You can do requests for the candle-lighting so that, say, Cousin Ruth, who likes Sting, or Uncle Robert, the Dead Head, gets their song when they come up to a light a candle."

"That sounds fine," said Carla, feeling dizzy. "We'll give you a list of what the family likes."

"Okay, then," said Griffin, "so all we have to do now is review the favors and prizes and we're set." He gave them a sidelong glance, as if daring them to question him on this point, then took out some samples from his valise. "The CD prize"—he held up a CD imprinted with the *Griffin* logo—"very big right now. The kids like to have personalized mixes—we can do that to your specifications, for a modest additional fee. We also have the inflatable favors which are very big." He produced a brightly colored laminated sheet. "Blow-up guitars, saxophones, trumpets, even a full set of inflatable drums—great at the beach. Then there's the basic filler: glitter sticks, hula hoops, top hats, sunglasses, leis—"

"Do we really need to have any of this stuff?" asked Mark. "Isn't it enough that the kids are having a great party?"

Griffin paused for a moment and looked over at Mark as though he were crazy. "Where have you been, man? Kids aren't satisfied anymore unless they have this stuff. Sure, they get thrown out the next day, but it's the energy, the sense of things happening that's important. If you don't do it, they're going to ask your daughter, 'Where are the prizes, where are the favors?' What's she going to say—'My folks were too cheap to have them'?"

Mark was silent.

"A few favors," said Carla. "Maybe one or two."

"One or two? Better have nothing," said Griffin. Then, waving his hand as if to say he'd have to take things into his own hands, he added, "I'd recommend our three-star package: five favors, two CD prizes—that's the one for those, like you, that don't like to be flashy."

"Sounds fine," said Carla, not looking at Mark. "We'll do the three-star package then."

"That settles it," said Griffin. "We have a two-entertainment-facilitator presentation and a three-star prize-and-favor package. Very elegant and low-key."

"And the cost?" asked Mark. "What does that combination run to?"

"That's, let's see, three thousand ballpark," said Griffin, checking through a variety of Xeroxed sheets in the valise. "The CD prices fluctuate, as do the favors. So it's give or take a few hundred. I'll have the exact estimate for you a few weeks before the affair."

"Three thousand dollars," said Mark. "I had no idea . . ."

"Well, perhaps you've got the wrong person," said Griffin, his good cheer beginning to evaporate. He was someone who clearly did not like to nickel-and-dime, and Mark, for whom questions of cost were the bane of his existence as a physician, was struck by the fact that the entertainment motivator seemed far more able to call the shots than he could as a physician with ten years of practice under his belt.

"I'm afraid anything less would compromise my standards," said Griffin in a huffy tone. "You see, I have a reputation to maintain. I'm considered the best deejay in the Delaware Valley—chosen by *Philadelphia* magazine." He extracted another Xeroxed sheet to this effect from the recesses of the valise. "If you want something second-rate, I suggest you go elsewhere."

"No, no," said Carla, frightened that he would throw them over and they would be left without a deejay three months before the bat mitzvah—akin to being left on Thanksgiving without a turkey. "I'm sure that the package you suggest will be just fine." She darted Mark a warning look. "Three thousand dollars seems reasonable."

"Then that's settled. I'll draft the contract and have it in to you in a jiffy," said Griffin, snapping the suitcase shut and regaining his ebullient mood. "You have the bat mitzvah girl draw up a list of her favorite songs. Don't you worry, you won't regret it; everyone will have a blast. Now, if you'll excuse me, I'm off to the Rothsteins. They're going for a big blow-out. Ten entertainment facilitators and a full reenactment of the highlights from three Broadway shows: *A Chorus Line, Chicago*, and *42nd Street*—not to mention the full roster of favors, including tag bracelets from Tiffany's for the young ladies and money clips for the young men. But that's high-end, top-of-the-line stuff—he's in sporting goods." Doctors were obviously very low on the totem pole with bar mitzvah motivators these days. "But each event," he qualified, "is special, no matter what the size. You're going to love every minute of it, believe me."

Chapter Twenty-six

*H*al *sat* WITH JESSIE IN A CORNER BOOTH OF PONZIO'S, A Cherry Hill diner where everyone in the area, from mob bosses to politicians to members of the Hadassah Sisterhood, met for lunch. Ponzio's was located at the epicenter of Cherry Hill on the Ellisburg Circle. The Circle itself had long disappeared, redesigned to allow for less treacherous traversing, but the name remained out of sentimental affection for that deadly South Jersey traffic pattern.

Hal arranged the lunch without Carla's knowledge, calling at a time during midday when he figured Jessie would be alone. He knew that if Carla answered she would try to dissuade him from talking with her mother. Not that he didn't think that Jessie would tell her daughters about their appointment. He was in fact expecting an annoyed call from Carla or an angrier one from Margot complaining that it was a bad idea to encourage their mother in her delusions. He had already prepared a response to them: "Your mother is a grown person," he heard himself saying. "Okay, she's not exactly of sound mind, but she's not helpless or incoherent either. I just want to get the full story." Truth be told, he was hoping that Margot, in particular, would call; he would have liked to hear her voice.

But no call had come. This led Hal to believe that Jessie, aware of her daughters' views, had not mentioned anything about the meeting—a degree of foresight that led him to the conclusion that, as with Hamlet, "Though this be madness, yet there is method in't."

It happened that on Tuesdays and Thursdays Carla helped Mark in the office, not only with the HMO paperwork but with the media calls that were now pouring in as a result of his *Courier Post* column and *Action News* appearance. (Yvette, the Drexel co-op student, had to go back to school, so Carla had taken over the outreach effort.)

This left Jessie on her own. Usually, when she wasn't engaged in household chores like cooking and cleaning, she liked to cruise the malls and do some serious bargain shopping—and Cherry Hill is a mecca for the bargain hunter. Although most of the area's residents make a comfortable living, they see buying at full price as a kind of moral backsliding, like sleeping past noon or eating a whole container of Ben & Jerry's ice cream. It happens, but one feels bad about it afterward.

Jessie was no exception in this regard. She greatly appreciated the cornucopia of discount stores and factory outlets. She took pains to comparative shop, even among the various bargain stores themselves, and felt that to discover a pillow that was two dollars cheaper at Marshalls than at T. J. Maxx was an achievement to be proud of. Her skills as a bargain hunter were all part of the package that Milt Kaplan had found so captivating: a beautiful woman who cooked and cleaned like a dream, and who also shopped so as to save her husband money. Such a thing was unheard of—"as a rare as a snowstorm in July," Milt liked to say, "but there's my Jessie, making snowballs in a sundress."

In short, Jessie's shopping habits meant that if Carla called from Mark's office and found that no one was home, she would assume that her mother was traipsing through the malls, looking for markdowns. She would have no reason to suspect a more covert errand.

After Hal greeted Jessie in the reception area of Ponzio's, he asked the hostess to seat them in one of the smaller rooms in the back. They were led to the Barclay Room, where, though it was lunchtime and the place was buzzing, they could still find a relatively quiet spot in the corner. Ponzio's was spacious enough that privacy was possible, even though everyone went there.

The diner was also noteworthy for its staff of competent, mature waitresses—a far cry from the inept high-school girls who staffed Friendly's. Ponzio waitresses were always on hand, lounging near the coffee urns, prepared to saunter over at the slightest gesture and call you "sweetie" or "hon." Hal had barely crooked a finger when one appeared at his elbow.

Jessie ordered the chopped Greek salad, a Ponzio's specialty, and Hal, a Reuben sandwich. After scratching a few marks on a pad, the waitress sashayed off, only to sashay back, a few minutes later, with their order. The rapidity of service at Ponzio's was another mystery. Given the size of the place and the extent of the menu, no one could fathom how the food could be prepared so quickly.

"Now," said Hal, addressing Jessie with gentle seriousness, "you have certainly piqued my interest, and I'd like to hear more. I have an hour before I have to get back for my sixth-period class, and I wonder if you could answer some questions."

Jessie said that this would be fine, but he should eat his Reuben before it got cold.

Hal took a bite from his sandwich, then extracted a pad and pencil from his pocket and prepared to take notes. "First, if you could tell me about the kind of life you led in Venice during that other time . . . Where you lived in the city, for example, might be a good place to start."

"We all lived in one area," said Jessie. "Crowded in. It was a tight fit."

"The Jews, you're talking about," clarified Hal. He'd been

reading up on the subject and had learned that during the Renaissance, Jews in Venice had been segregated to one part of the city—an island of its own, itself divided into two areas. "From what I read," he explained to Jessie, "the Old Ghetto, also known as the Getto Vecchio, was settled later than the New Ghetto, but was called the Old Ghetto because it was located near an old foundry—*getto*, its seems, means 'foundry' in Italian."

"So what?" said Jessie impatiently.

"Okay, okay. My question is, were you in the Old Ghetto or the New?"

"The Old," Jessie responded without hesitation. "The riffraff Ashkenazim were in the New. We were Sephardim—more high-class. From Spain by way of the Levant."

"I see," said Hal, jotting this down. "Your family left Spain for the Ottoman Empire before settling in Venice?"

"Yes. In Spain, they made Father's family say they'd give up being Jews—that's why they left. The Church had gotten so they couldn't take a breath."

"The Inquisition: forced conversion, torture, burning at the stake for heresy?"

"All that—and more."

"So your family were Marranos, secret Jews?"

"Yes, but they stopped being secret when they came to the Levant. The Turks didn't care—what did they know from the Church? You see, Jews and Arabs got along back then. They were both being pushed around, so they decided, why not get together and make like a partnership? The Christians would have to treat us right if they wanted to get their ships through. And that's how Poppa became such a big *macher*. The doge needed him to make the negotiations with the Turks and work out the trade routes to the East."

"So he made his money from foreign trade negotiations, not by loaning at interest to individuals?"

"That's right. He lent money mostly as a favor. Three percent or less, he charged. It was the German and Italian Jews in the New Ghetto who charged more. Not that they had a choice. They didn't have connections like we did. It was their living."

"But you were all confined to one area—the two ghettos surrounded by the canals?"

"Yes, there was only one entrance and it was guarded by Christians. They used to lock up the gates to our part of town at night. I don't know where they were afraid we would go. But it didn't really mean anything to us. We paid the guards and did what we pleased. It was crowded, I grant you—everything on top of everything, six stories or more to the buildings. But we didn't mind so much; it was snug, that's all. There were plenty of synagogues and other things too: bookstores and *salonieri*, which were like our book clubs today; doctors and dentists to beat the band. A music school, very well thought of, even the gentiles came for lessons. And the shops—you name it, we had it. Jews weren't allowed to make things but we could sell them. *Strazzaria-shmatta* stores, it meant—but high-quality merchandise. Also very popular with the gentiles. They came to shop or get a tooth pulled, maybe. For gambling too; that was very big."

"They had gambling in the ghetto?"

"Sure. They used to come from all over, a regular Atlantic City. When they ran out of money, they came to Poppa for a loan. They knew he was generous and wouldn't take advantage."

"It sounds like maybe your father shared more qualities with Antonio in *The Merchant of Venice* than with Shylock. Antonio was the character who lent the young man money in the play and from whom Shylock wanted to take his pound of flesh. He was supposed to be prosperous, generous, a good businessman, and a good friend."

"I suppose," said Jessie doubtfully. "But he was a gentile; Shylock was a Jew."

"Yes, but authors sometimes spread qualities around among

different characters. It could be that Shakespeare put some of your father into Antonio, even though the character was a gentile, and some of himself into Shylock, even though Shylock was a Jew. Maybe he felt cheated out of his bond—his right to you—and wanted to seek revenge on your father, the way Shylock wanted revenge on Antonio."

Jessie ruminated on this for a moment. "It's a thought," she said, "but I don't buy it."

"All right," continued Hal, taking another tack. "What about your mother? You haven't mentioned her. What was she like?"

"My mother died of typhoid when I was four. It was common to die young then, especially the women—some died of typhoid, some in childbirth, some from other things we didn't even have names for. I barely remember her. As far as I knew, it was always Poppa and me. I ruled the roost. Nothing like the way it was made out in the play."

Hal nodded. "So you and your father lived alone. What was your relationship to the rest of the community?"

"We were looked up to. Poppa was rich and had connections. We mixed mostly with the wealthiest families and of course with the rebbe. The rebbe's son was a nice boy—they were going to send him to Padua to train in medicine, but later he decided he'd follow in his father's footsteps and be a rebbe, too. His name was Leon Modena—maybe you heard of him? He became chief rabbi and had a big reputation for new ideas. He married my girlfriend Rivkah, though it was me he really liked. That's what set Will off the first time."

"He was jealous of the rabbi's son?"

"Yes, he saw me walking with Leon in the Campiello and he assumed . . . that's where the nasty sonnets came from. Later he wrote the others to make up for them."

"The others?"

"I told you he wrote more to the lady than what you said."

"More than the twenty-seven we have?"

"Way more than that. It was more like a hundred and twenty-seven."

Hal scribbled in the pad. "You mean as many as to the young man?"

"At least as many. As I said, the young man was just a concoction."

"A conceit?"

"Whatever. It was to make me jealous. And for spite."

"I see," said Hal. "But let's backtrack. You haven't explained how you and—Will—met. I would have thought that as a woman and a Jew, you wouldn't have had much opportunity to meet new people, no less famous London playwrights."

"You would think so, but you'd be wrong. Not having a mother was part of it. And of course Poppa being such a big *macher* and so fond of me, he let me do whatever I wanted and no one said anything. Let's face it; I was spoiled. Like Margot." She gave Hal a knowing look. "What did you think of Margot? Have you asked her out on a date yet?"

"She seemed like a nice woman," replied Hal, wincing slightly, "but no, I haven't asked her out."

"She's not so nice," said Jessie, "but you should. She's an interesting girl and very sharp. She'd liven things up for you, and you might help make her nicer."

"That's very thoughtful of you to say," said Hal brusquely, "but if you don't mind, let's get back to your story."

"Okay, okay. So I met Will one day when he came to the house with Kit Marlowe and one of their friends who'd gambled away his money and wanted Poppa to give him a loan. Kit had been by before and we knew his story. He was a *feigeleh*, but talented, and had to leave England owing to some sort of political *mishegoss*. Poppa took him under his wing, lent him money, introduced him to people. Kit was educated but an outsider too, like us, so we could relate. Poppa liked to argue with him the way he did with the rebbe: 'Is the Bible true or made up?' 'Why did God do this and not that?

'Who knows even if there is a God?'—that kind of thing. Then Kit started bringing his friends. Some wanted to borrow money, some wanted to look at me."

"So you were an attraction?"

"I was nice to look at, yes," said Jessie frankly. "I looked like Margot, but not as sharp-tongued. So everyone liked me."

Hal nodded.

"So, like I said, one day they brought Will along. He'd just come in from London to meet with Kit about the plays. Kit was better educated and Will had him add some touches to make them more high-class. In those days, you had to appeal to high and low together. Very demanding. So Kit would add a fancy word here, a quotation there, some Latin maybe, and Will would give him a little money and take him to dinner. So one day, one of their friends had some bad luck with the dice and they came to Poppa for help, and maybe to show me off—they knew Will had an eye for the ladies. I was crossing to the rebbe's house as they came and they stopped me and said, 'This is our friend Will, just come from London. Won't you give him a nice smile?' Since when am I stingy with smiles? So I did, and the next thing you know, he was hanging around writing me the sonnets and telling Poppa how we should come to London for the business opportunities."

"Did you go to London?"

"A few trips. I was already fluent in English—Poppa had had in tutors. And when we went, I even made some friends with the women there. They gave me their recipes and some pointers on how to dress. Will was very much the gentleman—took us to all the fancy places and to see a play he'd written about two families that hated each other."

"*Romeo and Juliet?*"

"Yes. Stephanie did a beautiful job with that scene on the balcony. But who needs so much fighting? Like the Feldsteins and the Cutlers in Vineland: Rhona Feldstein fell for Michael Cutler, and her father said he'd kill them both if she didn't break off with that lousy nogoodnik whose father had dented his Lincoln. Well, they eloped and of course the family got over it. Once the grandchild came, it was water under the bridge. Will's play didn't end so happy, which was a mistake, if you ask me. I told him, 'People don't want the children dying; it's gloomy.' At first he was offended, but later he said I had a point. So there you have it; we fell in love."

"And your father didn't mind?"

"He did. He said, 'The man's a fine man, a genius even, but you can't like a nice Jewish boy, the rebbe's son, he's crazy for you? Take him; leave this playwright alone.' So I tried to take his advice. Went out with Leon a few times. It didn't take. But Will heard and so he wrote the nasty sonnets and the concoctions to the young man."

"And then?"

"We got back together. Poppa said, 'Okay, if it's what you want. Maybe we can get him to convert.' Will, you see, claimed he had some Jewish blood on his mother's side, way back. It might have been made up, who knows? Making things up was his profession. But it played well with Poppa. 'A little Jewish blood goes a long way,' he liked to say."

"Hmm," said Hal. "I've heard stories that Shakespeare had Jewish blood—but then again, there are stories that everyone has Jewish blood."

"That's true," admitted Jessie.

"Though it would help my theory about his putting himself into the Shylock character," noted Hal.

"But Shylock was very Jewish, not just a little," objected Jessie.

"So then what?" prompted Hal, feeling that they weren't getting anywhere discussing precisely how Jewish Shakespeare might have been.

"And so it went on for a while. We had a good time: I'm happy, he's happy. That's when he wrote the other sonnets, the ones you don't know about. He gave them to me for my birthday. I kept them under the floorboard of my room in a special box. A hundred of them, at least."

"Hmmm," said Hal, "a stash of lost Shakespeare sonnets. . . . Very interesting." He jotted something in his notebook, and they were both silent for a moment.

"And then?" asked Hal, finally breaking the silence.

"And then, I get the letter from the Stratford woman. Said how she was his wife, married him years ago, three children, one died. Called me a 'Hebrew harridan'—that was the phrase. I remember because it had a ring to it."

"You felt lied to, betrayed?"

"Yes," murmured Jessie, seeming for a moment to drift off. "And to think of Saul Millman kissing that girl," she remarked, out of the blue.

"What?" said Hal. "Saul who?"

"No, no," said Jessie, shaking herself, "it's Will I'm talking about. He'd been married to that woman and never told me. Hathaway, her name was—the English had names like that. They sound made up, but they're real. Her letter came as a shock, as you can imagine."

"And what then?"

"I broke off, what do you think—I'm going to be with a married man? A gentile was bad enough, but married with kids?" Jessie had grown agitated. "What do you take me for?"

"No, no," said Hal, trying to calm her. "I understand."

"That's when he wrote the play smearing Poppa and me. I know it was because he was hurt and wanted to get back—but still, it was a low blow. I never spoke to him again."

"He tried to get back together?"

"He tried. He had Kit Marlowe come by with some sort of *fachochta* story: it wasn't us, just a coincidence, happens all the time, like his play, *The Jew of Malta*." She paused here to explain: "That was a play Kit wrote about a nasty Jew and his daughter—he told

Poppa when they first met that it wasn't so much against Jews as we might think and that besides, he wrote it before he met us. We gave him the benefit of the doubt."

Hal nodded, obviously familiar with *The Jew of Malta*.

"Anyway," continued Jessie, "Kit said that Will was just stealing from his play: 'Just because he never went to Cambridge, he thinks he has to write everybody else's plays better,' Kit said. 'Don't take it so personal; it's not about you. I'm the one should be insulted.' But he couldn't convince me. I knew what it was about. It was smearing Poppa and me out of spite."

"And that was the end?"

"Oh, I heard through the grapevine how he felt bad and added that speech for the Jew, which they said was a great thing for the time. It was a good speech, I grant you, but it didn't cancel the rest."

"So you kept track of him? You watched his career?"

"I kept abreast. We went to London again a few times for Poppa's business, and I made a point to slip away to see the plays. I knew what he was saying in them. The one in Denmark with the Jewish characters—that was spite again. My cousin Golda's husband was Guildenstern, and Poppa's partner was Rosencrantz. In the play, they betrayed the hero, didn't they, and he had them killed? Just another way of getting back. Guildenstern was a very nice man; traded in fine fabrics. We used to visit sometimes on Sunday afternoon. . . ."

"To get back," said Hal.

"Oh, yes, as I said—eventually he softened. Had enough with the spite. Wanted to make peace. In the one with the black man: He shows how you can get carried away and how being an outsider makes for problems."

"*Othello.*"

"And the plays he wrote at the end were his way of saying: 'I'm sorry, I wish I'd done different.'"

"The late romances: plots of contrition and reconciliation."

"The girl on the island, that was his picture of me from another angle. Poppa was the magician and Will was the wild animal that tried to take advantage. And the other one, with the jealous king who kills his wife and then has her come back to life—that was saying he was sorry for being jealous and wishing there was a second chance."

"*The Tempest* and *The Winter's Tale*." Hal nodded.

"He wrote me kind letters then. He was, when all was said and done, a decent man. It just wasn't meant to be between us. Who knows, but maybe I served him better by having broken off. He could make with me whatever he wanted."

Hal nodded. "You were his Dark Lady, his muse: Jessica, betrayer of her father; Miranda, loyal to her father."

"Yes—but always underneath it was the Jewish girl from Venice." Jessie wiped her eyes with the corner of her napkin. She looked across at Hal and then down at his plate. "What's the matter," she said, pointing to his sandwich, "you don't like your Reuben?"

Chapter Twenty-seven

*I*t *gradually* DAWNED ON CARLA THAT THE BAT MITZVAH WAS meant to exist in two kinds of time: real time, which was fleeting and unpredictable, and recorded time, which was fixed and eternal. The whole point in hiring a photographer and a videographer was to embalm the thing in the process of its taking place—a strange, even morbid paradox that she tried not to dwell upon too closely.

She had originally thought of asking an orderly at Mark's hospital, known to be good with a digital camera, to take the photographs, and have some of the cousins pass around the family's camcorder for the video. But that idea had been nixed by her friend Jill.

"You can't have just anyone do the photography and video," said Jill. "You're going to have this forever. Stephanie will want to show it to her children and grandchildren." (The words *forever, children,* and *grandchildren* seemed to crop up again and again in the planning of the bat mitzvah).

When it was put that way, Carla felt obliged to consider the professional options available.

For the photographer, two candidates appeared to dominate the field. One was a middle-aged man who had been doing Cherry

Hill bar mitzvahs for a hundred years and who took photos in the conventional mode (Grandma crying with pride while hugging embarrassed bat mitzvah girl; bar mitzvah boy sloppily cutting cake under mother's distressed eye; friends of bar mitzvah boy, grinning malevolently, holding him aloft in a chair, etc., etc.). This photographer's work was predictable, but predictable had its merits. Besides, he was known to be a genius with an airbrush. A couple of women at the JCC, no beauties, had praised him for making them look stunning.

The other candidate had a smaller but more vocal following, including the support of Jill Rosenberg, known to favor the cutting edge. This photographer was a young girl just out of Bennington College, a small and agile creature who could slip into nooks and crannies without being seen. Her photos were less polished than those of the veteran photographer, but they had the virtue of originality and candor. According to her supporters, she was adept at capturing moments that "summed up the essence of the event." Typical was the photograph in Jill's album that showed her, arm lifted in admonishing gesture, mouth open, as an implacable Josh sat slumped in a chair. "I look at that photograph," said Jill, "and everything comes back." Carla had perused Jill's album (which included a shot of herself and Mark staring straight at the camera as if hit by a stun gun, a piece of bar mitzvah cake still clinging to the side of Mark's mouth), agreed that the young photographer was enormously gifted (her work resembling that of the famed, if also famously troubled, Diane Arbus), and quickly decided to go with the boring, middle-aged photographer.

With the videographer the choice had been simpler. In this area, there was only one name that could be considered—everyone said so: the Steven Spielberg of bar mitzvah video, Cass Sunshine. Sunshine, originally Charlie Sunberg, had graduated from Cherry Hill East High School fifteen years ago and enrolled in the USC film program in the hope of cracking the Hollywood nut. Finding that nut harder to crack than expected, he returned home with the more modest ambition of cracking the Cherry Hill nut. Here he was successful with a vengeance. He had, as the saying goes, turned bar mitzvah videography on its head.

To begin with, in order to make the service in the synagogue interesting, he had hit on a brilliant technique: the reaction shot.

"The reaction shot," he explained to his clients, who liked being on the inside of the cinematic process, "is the key to pulling you through the service. Usually, they show you the kid up there droning away: *Baruch ata Adonoi*, blah, blah, blah. What a drag!" (It was understood that Cass was woefully detached from his Jewish roots and had no interest in the bar mitzvah as such, but this was vaguely seen to be a mark in his favor. It demonstrated his devotion to "pure cinema.") He continued, "You have to liven it up, show there's somebody out there—maybe listening, maybe not—who cares? You need visuals, not just the kid—*snore*."

Cass had brought along a shopping bag full of tapes to demonstrate, and Carla realized how wise she had been to schedule the visit for the afternoon, when Mark was at the office. Her husband might have lacked patience with the Steven Spielberg of bar mitzvah video, whose artistic tendencies, it was said, needed to be indulged if he was to do right by an affair.

Eager to show Carla the livening effects of the reaction shot, Cass pulled out a tape and cued to an appropriate spot. A bar mitzvah boy was shown droning for a second or two, then the camera panned to the congregation, revealing a series of interesting vignettes—a mother fiercely chastising an unruly child; an uncle asleep, mouth open, yarmulke askew; a line of gentile faces, glazed with incomprehension, trying not to register any response for fear it might be the wrong one.

"You get the idea," Cass drawled, popping the tape out of the VCR. "We show you what's really going on. It lightens the mood, gives you some visual interest, not just the kid with his *Baruch ata Adonai*."

Carla had wanted to ask whether Cass had to get permissions

from the congregants so indecorously represented, but he had already moved on to a more crucial part of the video: the party following the service—which is to say, the meat of the event. He now handed Carla a card that resembled a menu in one of those restaurants where sandwiches are named for famous people or places. In this case, the listings were of great movies in the cinematic tradition that could serve as stylistic models in filming the bat mitzvah.

The Godfather:

A festive but magisterial record of your event. Maintains a sense of family dignity and holds to old-fashioned notions of decorum and prescribed liveliness.

The Fiddler on the Roof:

A boisterous rendering. Makes much of the Jewish elements of your event, focusing on tradition and on the charm of the elderly and the very young. Note: A *Fiddler* video often works best with a klezmer band.

The Annie Hall:

A whimsical approach that chooses one character, say Uncle Phil, who has a big mouth or tells a lot of jokes, and weaves his comments throughout. Adds continuity and humor to the record of the event.

The Nashville:

A stylish montage effect. Lots of cross-cutting between, say, Grandma dancing the hora and Aunt Jennie flirting with the bartender. Makes for interest and originality.

Cass had hit on the idea of cinematic models when he returned to Cherry Hill after his hiatus on the West Coast and toured some of the new housing developments that had sprung up in his absence. It was the era of semicustom homes that were being marketed according to celebrated edifices or styles in the architectural tradition: the Sienna, the Fontainebleau, the Blenheim, etc. He realized that he might do the same semicustom marketing with the great cinematic tradition.

Cass showed Carla snippets of the sample tapes for each of the stylistic options, taking time to explain the techniques involved. After viewing the tapes, her conclusion was that the *Godfather* style was most in keeping with their family's sensibility.

"*Godfather*'s classy," pronounced Cass approvingly. "Go for it."

"But we are having a klezmer band," Carla noted, glancing at the menu that associated klezmer with the *Fiddler on the Roof* option.

"No problem," said Cass. "We can customize and do a *Godfather* with *Fiddler* overtones."

Carla said she'd consider this suggestion—along with the price tag (which approached that of a modest independent feature film)—and get back to him.

Chapter Twenty-eight

*A*fter *Cass* LEFT, CARLA PREPARED TO RUN OVER TO THE geriatric center, where she wanted to discuss the videographer's options with Mr. O'Hare.

O'Hare's knowledge of the mechanics of the bat mitzvah had become veritably encyclopedic in the past few weeks. He now had definite opinions on such things as the timing between the dancing of the hora and the serving of the matzo ball soup, not to mention the niceties of whether Mark's father, Charles Goodman, should perform the *Motzi* alone, or whether a male relative from the Kaplan side should perhaps be brought in as well, to balance things out. "Families can get testy that way," said O'Hare. "What about that Uncle Sid you mentioned? Is he mobile? Does he have his faculties? Maybe he might do the wine prayer in a pinch."

Carla agreed that there was wisdom in this advice. Perhaps, she said, O'Hare might want to consider a career in bar mitzvah planning; he seemed to have a flair for it.

Before she left for the geriatric center, however, Carla went to check on her mother. Jessie had not been puttering around the kitchen or straightening up the den, which was her usual occupation at this hour, and Carla wondered if perhaps she was feeling under the weather and had gone upstairs to lie down. She found

Jessie in her bedroom, not napping but watching a videotape on the small TV on her night table. This was strange, since Carla didn't recall having rented anything in the past week.

"What are you watching, Mom?" she asked curiously. The tape was clearly not one of the musicals or '40s melodramas that her mother tended to favor.

"It's a tape of *The Merchant of Venice*," said Jessie in a rather supercilious tone, "with that famous English actor, what's his name?—I think he's dead now."

"Laurence Olivier?" Carla glanced at the screen, where Olivier was indeed recognizable in a frock coat talking to two other men in frock coats in what was unmistakably Shakespearean language.

"It was made for English television," Jessie explained. "They have higher-class taste over there."

"I see," said Carla, unused to being lectured by her mother on British taste.

"This one is set in a different period," continued Jessie. "You see the costumes aren't what you'd expect." She gestured to the frock coats. "But it's the play all the same. And I have to admit that this what's-his-name does a lot with the Jewish moneylender part. I don't like the daughter, though—but then I'm prejudiced."

Carla, ignoring this critical evaluation, asked, "Where, might I ask, did you get this copy of *The Merchant of Venice*?"

"Oh"—Jessie faltered a moment—"from the new video store up the way." (In point of fact, Hal had gotten the tape for her from the new video store, and she planned to return it to him at their lunch tomorrow.)

"Are you telling me you drove all the way down Route 73 to that new store, Videos Unlimited?" Carla knew that Jessie was a fearful driver, not inclined to venture anywhere that she hadn't been before.

"And why not?" said Jessie, growing huffy. "I'm not helpless, you know."

"Okay, okay," said Carla, assuming that her mother's imagined fling with Shakespeare had emboldened her as a driver. "My mistake. I just thought you didn't like to drive out that far, that's all."

"Shh!" said Jessie suddenly. "This is the part I wanted to hear."

It was Shylock embarking on the famous speech that explained why he was seeking revenge against the Christian who owed him money. Carla and Jessie sat without speaking as Olivier took flight, the lines rendering him at once noble and pitiful.

"'Hath not a Jew eyes?'" intoned Olivier, his voice rising to an epic lament. "'Hath not a Jew hands, organs, dimensions, senses, affections, passions?—fed with the same food, hurt with the same weapons, subject to the same diseases, healed by the same means, warmed and cooled by the same winter and summer as a Christian is? If you prick us, do we not bleed? If you tickle us, do we not laugh? If you poison us, do we not die? And if you wrong us, shall we not revenge? If we are like you in the rest, we will resemble you in that. If a Jew wrong a Christian, what is his humility? Revenge. If a Christian wrong a Jew, what should his sufferance be by Christian example? Why, revenge. The villainy you teach me I will execute, and it shall go hard but I will better the instruction.'"

"Powerful," murmured Carla.

"Yes," sighed Jessie, turning off the TV and standing up, "he did himself credit there. The rest—fch!—but that speech was something. But enough with the Shakespeare already," she pronounced, to Carla's relief. "It's time I started dinner."

Chapter Twenty-nine

This is AMAZING STUFF!"

Hal Pearson was sitting in a corner of the roof dining room at the Yale Club in New York City with his old college friend Anish Patel. Anish had been Hal's roommate at Yale and was now an assistant professor of English there. His exclamation was in response to a paper Hal had e-mailed him the night before.

In the context of contemporary academic life, Anish was an odd bird. He was a literary conservative at a time when most rising academics were liberals, and an ethnic minority who not only didn't champion contemporary ethnic literature but believed that the literary canon effectively ended with Dr. Johnson.

Anish could buck the multicultural trend because his background placed him technically out of bounds. Born into the lower castes of Indian society in one of the poorest neighborhoods in Calcutta, he had applied himself to his studies with a tenacity and vigor that had earned him scholarships to Andover and Yale. In the end, despite being the descendent of a people who had suffered the yoke of imperialist oppression, he had become a rabid Anglophile—in Hal's words, "more jingoist than Kipling."

"Personally, I don't care what the politically correct types think," Anish often declared to Hal, "I like the great old books and I don't take their authors to task for prejudices and limitations they had no way of recognizing. I'm fed up with you guys who insist that the geniuses of the past should share your enlightened views. You conveniently ignore the fact that it takes time—and great writing—to prepare the way for enlightened views."

As Anish's words suggested, Hal's tastes in literature and in politics were more ecumenical than his friend's, and they often became embroiled in heated debates in which Hal argued that a particular author (say, James Joyce, Gertrude Stein, or Vladimir Nabokov—not to mention Philip Roth or Toni Morrison) belonged in the pantheon of literary greats, while Anish argued that said author was an overhyped piece of garbage. What they shared, however—and what kept the friendship strong—was a mutual devotion to Shakespeare. They never quarreled about that, and it was the reason why they were meeting at the Yale Club today.

Anish was thumbing excitedly through the sheaf of pages that Hal had e-mailed him. The two men had often shared ideas during college and graduate school, though they had ultimately taken different career paths. Anish had accepted a professorial position at Yale, while Hal had gone on to teach the great unwashed—i.e., the middle-schoolers of Cherry Hill, New Jersey. Anish said he didn't understand Hal's choice. He had seen dirt and ignorance enough in Calcutta, and couldn't imagine wanting to see more of it in the New Jersey suburbs. He was pleased to have a wood-paneled office, a few prissy graduate students to advise, and plenty of time to peruse the quartos and folios of his beloved bard in Yale's Beinecke Library. Hal, for his part, said he didn't care about wood paneling. He wanted to bring Shakespeare "to the people"— and Cherry Hill middle-schoolers seemed as good a sample of that group as you were likely to find anywhere. Besides, he happened to be one of those rare adults who liked kids. He thought they were amusing and interesting—something that Anish found impossible to comprehend.

But in the present instance, such differences were forgotten.

Anish was excitedly turning over the pages in his hands while Hal looked on with pleasure.

"It's amazing!" Anish exclaimed again. "It'll turn Shakespeare scholarship on its head. The journal will never hear the end of it."

"The journal" was the *Shakespeare Biannual Review*, an academic journal that no one read but that was highly respected in certain circles, albeit very small ones. Anish was its editor.

"The idea that we can trace Jessica's betrayal of her father in *The Merchant of Venice* to a real woman of Hebrew persuasion who rejected Shakespeare's advances sheds light on the entire development of his career," Anish continued enthusiastically. "It makes *The Merchant*, as you say"—he flipped through the article and read from one of the pages—"'a nodal point in the canon, from which the other plays spring rather in the manner of a theme and variations.' All Shakespeare scholarship will have to be revised in the face of it." (In making his case, Hal had adopted the academic tone of the world he had left behind.)

"It *is* good, isn't it?" agreed Hal exultantly. The more he had mulled over Jessie's story, the more interesting and exciting the implications seemed to be.

"It's sensational! Altogether without precedent!" Anish exclaimed, then paused and gave his friend a penetrating look. "I assume you have sources to support your ideas?" His voice had suddenly taken on a concerned note. "You didn't just make the whole thing up, did you? If you did, it's an impressive leap of imagination, I grant you, but no use to us."

"No," said Hal slowly. "I didn't make it up. But the source is unorthodox."

"Unorthodox is all right," said Anish hopefully. "We're none of us High Church here, are we?"

"I should say not," said Hal. "You're Hindu and I'm a Methodist, which leaves Church of England more or less beside the point."

"Not that there's anything wrong with the Church of England,"

Anish noted. "But I assume some sort of evidence stands behind this."

"As a matter of fact," said Hal tentatively, "the source hardly counts as a source at all."

Anish frowned more deeply. "A source that is not a source—sounds mysterious."

"Yes," admitted Hal, "I suppose it is."

"Don't tell me you are going to present me with three caskets and ask me to solve riddles in the manner of poor Portia's lover. I could never understand what Shakespeare saw in that selfish bastard Bassanio—"

"And now you know why," Hal jumped in enthusiastically. "Shakespeare created him to get back at his beloved and her father, Jews who had turned their backs on him. It was Bassanio, as I argue"—he pointed to his paper—"who was Shakespeare's own alter-ego—a figure of self-loathing thinly disguised as a leading man. Not that elements of Shakespeare aren't present in the character of Shylock as well, as I explain here on page nine."

"Yes, yes, very ingenious," said Anish impatiently. "The characters are predictably overdetermined, all stemming from the traumatic rejection by the Jewish woman—that's clear enough. But how do you come by it—that's the question?"

"I'd rather hold off on any further explanation," said Hal in a tone Anish knew meant the case was closed. "I'm not sure I'm in a position to reveal my source—and you'd probably be inclined to discount it anyway. The point is whether the theory makes sense."

"It holds together wonderfully," said Anish, "but without hard evidence, what's the point? You might as well write a novel. I realize that for many in our field the distinction is inconsequential. They write theories and say they're as good as facts, then they hogtie the facts and make them serve the theories. Their rationale: Since we can't know anything for certain, who cares what the particular proportion of truth to fiction happens to be? But we at *Shakespeare Biannual* hold to that unfashionable thing known as truth. Which is only to say, we don't publish anything without footnotes."

"I know that," said Hal. "I hope in time to collect the evidence and provide you with the footnotes you need."

"That's what I like to hear," said Anish, appearing to relax and smiling fondly at his friend. "Add the footnotes to this"—he slapped the paper with his hand—"and you make an invaluable contribution to Shakespeare studies and a name for yourself."

"I'm not interested in making a name for myself." Hal shrugged. "But I do want to follow this thing through as far as I can."

"Of course you do. You are pursuing important scholarship here that is bound to make a difference—"

"Let me clarify," said Hal, interrupting his friend. "The thesis I gave you is not the result of laborious research. It was more or less handed to me."

"An elaborate theory about Shakespeare's Dark Lady simply fell in your lap?"

"In a manner of speaking, yes."

"Curiouser and curiouser."

"As you said, the difficulty now lies in the proof."

"But you believe the proof can be had?"

"I do."

"Am I to assume from what you have written here that it involves a visit to Venice?"

"You are correct."

"And the unearthing of the lost sonnets to the Dark Lady?"

"Yes."

"And you have some idea where they can be located?"

"Not I, but my source may be able to locate them."

"A source that is not a source?"

"Correct again."

"Perhaps I can be of help." Anish considered. "I have access to a substantial grant for locating and studying old manuscripts. It's the sort of thing they give out freely at Yale. Money, you know, flows copiously here; you have only to stand still and allow the waters to lap over you. I suppose it would be nice to divert the tide to my poor cousins in Calcutta"—he paused to consider this novel idea for a moment, then gave it up—"but these are literary funds, you know, not intended for humanitarian purposes. Such things must be kept distinct or we might as well all run off and join the Peace Corps. But we can certainly use the money for your project, which fits the grant outline to the letter."

"Absolutely!" exclaimed Hal. "A grant for locating and studying rare manuscripts sounds like just what we need!"

"I'll get on to it tomorrow and take care of the paperwork and logistics," said Anish. "We can travel during your winter break when I'm between semesters. Meanwhile, arrange things on your end. Hopefully, all of us—your dubious source included—can be off to Venice in December."

Chapter Thirty

*C*arla and MARK SAT AT THEIR KITCHEN TABLE SHARING A bottle of wine. It was an uncharacteristic event. Mark's drink of preference was scotch, and Carla normally avoided alcohol on two counts: the undeclared premise of her Jewish upbringing that one drink would lead inexorably to alcoholism and Skid Row, and the practical fact that she never knew when she might have to pick Stephanie up from a late field hockey practice or run out for a bottle of Kaopectate for Jeffrey's upset stomach.

Today, however, marked an exception. She was celebrating the transformation of Mark Goodman from a miserable schlepper into a happy and prosperous physician.

Mark's PR efforts had been a success, yielding a considerable increase in patient volume. This new clientele was apparently drawn by the idea that a doctor who could write an essay and appear on TV with a good haircut must have a way with a scoping device. Mark had been inspired by this success to take a more proactive approach to the practice (in Yvette's communications parlance). He had replaced the old office computer with a new top-of-the-line system. He had also hosted a seminar at the local JCC, part of a potential series, on the stress factors behind many gastric disturbances.

But a major improvement had come once again via Carla, who had taken to surfing the Web on the subject of medical office management. One of the sites she discovered contained a detailed analysis of the CTB and E&M codes, the rubrics by which doctors identified what they'd done when submitting reimbursement requests to insurance companies and Medicare. Carla pointed out the site to Mark, who, after a few days studying the codes as they applied to gastroenterology, was shocked to find how often he failed to bill for legitimate work.

"I've simply been a dope," he declared, pleased to acknowledge his former imbecility now that it had been rectified. "I've been sloppy about learning the codes and taking advantage of them. It's like a restaurant charging for a meal that includes only the price of the main course but not the appetizer and the dessert. That's cheating yourself—and that's what I've been doing. It's a case of knowing the system and not being screwed by it."

"Great!" said Carla, relieved to think they were no longer being screwed by the system. She took a sip from her glass of white Zinfandel and beamed across the table at her husband.

"By the way," said Mark sheepishly, reaching into his pocket and taking out a small box with the name of a notable Cherry Hill jeweler emblazoned on the front. "I have something for you. A token of my appreciation and love," he said in tones that were mocking and serious at the same time.

Mark knew it was customary for the husband to give the wife a "nice piece of jewelry" on the occasion of the child's bar mitzvah. He vaguely remembered his father giving his mother such an ornament on the occasion of his own, twenty-five years ago. It embarrassed him to think that he was doing what his father had done—especially given his skepticism in matters of religious custom. But somehow, when it came down to it, he wanted to do the customary thing—an inclination that might help explain why things became customary in the first place.

Carla opened the box. Inside was a bracelet with a little heart dangling from it, with a diamond at its center. The diamond was not large, but it was quite sparkly.

"Do you like it?" asked Mark a bit anxiously. He knew that his wife was not one for expensive jewelry and was prone to say that a cubic zirconia was as good as a diamond.

"Like it? I love it!" exclaimed Carla. She suddenly found there was a discernible difference between a CZ and a diamond—or at least she was determined in this case to think so.

"Let's go out and celebrate," Mark exclaimed—buoyed by the sense that he had done well with the gift. "Let's go into Philly and have dinner. I think we have reason to treat ourselves."

Carla looked up from admiring the bracelet and considered what her husband had said. It was true. Things were going surprisingly well. Not only was Mark's practice humming along, but other family members seemed to be nicely on course.

Jeffrey, off chocolate milk for three weeks, was no longer more obnoxious than any average ten-year-old. He did his homework, was reasonably attentive in class, and had, as Dr. Samuels had promised, more friends. The latter fact had made such an impression on him that he not only stopped whining for chocolate milk but turned against the beverage entirely. The very sight of chocolate now had a violently antithetical effect—like the sight of a cross to a vampire.

Stephanie, too, had become more manageable. Carla had taken Samuels's advice and dropped her daughter off at the King of Prussia Mall to search for a dress. Two weeks ago, the first time this course of action was implemented, a dress was not found but Stephanie did emerge from the mall with a pair of shoes. Carla could only take her daughter's word that her feet, already a size 9, would not continue to grow in the interval between now and the bat mitzvah. (Stephanie had promised they wouldn't, as though she had special powers to prevent this.)

"And what if the shoes don't go with the dress?" Carla had asked. But Stephanie had reassured her that *these* shoes—black

Nine West heels—would go with everything; Stephanie's best friend, Elaine, seconded this.

"And are you sure you can walk in them?" asked Carla. The heels were very high and oddly shaped, giving the appearance of exotic stilts. One wrong step, Carla thought, might result in a serious injury.

"They're just for the service," Stephanie explained reassuringly. "I'll take them off at the party." Carla was reminded that bar mitzvah etiquette dictated that girls immediately shed their high heels as soon as the dancing began. She made a mental note to pick up several dozen pair of sweatsocks at Marshalls. (A basket of socks, to guard against splinters and pneumonia for the unshod girls, had become a bar mitzvah staple.)

Then, a week after the shoes were discovered, came the dress. Carla was sitting in the King of Prussia food court, reading an article on effective feeding techniques for stroke patients, when suddenly Stephanie and Elaine came running toward her.

"I found it!" Stephanie exclaimed, holding up a Bloomingdale's shopping bag. "I found the dress!"

"It's awesome," seconded Elaine. "It's even nicer than Lisa's."

"Come on," said Stephanie modestly. "There's no way it's nicer than Lisa's," she said—her tone suggesting that she really believed otherwise.

"Let's see," said Carla, curious to see the dress that so pleased her exacting daughter and her friend.

Stephanie gently extracted the garment from the bag. Out came the same black dress that Carla had presented for Stephanie's inspection several months earlier.

"What do you think?" asked Stephanie happily. "Don't you love the sleeves?"

Carla agreed that the sleeves were the dress's finest feature, and gave a silent prayer of thanksgiving to Dr. Samuels for his excellent advice.

As for Jessie, Carla believed that Samuels's prediction that the delusions would dissipate was beginning to come to pass. There had been the incident with *The Merchant of Venice* tape, to be sure, but that could actually be viewed as a good sign: It suggested that her mother was detaching from her fantasy life and exploring her interest in Shakespeare in a more realistic way.

"The next thing you know, she'll be off to graduate school to get a Ph.D. in English literature," noted Mark. "Now, there would be a useful outlet for her energy!"

Chapter Thirty-one

Have you TOLD YOUR DAUGHTERS YET?" ASKED HAL. HE and Jessie were seated, as usual, in the Barclay Room of Ponzio's. A hard-bitten waitress named Margie with a red beehive harido had, without bothering to consult them, brought a chopped Greek salad and a Reuben.

"Eat your sandwich," said Jessie, avoiding a response to his question.

"If you won't tell them, I will," said Hal seriously. "We can't keep meeting in secret like this. It's not right."

"Are you afraid for my reputation, maybe?" asked Jessie. "You didn't care so much about it back then."

"Jessie—how many times do I have to tell you that I am not that person? Or if I am, I have no knowledge of it, so you can't make those kinds of statements."

"I know, I know. I'm sorry. It just slipped out."

"Getting back to the point," said Hal. "Would you like me to call Carla and Margot and tell them what we have planned?"

"I'd like you to call Margot."

"Okay," said Hal. "I'll call her tonight."

"And ask her out?"

Hal stiffened slightly; Jessie had hit a nerve. He had wanted to ask Margot out—the thought hadn't left his mind since Jessie's Shabbos dinner. He had even, finally, determined to do so last weekend. But before he had a chance, he actually ran into her by accident.

It was a Thursday evening at the Pennsylvania Academy of Art, which was having one of its exhibitions of student work. He had gone to see the painting of a former student. Many of Hal's former students kept in touch, and his social calendar was crowded with graduation parties, recitals, plays, and sundry other events involving people who had once been members of his seventh-grade class. One former student had even insisted that he attend the premiere of a porn film in which she had landed a role (and where the best that could be said was that the role was small and the porn, soft—though he had duly praised the performance for its "expressiveness").

On this particular day, he had entered the mausoleum-like Academy of Art, climbed the wide stone steps to the main exhibition floor, and been confronted by the sight of Margot Kaplan standing directly in front of him.

She was wearing a red dress, and her copious dark hair was twisted at the back of her head in a loose chignon. She was, he thought, worthy of taking her place beside the women in the John Singer Sargent and William Merritt Chase paintings that were scattered throughout the museum.

She was standing by the side of a tall, thin man in an expensive suit whose hair was brushed straight back in the European style. They were examining a canvas, obviously one of the more experimental pieces of student work, in which the edges had been charred as though rescued from a fire.

Margot, always acutely aware of being looked at, had turned to face Hal almost as soon as he reached the top of the stairs. As he approached, a look of surprise and pleasure flitted across her face. She put out her hand. "If it isn't William Shakespeare," she said.

"Fancy meeting you in a modern picture gallery. Pierre de Villiers, meet—Hal."

"Hal Pearson," said Hal, taking her hand and then, reluctantly, letting it go. He was pleased that she remembered his first name but irritated that she had forgotten his last (or pretended that she had).

Pierre gave Hal a quick glance but did not extend his hand. "You are an artist," he declared, as though he couldn't be bothered with the inflection required for a question.

"No," said Margot, who was examining Hal closely, as though his presence held a certain fascination for her, despite herself. "He's my niece's seventh-grade English teacher."

"Ah!" said Pierre, as if this now rendered Hal completely insignificant, and turned back to the canvas on the wall.

"Pierre's a friend," said Margot vaguely, "and a serious art collector. He wanted to see what our young American artists were up to."

"And what do you think our young American artists are up to?" asked Hal, addressing himself to Pierre's back since Pierre continued to look at the canvas on the wall.

"Not much," said Pierre, still not turning around but making a slight wave with his hand. "Very derivative."

"Pierre collects cutting-edge art," explained Margot. It wasn't clear whether she agreed with his assessment about young American artists or was perhaps apologizing for it. "He's found some wonderful things in Soho."

"I'm sure he has exquisite taste," said Hal. He had begun to grow annoyed at the idea that Margot was in any way attached to this appalling person.

She must have sensed his feeling, because her manner grew more brittle. "As a matter of fact, he has," she declared. "He has one of the most celebrated collections of contemporary art in Paris and lends regularly to the Beaubourg for exhibition."

"Then it must be a great honor to be part of his collection," said Hal, giving her a pointed look. It was not in his nature to be ungallant, but something was pushing him in a dangerous direction.

Hal saw her eyes flash in the way they had at dinner, when they had quarreled—about what he couldn't remember—and he was bracing himself for an acid reply when his student, a waiflike blond named Caroline, who had won a prize for a large canvas that depicted the war in Iraq using motifs from Picasso's *Guernica*, ran over and pulled him across the room to meet her painting instructor. "The two people who most influenced my imaginative development," she said, as she brought them together. "Mr. Pearson taught me to think, and Mr. Steinberg taught me to paint—not that the two things are really different." Hal tried to pay attention to what Caroline and her instructor were saying about how thinking and painting were the same, but his mind remained fastened on the encounter with Margot. For days afterward, he replayed the scene, considering what he should have said to show himself to advantage in Margot's eyes.

"All art is derivative," he might have told Pierre. "Look at Shakespeare. He borrowed from everyone. If you can't see the energy and potential in a painting like Caroline's, then you have no right to be looking at these pictures at all." He wished he had said this, if only to make clear to Margot where he stood—and also, he realized, because he would have liked to fight a duel with Pierre. Given they had no swords, words would have had to suffice.

"So will you ask Margot out?" Jessie repeated the question, since Hal had been daydreaming about skewering Pierre with his words and had not responded the first time.

He now answered with uncharacteristic sharpness: "Your daughter wouldn't go out with a lowly middle-school teacher, so I'm not going to humiliate myself by asking."

"I think you sell Margot short," said Jessie with a touch of maternal indignation. Then she shook her head sadly. "And one thing you weren't before was a coward."

"You're doing it!"

"I'm sorry."

Hal now assumed a gentler tone, though he spoke firmly: "I will call Margot *and* Carla and tell them about the trip, if you won't. So make up your mind."

Jessie took her fork and picked at her Greek salad for a moment. "They won't let me go."

"How can they prevent you? Anish is covering the expenses. They're not going to hold you against your will or put you into an institution or something, are they?"

"No," said Jessie slowly. "At least I don't think so. But they'll disapprove."

"So let them."

"And they'll bad-mouth you. They'll say you're trying to take advantage. Or that you're crazy too."

"So what? Maybe I am. If I don't care, why should you? But you have to tell them."

"I suppose you're right," said Jessie, sighing. "I'll tell them tonight. Margot is coming to dinner." She gave Hal a knowing look. "You could come too, if you want."

He shifted in his chair. "I don't think that would be a good idea. I've already been to dinner once. It would look a bit strange to have me again, especially since you haven't told them."

"Okay, okay, I'll tell them tonight," Jessie sighed.

"Good," said Hal. "Anish says he'll have the tickets for us by next week. He'll be bringing along a colleague who knows the ins and outs of the city going back to the doges, so you'll have plenty of help in finding your way."

"I won't need any help," said Jessie. "I know that city like the back of my hand."

"Well, a lot may have changed since the 1590s. Flooding and earthquakes; all sorts of rebuilding and renovation. There's no telling if your house is still standing."

Jessie looked at Hal and became quiet for a moment. "You

know," she finally said, "it's like I'm preparing to go on the stage for a performance, but it's one that happened a long time ago. Will always said the best actors always looked forward and never back. That's why it didn't upset them if they missed a line; they were thinking about what was coming next."

"You don't have to go back, you know," noted Hal, catching the implicit meaning in what she said. "Sometimes I think maybe you shouldn't. Feel free to cancel, if you have any doubts at all. Anish can always use the tickets to take some graduate students over. He has plenty of other work he can do in Venice."

Hal was speaking truthfully. He had grown very fond of Jessie, and he often felt himself siding with her daughters—wanting her to simply give up on the whole harebrained scheme, to try to forget whatever she thought she remembered, and to move forward rather than back in her life.

"But I must go back," countered Jessie with vehemence. "It's not just to find my birthday sonnets. It's more than that—or maybe something entirely different. All I know is that it's a trip I need to make. You mustn't try to talk me out of it," she said, clearly upset at the prospect that he might.

"If it's what you want, I won't try to talk you out of it," said Hal reassuringly.

Jessie sighed and patted his hand. "Such a sweet and loyal boy. Don't worry, I'll do what you said and tell the girls tonight." She paused and gave Hal a look. "But that doesn't mean you can't pick up the phone and ask Margot out."

Chapter Thirty-two

You haven't COMPLAINED LATELY, SO I TAKE IT MOM'S better," said Margot, who had come over for Friday dinner and was helping Carla take the good dishes out of the breakfront and set the table. Jessie could be heard in the kitchen humming "Now I See Thy Looks Were Feigned." "By the way, what's that song she's singing?"

Carla ignored the second question and addressed herself to the first. "She seems to be better," she responded with some deliberation. "She makes fewer odd references, but then she's talking less in general. She's keeping herself busy, though. When I'm at Mark's office on Tuesdays and Thursdays, she's always out when I call."

"What does she do the rest of the week?" asked Margot.

"Oh, the usual. Putters around the house. Cooks and sews. Watches some TV."

"So she only goes out on Tuesdays and Thursdays?"

"Come to think of it, yes. At least for the past few weeks, it's been that way. Goes to the mall, she says—not that she ever buys anything. But you know how she likes to look for bargains and compare prices. And I suppose she doesn't like being home alone."

"I suppose," said Margot, who, as an experienced trial lawyer, had a tendency to look for patterns and be suspicious about them.

Not that she could think of anything to be suspicious about in the case of Jessie's outings.

Carla had moved on to tell Margot about the windfall of the bat mitzvah dress that now rendered Margot's help in this area unnecessary.

"But I can at least do her makeup," said Margot. She seemed disappointed at losing the chance to shop with Stephanie for the dress—a typical example of the naiveté of the childless, Carla thought.

Carla had invited several guests for dinner that evening. Along with Margot, there was her friend Jill Rosenberg and her husband, Adam, a dentist, as well as her supervisor and friend from the Golden Pond Geriatric Center, Susie Wilson. Jill and Susie were superficially opposing types. Susie was in the martyr mold: a visionary Saint Joan willing to be burned at the stake for her beliefs. Jill was more like the hostess at an awards ceremony, determined that the lighting flatter everyone's makeup. Carla thought there were virtues and limitations to both approaches. Margot, she thought, would be a helpful bridge between them. Were the three women ever to consolidate their skills, they would truly be a force to be reckoned with. As it was, their combined presence would make for a diverting evening.

"Margot, you look stunning," said Jill as she entered the house, her eyes darting with lightning speed from Margot's shoes to her hair. The ability to appraise the physical packaging of another woman in a nanosecond may well have survival benefits for the evolution of the species. Certain women, of which Jill was one, had perfected it to a high degree.

Jill herself was wearing a wildly flapping silk ensemble with multiple bangles, and Adam, an outfit clearly picked out by his wife—the sweater had a garish cheerfulness at odds with his lethargic disposition. Even at this early stage in the evening, he looked as though he wanted to take a nap.

"We were so excited to hear that Mark's practice is going so well. I hope he can get an associate," said Jill. "Adam got a whole new lease on life when he got his two years ago, didn't you, dear?"

Adam nodded soporifically. For his present state to represent a new lease was to make his former one akin to being six feet under.

Susie came in next, looking harried. She was a handsome but disheveled-looking woman, always struggling with some new crisis involving care for the elderly. At the moment, she was worried about cuts in funding for the nonprofit Golden Pond Geriatric Center. Lately, government money had decreased and a promised stipend from headquarters had not materialized. This meant that the Center might have to reduce the number of beds, a prospect that would essentially mean throwing ten debilitated eighty-five-year-olds into the street. It was the sort of thing that kept Susie lying awake nights.

When she explained the problem to the assembled group, Jill became incensed. "How dare they?" she exclaimed. "I'm a taxpayer and have the right to expect that the elderly in my community are properly cared for."

"It's politics, that's all," said Susie wearily.

"I'm going to call your boss and give him a piece of my mind," said Jill. Calling and giving someone a piece of her mind was one of Jill's favorite occupations.

Carla, who knew Jill's ability to make adult men cower in fear, saw this as an opportunity for the Center. "Why don't you drop by the facility with me on Monday?" she suggested. "You can have a look around and get a sense of the problems a funding cut would cause."

"Excellent idea." Jill nodded.

Carla knew that, when activated, her friend was a formidable force for good. Otherwise, she tended to spend her day getting manicures, shopping for the perfect push-up bra, and nagging her son Josh. Not that Carla faulted Jill for this. The mix of narcissism and altruism in her friend's nature was part of her charm and made her a kind of mascot for the richly contradictory nature of suburban life.

"Feel free to take a look," said Susie, not sure what to make of Jill's on-the-spot devotion to her cause, but prepared to take any help she could get. "If you're really serious, I'll send you a prospectus on the company and some background articles on adult care that might be helpful."

"Please do," said Jill, who was already looking forward to browbeating the CEO of Golden Pond, Inc.

At this moment, Mark strode buoyantly into the house. He had begun to exude the cheerful bonhomie and mild pomposity that characterized successful physicians a few decades back, but that one rarely saw nowadays. He had grown far more affable and interested in others in the wake of his own success, and now, given that there was only one other man present, took to questioning the soporific Adam Rosenberg.

He began asking about a new dental bonding technique he had read about, and Adam, to everyone's surprise, perked up. Dental innovation happened to be Adam's passion, but since no one ever cared about the subject, he never had the opportunity to expound on it.

Mark's question also opened the floodgates to Adam's view of the field in general. "Used to be you could relax and make a good living with a dental degree," he observed crankily. "Now you have the cut-rate clinics stealing your patients and the insurance refusing to pay for the specialty dental work."

"Don't I know it," said Mark. "But I've been doing some creative marketing. You have to tie innovation to a public information campaign—get the word out so people know what's available."

Adam nodded, and Jill piped in to the effect that the doctors and dentists on Long Island, where she had grown up, had a good grasp of promotion. "Remember the ads that Ronnie Feldman put on the back of the phone books?"

"No!" said Adam, with surprising vehemence—he had never disagreed with his wife in public before. "Phone book advertising is tacky!"

"There are better ways," agreed Mark, translating this into a gentler vocabulary. "In the health-related fields you need to be subtle or you lose your credibility. For dentists, I'd say, maybe host a tooth-whitening seminar. Or a luncheon for area ENT docs, potential referring sources, on the importance of good bridgework to sinus health."

"Nice idea," said Adam, taking out a pencil. "Let me jot that down."

"I wish you could come up with some PR ideas for me," said Susie Wilson dejectedly. "I'm in a field that just doesn't lend itself to sexy promotional literature or video spots. Shakespeare said it best: The end is 'second childishness—Sans teeth, sans eyes, sans taste, sans every thing.' We've got the 'sans' stuff at the center in spades, but who wants to look? Maybe if people read more they'd understand."

"Please don't talk to me about Shakespeare," said Carla—anything related to the Bard had a tendency to give her a headache.

"I don't know that reading is the answer," said Margot, considering Susie's point more objectively. "I just think most people would rather not think about such things. Life is hard enough without concentrating on what's going to happen when we get older."

"But that's exactly the point," declared Susie. "It's in facing mortality that we can see our lives in some perspective. How can I cry about my big butt or even my bastard of an ex-husband when I see Mrs. Carmine, once the most beautiful woman in Brooklyn (or so her daughter told me), incapable of going to the bathroom by herself, much less recognizing her darling grandson? It breaks my heart but it also makes it stronger."

"So we need to require everyone to spend time working at the Golden Pond Geriatric Center?" asked Carla.

"That seems a bit extreme," noted Margot. Such work would not have agreed with her.

"Then I still maintain that reading is the next best thing," argued Susie. She herself had majored in English at Smith and had appeared destined for a career as a society hostess—that is, until her husband's infidelities had propelled her into the workplace and the discovery of a calling in geriatric care. "It's the human condition, in the end, that we have to deal with," she continued, "and literature teaches about that."

"That was the argument that Jessie's friend Mr. Pearson made," said Carla, glancing at Margot. "He's Stephanie's English teacher," she clarified for the other guests.

"And he majored in English at Yale," interjected Jessie to everyone's surprise. She had just brought out the appetizers—liver knishes, one of her specialties.

"I didn't know Mr. Pearson went to Yale," said Carla. "I don't remember him mentioning it when he came to dinner."

"Oh, we talked a bit in the kitchen when he was helping to clear the table," said Jessie quickly.

"You'd think he'd do more than teach middle school with a Yale degree," said Margot.

"And what's wrong with teaching middle school?" demanded Susie. "I say it's a noble choice of career. If we had more good teachers for kids at that age, the world would be a better place."

"Granted," acknowledged Margot. "It's just that a Yale degree is a commodity that generally brings with it a big job and a big salary."

"All the more reason to applaud the fellow for bypassing those rewards," insisted Susie.

Her point struck home. There was, Margot felt—though she had tried not to feel it—something admirable about Hal Pearson that seemed to place her in the wrong, a position she didn't enjoy occupying. This was, if she were to be perfectly honest about it, part of her irritation with him.

"It's a sign of heroism not to care about money," continued Susie. "Think of Isabel Archer in Henry James's *Portrait of a Lady*. She didn't care about money; that's why James made her the heroine."

"And look what happened to her," pointed out Margot, who had read that novel in college and identified with the strong-willed heroine while being exasperated with her for her disastrous taste in men. "She threw away her inheritance by falling for a bastard." It occurred to her as she said this that she had fallen for quite a number of bastards herself.

"We showed the film version of that book at the geriatric center the other night," noted Carla, hoping to divert the conversation to a lighter subject, "the one with Nicole Kidman. But the sex scene was much too explicit. Mr. O'Hare liked it, of course, but it shocked some of the others. It wasn't in the original, was it?"

"God no," said Margot, laughing. "The whole point of Henry James is to leave the sex out."

"It depends on how you read him," amended Susie. "For me, James is very sexy. He incites the imagination."

"My problem," said Mark, happily taking the philistine view, "was that Henry James always put me to sleep before my imagination had a chance to kick in. I'll never forget feeling screwed by *The Turn of the Screw* in college. That was an ordeal that may have driven me into medicine."

"Then I suppose we have Henry James to thank for an excellent physician," said Margot dryly.

While this conversation was transpiring, Jessie got up from the table and began clearing away the appetizer plates and bringing out the main course (a succulent veal chop with a very nice rice pilaf). With the exception of urging everyone to have seconds of everything, she remained quiet for the rest of the evening.

Chapter Thirty-three

After the GUESTS LEFT, MARGOT AND CARLA DEBRIEFED AS they cleared the dining room table. "Mom was good, don't you think?" asked Carla.

"Good, I don't know," replied Margot, appearing to consider the question. "She didn't say anything odd, if that's what you mean. But she was kind of quiet."

Before they could continue their analysis of their mother, Jessie herself came out of the kitchen. She stood near the door for a moment, wiping her hands on a dishtowel, and then proceeded to sit down at the head of the table and fold her hands. "Can I have a word with you girls before Margot leaves?" she asked.

Her daughters sat down on either side. "You were kind of quiet tonight," said Margot, seeing that her mother, though clearly wanting to speak, seemed at a loss for words. "It was a great dinner, but you didn't seem to be involved."

"Except when you reminded us that Hal Pearson went to Yale. That was a surprise," added Carla with amusement.

Jessie cleared her throat at this. "Which brings me to what I have to tell you. I have an announcement."

"There you are!" said Margot to Carla. "I knew there was

something up her sleeve. She's been acting very sly and secretive lately."

Jessie ignored this and continued. "I want you to know that I've been meeting Hal Pearson for lunch for the past few weeks. Tuesdays and Thursdays," she clarified, "when Carla was at the office."

The sisters looked at Jessie, stupefied. "You've been meeting Stephanie's English teacher for lunch!" exclaimed Carla. "What is this, *Harold and Maude*? The man's forty years younger than you are, for God's sake. It's perverse!"

"Carla," said Jessie with exasperation, "I have not been meeting Mr. Pearson that way. What do you take me for?"

Both women relaxed perceptibly. "Okay," said Margot, the first to take the measure of the situation. "Obviously you've been meeting that man to discuss your delusions about Shakespeare. He's probably been encouraging them. I think that's highly irresponsible, if not outright criminal. I thought he was odd, but I didn't think he would exploit the fantasies of an elderly woman behind her family's back."

"He's not exploiting," protested Jessie. "He's interested in what happened, and he's helped me put it all together very nicely. I owe a great deal to him."

"Yeah, you owe him a ticket to the loony bin along with you," said Margot angrily.

Carla cut in at this point. She, too, was appalled that her mother would sneak around behind her back, but she could not feel as outraged as Margot. She felt partly responsible for leaving her mother alone two days a week. "Mom, I realize you were lonely, but you could have asked me to stay home. It's not absolutely necessary that I help Mark at the office, especially now that things are going so well."

"It has nothing to do with you staying home," said Jessie in an irritable tone. "I needed to talk to Hal about what I remembered. And then, of course, we had to make plans."

"Plans?" said Carla with trepidation.

"For the trip. That's why I felt I had to finally speak to you. We're going to Venice in three weeks. Just a short trip—four days. It's all I'll need. But I can't tell you what it will mean for me to go back."

"Okay, now I get it," exclaimed Margot, growing more irate. "The man's a fortune hunter. He wants to bilk you of your savings. You take him on a nice trip to Venice to explore your roots, and he gets to go along."

"He's not taking my money," said Jessie calmly. "His friend has a grant that's covering everything."

"His friend? It must be some sort of kidnapping racket," said Margot, turning to Carla. Then, to her mother: "Who's his friend?"

"His friend is a professor of Renaissance literature at Yale," Jessie sniffed. "Professor Patel is not kidnapping anyone. He happens to have research money that can pay for the trip. If we find them, he can write about them for his journal."

"Find *them*?"

"The lost sonnets. The ones Will wrote me for my birthday, after the mean ones and before that nasty play."

Carla and Margot looked at each other. "So Mr. Pearson and the alleged Yale professor think you can lead them to some lost sonnets in Venice," Margot said. "Do I have this right?"

"Yes," said Jessie. "And I must say it's rather sad that people as important as Hal and Professor Patel take me seriously when my own family doesn't."

Her daughters were silent for a moment. Then Carla spoke: "I'm sorry, Mom, if we've been neglectful or—dismissive—of your ideas. But put yourself in our shoes. It's not reasonable to believe in what you're saying. Mr. Pearson and this professor, if he is one, perhaps have their reasons for wanting to. They've made the study of Shakespeare their life's work. Perhaps they're willing to grasp at straws. But it's hard for us. And to have you trekking off to Venice less than two weeks before the bat mitzvah, at your age, with some men you barely know, well, we can't very well support it."

"I'm sorry, Carla," said Jessie, pulling herself up into a posture not unlike the one Margot took in court after putting forward a risky line of defense that she was determined to stand behind. "I'm sorry, but I don't care what you think. I'm going to Venice with Hal and his friend, and that's the end of the story." With this, she got up from the table and went upstairs to bed.

Chapter Thirty-four

*C*an you BELIEVE THAT MOM IS GOING TO VENICE NEXT
week?" Carla asked Mark as they stood in the florist shop in
the upscale strip mall. It was not the same upscale strip mall in
which the stationery shop was located, but a similar one—upscale
strip malls being as plentiful in Cherry Hill as cherries and hills
were scarce.

Mark, realizing that Carla was asking a rhetorical question—a
common tendency when she was tense—did not reply, allowing her
to vent on the subject.

"Mother hasn't been out of the country since she and Dad went
to Paris on an ABC tour when we were in high school, and then she
said she liked Epcot better. So now, all of a sudden, she decides to
go to Venice to dig around some old building that's probably sinking into a canal? I just can't wrap my brain around it!" Carla's voice
had taken on the quasihysterical note that Mark hadn't heard since
Jeffrey was high on chocolate milk.

"Margot's going to try to talk Mr. Pearson out of it," he reassured her.

"That's true," said Carla, taking a breath. Margot's powers of
persuasion were legendary in the family and, indeed, in the entire
Delaware Valley, where she was known to have persuaded juries to

acquit individuals where motive, opportunity, and evidence seemed to argue forcefully against them. Certainly Margot would be able to nip this thing in the bud if she applied herself.

And yet Jessie could be stubborn. She was, after all, Margot's mother, and had a bit of the same stuff in her. And there was that Hal Pearson to contend with. Who knew what kind of steely heart might lie beneath the seemingly gentle, teacherly facade.

"But what if she doesn't convince him? What if Mom insists on going anyway?" Carla wailed.

"If Margot doesn't convince her, so what?" Mark shrugged. "Then—big deal—she'll go."

This had essentially been Dr. Samuels's take on the matter. Carla had made an emergency visit to Samuels after lying awake for three nights running, thinking of her mother with a bunch of goofy Shakespeareans in search of her sixteenth-century roots.

"She wants to go to Venice, let her go," Samuels had pronounced after Carla filled him in on the situation. "Why shouldn't she see the world at her age? Venice is a beautiful city. St. Mark's, the Doge's Palace. Sylvia and I spent hours in the Academia. The Bellinis and Titians knocked our socks off. And talk about good food. We didn't eat for a week when we got back."

"But she's not going for sightseeing or food," protested Carla. "She's going, she says, to find some sonnets that Shakespeare wrote to her and that she stashed under the floor of her room in 1597."

"So she wants to make it into a scavenger hunt; what's the harm?"

Samuels's nonchalance had calmed Carla for a time, but as her mother's trip approached, she became agitated again. Fortunately, the chores attached to the bat mitzvah were a distraction. Now, for example, she had to put her worrying aside and concentrate on the flowers for the centerpieces.

Flowers had not been part of the bat mitzvah equation until four weeks ago, when the caterer called to say the magenta tablecloths were out of stock and they would have to go with something called "scarlet sunset," a similar color, though a tad brighter. "What are the flowers going to be?" he asked. "You probably want to take it down a notch; scarlet sunset makes a bold statement and you don't want to compete."

Carla said that she hadn't thought about flowers. Were they really necessary?

"Necessary, I don't know," said Moishe in the tone of a philosopher. "If you went with necessary, you'd have paper plates and baked beans." (The desirability of paper plates and baked beans flitted momentarily through Carla's head.) "Without a centerpiece," Moishe continued, feeling inclined to take the argument further, "the tables look naked. Besides, lots of the guests don't really want to look at each other. Put some irises and some baby's breath in there—or some balloons, if you want to go in that direction—it's much better than staring straight across at some *farbissener* you haven't seen in thirty years. Helps the digestion, if nothing else."

Carla had put the question to Mr. O'Hare, who had become her sounding board and touchstone for almost everything regarding the bat mitzvah. O'Hare agreed with Moishe on the importance of a centerpiece and came down strongly on the side of flowers.

"Flowers are alive," he said. "Balloons are goddamn synthetic. Your daughter's not a cheap plastic balloon; she's a delicate flower, growing and blossoming. Use your head; flowers are the way to go, goddammit."

Mr. O'Hare had a way of making things seem crystal clear.

Once the necessity of floral centerpieces had been established, Carla made an appointment with the premier Cherry Hill florist, Bennet, who had trained on Sixth Avenue in Manhattan, known as the Cordon Bleu of floral design. Bennet wore a striped T-shirt and a small kerchief knotted around his neck, a look Carla thought might be some sort of tribute to Audrey Hepburn.

His eyes widened in theatrical disbelief when he heard that the bat mitzvah was only seven weeks away. "Don't you know that flowers take time?" he exclaimed, as if hair and makeup were somehow involved.

Nonetheless, he called jubilantly two days later: They were in luck! (Carla had at first thought they had won the Publishers Clearinghouse Sweepstakes.) A wedding scheduled for the same date as the bat mitzvah had been suddenly canceled when the groom was indicted for insider trading. "Sad for them, marvelous for you," said Bennet succinctly, encapsulating the lessons of Darwinian struggle embedded in this floral transaction.

He promised to have a sample centerpiece ready for their inspection in a month or so. That time having collapsed, Carla and Mark were presently waiting in the fetid atmosphere of the florist shop to view his handiwork.

Bennet now appeared, looking agitated. "The lilies are so difficult this time of year," he pronounced. (Carla imagined the flowers throwing tantrums and Bennet having to administer Valium.) He ushered them into the back of the shop. In a small alcove on a table in the center sat a large, scary looking constellation of twigs, leaves, and waxy, angular forms in unnatural colors that Carla supposed must be flowers, though they resembled none that she had ever seen before.

"There she is!" said Bennet, as though the display were a debutante making an appearance at a cotillion ball. "Isn't she exquisite?"

Carla and Mark stared at the arrangement. "This," said Mark in an authoritative tone (ever since his practice had begun to improve, he had become more forceful in his manner), "is not what we want!"

Bennet drew back huffily. "You don't like her?" he said in disbelief.

"No!" said Mark. He turned to Carla for clarification.

"It's not that we don't like—her," said Carla, always the diplomat. "It's that we're going for a simpler look. Maybe some wildflowers," she said, making a stab at describing the opposite of what stood before them. "Nothing so—modern."

"Ah!" said Bennet, with the air of an artist with an illumination. "You want the natural, just-picked look; the ran-out-to-the-meadow-found-some-daisies look; the wandering-through-the-English-countryside-and-gathered-these-in-my-apron look."

"Yes," said Carla, "something along those lines."

"I understand," said Bennet, gazing at his monstrous creation wistfully. "The insider trader and his bride loved this one. But to each his own. I'll whip you up a new sample for tomorrow. But keep in mind," he sniffed with artistic disdain, "the just-picked look is one of our most labor-intensive arrangements. It won't cost you any less."

Chapter Thirty-five

*M*argot decided THAT THE BEST WAY TO TALK HAL
Pearson out of the Venice trip was to attack him with
the full arsenal of her persuasive skills while garbed in a tight
sweater. To this end, she prepared to surprise him in his classroom
directly after school.

On a Monday afternoon, Margot left her office early and drove
from downtown Philadelphia to Cherry Hill. Carla, who had
acted in the manner of an undercover detective planning a stake-
out, had informed her sister that middle-school classes ended at
2:58 P.M.—a time that neatly encapsulated the nature of middle
school itself, where the sense of counting minutes was combined
with the sense of their unutterable dullness. Carla had ascertained
that the first round of buses would have departed by 3:16, but that
teachers were obliged to remain in the school until the second (or
late) bus left. Thus, if Margot left her office at 2:17, she would,
barring a jackknifed tractor-trailer on Route 70, arrive at just the
right moment to catch poor, unsuspecting Hal Pearson alone in
his classroom, in a perfect position to be browbeaten.

As Margot entered the school at the designated time, having
parked her BMW in the spot marked *Assistant Vice Principal*, the
corridors had the desolate look of a recently abandoned war zone.

The pungent odor of adolescent sweat permeated the air, making it necessary for her to hold her breath for a few seconds to become acclimated. As she passed various rooms on the way to Hal's—she had gotten the precise location from Carla in a detailed map e-mailed to her the night before—she saw disheveled teachers erasing the boards, picking up stray papers on the floor, and shoving books into their briefcases in preparation for going home. The general feeling was one of lassitude and exhaustion—except as she approached Hal Pearson's room, where she could hear lively voices in conversation.

Carla had failed to interrogate Stephanie on the subject of Hal's after-school activity. Teachers had a policy that they would be briefly available at the end of the day for consultation—but the policy was a perfunctory one, students being generally disinclined to consult them. In Hal's case, however, they did, owing perhaps to the genuine pleasure he seemed to take in their presence. Children of middle-school age, not unlike people of any age, tend to be sensitive to the response of others and will be grateful and forthcoming to anyone who appears to like them. This simple but much-ignored rule of behavior could, if properly applied, transform the education of adolescents. Of course, it would require the difficult feat of liking a group of individuals who display very few obviously likable characteristics.

Hal Pearson was one of those rare souls who could see the freshness and wonder that lay beneath his students' surly, inarticulate facade. As a result, there was always a motley collection of young people milling about in his classroom after school. Today there were three who had draped themselves loosely over the desks and chairs.

Margot paused at the door, waiting for an opportune moment to announce her presence. She wondered at first if the students were there for some sort of club, and if Hal was their faculty adviser. But the absence of a clear agenda made this seem unlikely. It then occurred to her that perhaps the students were being punished for bad behavior or late homework. But the benign atmosphere belied this theory as well.

"So what is it you guys want to discuss?" Margot heard Hal ask. His tone threw her. Had she, during her own extensive academic career, ever heard a tone of such genuine goodwill expressed by a teacher toward a group of students? If so, she could not recall it.

"Commas," said a girl in low, very wide-leg jeans, a skull-and-crossbones T-shirt, and multiple piercings in ears, nose, and eyebrows. She looked like someone who, even at the age of thirteen, you wouldn't want to tangle with in a dark alley.

"Ah yes, the uses and abuses of the *virgule*," said Hal. "That's French for comma—you never know when you might want to impress the French. What don't you understand about commas?"

"Everything," said a large boy in a football jacket. "They say they taught us to use them somewhere back in, like, the third grade, but I must have been absent."

"Yeah," said the girl, "they always say they taught you stuff. That's how they get out of teaching it."

"They probably did teach it," said another boy wearing headphones, "only you were in the bathroom or something."

The girl glared at him. "So are you saying *you* learned it?"

"No, but that's 'cause I wasn't listening," said the headphoned boy.

"Enough with the origin of your ignorance," said Hal. "If we try to arrive at first causes we'll never accomplish anything. I'll explain commas if you want to listen. If not, you can just hang out."

"I'll listen," said the girl with the piercings.

"Gimme what you got on commas," said the husky boy.

"Okay, let's start by seeing what you know," said Hal. "When do you use a comma?"

"When you pause," said the girl. "'I saw him—pause—walking down the street.'"

"I wouldn't pause there," said the husky boy.

Hal nodded. "Not everyone would pause there."

"I thought a comma was supposed to mark a pause."

"Yes," said Hal. "But you can't decide to put in a comma just because you happen to pause. It has to be a generally agreed-on pause."

"So how do you know where a generally agreed-on pause is?"

"That's where the rules come in," said Hal with an air of triumph. "Rules generalize about things—like pausing. Which doesn't mean you might not pause somewhere else occasionally. It's just that you don't put in a comma unless the general pause rule holds."

"Sort of like a traffic light," said the boy with the headphones, who, though his ears were covered, appeared to be following the conversation closely.

Hal threw the boy a Jolly Rancher. "Excellent analogy, Spencer."

"But you would pause if, say, a rabbit ran across the road," said the girl, "even if there wasn't a traffic light. In that case, there'd be no comma."

"Right you are, Monica," said Hal, throwing another Jolly Rancher to the girl.

"Sometimes you have to stop at a traffic light even if there's no traffic coming in the other direction. Is that like using a comma even if you don't actually need to pause?" said the boy in the headphones, warming to the exercise.

Hal threw a third Jolly Rancher. "Fine extended analogy."

"I wouldn't stop if there wasn't traffic," said the husky boy. "I'd run the light."

"And you'd get a ticket," said the girl. "You'd get an F on the paper."

Hal threw both of them a Jolly Rancher. "One for you too, Greg, for your interesting insight into social transgression." He then looked out at the group with an expression of pure joy. "You guys blow me away," he said. "You gotta all go into philosophy. Promise me you'll take Intro Logic with Mr. Muller next year."

"Mr. Muller is a dick," said the headphoned boy.

"Perhaps he is," said Hal in a noncommittal tone, "but with your gift for the subject, it wouldn't matter." The students appeared to consider this for a moment. It had never occurred to them to separate the subject matter from the teacher. "But we haven't gotten into the rules of commas yet," Hal continued. "Where to put the traffic lights—that's the hard part."

"I like the analogy part better," said the husky boy.

"You gotta blend abstract thinking with concrete," said Hal, "or all you've got is bullshit."

"Good point," said the headphones. "Hit us with the comma rules."

Hal took a piece of chalk out of his pocket and was about to put some examples on the board when he happened to look toward the door.

"Margot Kaplan!" said Hal, shocked into stating the obvious.

The students looked over. Noting Margot's appearance and Hal's flustered manner, they picked up their backpacks and filed out of the room. Hal gave a distracted wave and muttered, "To be continued."

"You seem to have them in the palm of your hand," said Margot, walking into the room with a certain tentativeness. She had originally imagined striding forward and cowing him with a few sharp words. But the scene she had just witnessed had a humbling effect. Her own memories of middle school were of teachers who were always either castigating kids for not doing what they should or patting them on the head for regurgitating what had been taught to them by rote. The idea of lazing around for an impromptu philosophical discussion of comma usage was not within the parameters of her experience. That sort of learning—of knowledge examined and savored—was something she had known only in college and law school, and then only on very rare occasions. To see such a thing done with pleasure and affection in a seventh-grade classroom was, to borrow from Stephanie's vocabulary, awesome.

Hal meanwhile had regained his balance. "To what do I owe the honor of this visit?" he asked in a light tone that could not mask his obvious pleasure. "Don't tell me that you dropped by for a quick comma review."

"No," said Margot quickly, "I mastered punctuation on the job, where I discovered that a misplaced comma could cost my client thousands in bail."

"Maybe you can be a guest speaker in my class. You can explain how the comma can literally affect life and liberty. These kids like to see the practical aspects of what they learn."

"I'd say they do pretty well with the philosophical aspects," said Margot. "You certainly got a high-level discussion out of a rather pedestrian topic."

"There, I agree with you. I never stop being surprised by the wealth of analogies that students bring to bear on their experience. We talk about adolescence as the period of raging hormones. To me, it's more like the period of raging metaphor."

"Nice thought," said Margot. "You oughta be a teacher."

Hal smiled.

"But I'm here on other business. I need a favor." The phrasing slipped out; it wasn't the way she imagined the conversation going at all.

"At your service," said Hal, meaning it. He had thought to have effectively squashed the romantic in himself. Burned in love at some point in the distant past, he had had only casual relationships since. Usually they started as friendships, then dipped into something vaguely sexual, coming out on the other end as friendship again. He had begun to feel that this was the natural way of things in the modern world, romance having given way to comfort and convenience.

But Margot Kaplan had an entirely different effect on him. She brought the romantic impulse, long dormant, to the surface. He wished he could be assigned some difficult, even dangerous, task to perform on her behalf.

"'Come, bid me do anything for thee,'" he said, borrowing the lines that Benedict spoke to Beatrice in *Much Ado About Nothing* and making a broad, facetious bow as he said them.

Margot's look suggested that quoting Shakespeare might not be the best tack to take with her right now. Her tone grew more severe: "Then abandon this harebrained scheme of going to Venice with my mother."

Hal's expression changed. "That, I'm afraid, I cannot do," he replied. "It's something that involves more than just me. Your mother wants to go—she's counting on it. And I could never sleep at night if I let her down."

"So you're saying you're doing all this for her!"

"Not entirely. I grant that she's sparked my curiosity. But I wouldn't take the trip, and I'd cancel in a minute, if her heart weren't set on going."

"She's an old woman. You've gotten her worked up over a delusion."

"But is it harmful? Your mother is full of knowledgeable detail about the period and the city, not to mention the Bard. If nothing else, it would be a shame for her not to see Venice again."

"Again? You actually believe that she lived there in another life?"

"I don't believe or disbelieve," said Hal. "I suspend my disbelief."

"But digging around under the floorboards of some old house, searching for ridiculous artifacts?"

"Lost sonnets."

"Whatever—it's creepy. I can't condone it."

"I'm sorry," said Hal. "As I said, I could never bring myself to disappoint your mother. I don't think you could either, if you were in my position. So the least you can do is tell her it's okay—that you won't be angry at her for going."

Margot considered this. "Does she think I'm angry?"

"Yes—and she's a little afraid of you. More of you than of your sister."

"And do *you* think I'm scary?"

"No," he said carefully, "*scary* isn't the word I'd use."

"What word would you use?"

"*Formidable*, maybe."

"So you're saying that you want me, formidable woman that I am, to give you and my mother my blessing for this trip?"

"Yes," said Hal, "your blessing would be nice."

"Well, then," said Margot, taking a breath, and then speaking with uncharacteristic recklessness: "I'll do one better. I'll go along."

Hal stared at her.

"She'll need me there for support and to keep an eye on things," she continued hurriedly, "and I have a week coming to me at the firm, so I'll have no problem taking off." She paused and seemed to get better hold of herself, her voice assuming its more familiar sarcastic tone. "I was looking for a vacation spot, anyway," she added. "I always wanted to see Venice, and it will be nice to have a native show me around."

Chapter Thirty-six

They had GONE: JESSIE, HAL, AND MARGOT FROM PHILADEL-
phia Airport that afternoon, Anish Patel and his colleague
out of JFK.

Although Carla was initially disappointed that Margot had
failed in her mission to talk Hal Pearson out of the trip, she was
somewhat mollified by Margot's decision to go along. She had
great confidence in her sister. Margot Kaplan might not be lucky
in love, but she was successful in everything else. She was a
woman of eminent rationality and will—someone you could count
on to act effectively in a crisis, and whom one crossed at one's
peril.

Now at seven P.M., Carla imagined that her mother and sister
were somewhere over the Atlantic, winging their way to the Gritti
Palace, one of the foremost luxury hotels in Venice. The hotel had
been chosen by Anish, who said that his grant permitted him to
travel in style and that, having lived in squalor for so many years
during his childhood, he was not about to stint now, especially
when the luxury was paid for by someone else.

Margot had promised to call as soon as they arrived, which
would probably be in a few hours. Meanwhile, there was nothing
Carla could do, which placed her in a state of welcome calm. She

could concentrate for the time being on the last lap of the bat mitzvah, which was rounding the corner at breakneck speed.

Many things had been done. She and Mr. O'Hare had prepared a checklist and reviewed it together to their mutual satisfaction.

1. *The caterer—all wrapped up. Even if there were a world shortfall in soy products, Moishe assured them he had his black-market sources. Not to worry.*

2. *The band—confirmed for an evening of authentic klezmer tunes. This was the band that Mark had heard coming home from work on Philadelphia's public radio station. The members were ethnomusicology students at the University of Pennsylvania and turned out not to be Jewish—a fact that pleased Mark, since it assured that the ethnic temperature of the event would be maintained on a refined, academic level.*

3. *Griffin (aka the entertainment motivator)—on track, now that a small snag had been ironed out. It seemed that Uncle Sid, who had made a miraculous recovery, had wanted a song by Artie Shaw that no one ever heard of to accompany his candle-lighting. Griffin had pronounced that if he didn't know the song, it didn't exist, a pronouncement that incensed Sid and made him want it all the more. Fortunately, Stephanie's friend Zack, at twelve already an accomplished computer hacker, managed to locate the song on Kazaa on the Internet and duly burned a copy. This was passed on to Griffin, who conveniently forgot that the song didn't exist and agreed to play it when Sid came up to light his candle. Ergo, problem solved, short of a lawsuit from the Artie Shaw estate for unlicensed performance. But Mr. O'Hare said not to worry on this score: He once knew a girl who dated Artie Shaw (though in a rare deviation from the norm, didn't marry him), and was sure that he could parlay that connection to their benefit if absolutely necessary.*

4. *The photographer and videographer—getting along well. While planning his* Godfather-*with*-Fiddler-*overtones production, Cass Sunshine had decided that the photographs should resemble Hollywood stills (a new concept that he thought had great marketing potential). The Bennington photographer would certainly have balked at this directive, but the middle-aged photographer saw no problem with it, so long as he got paid on time.*

5. *The flowers—done. Bennet had gone back to the drawing board and created a just-picked-look centerpiece that was acceptable to Mark and Carla. Of course, as had been predicted, the price of said unpretentious arrangement had knocked the breath out of them.*

6. *The guest list—finalized! The cancerous growth of invitations had finally been staunched at 200 and now, with RSVPs in, had settled at a reasonable 150. The unexpected shortfall had come from two factors. Number one: A Florida friend of Carla's mother-in-law had suddenly gotten it into her head that the almanac augured a snowstorm for the bat mitzvah weekend, and had scared some of the others, who were terrified by the word "accumulation" (i.e., that they might be stranded up north for an indefinite period to battle the cold and their children). Number two: A popular nurse at Mark's hospital happened to have her baby shower fall on the day of the bat mitzvah. This obliged many of the nurses to choose between a cozy, familiar event and a possibly uncomfortable, unfamiliar one, with more opting for the former than the latter.*

The checklist reassured Carla that the celebratory component of the event was under control.

Less so, the religious aspect—or at least one crucial part of it. Stephanie was fine with her Torah and haftorah portions, the scriptural readings that made up the bulk of her ceremonial performance. The cantor had reported with gratitude that Stephanie actually had a lovely singing voice and an admirable sense of phrasing. The mumble and screech of many bar mitzvah children as they rushed headlong through their portions was the real strain of the cantor's job.

The problem lay with the *D'var Torah*, which is to say, Stephanie's speech. This was the section of the service when the bar mitzvah child was expected to demonstrate something more than pure rote learning. The *D'var Torah* was a commentary on the Torah portion, a kind of minisermon, and the one moment in the service when the formalized trappings of the event could be put aside for a glimpse of the child as an individual.

The *D'var Torah* requirement made sense on a theoretical level. On a practical one, however, it did not. To expect a newly minted thirteen-year-old to write a formal speech of any kind, no less one on a passage from the Bible difficult to fathom even by scholars rigorously trained in theological discourse, and then to expect said thirteen-year-old to perform it for a disparate group of relatives and friends who were itching to get their hands on the hot hors d'oeuvres whose odors were wafting in from the other room, was asking a lot.

The Education Committee at the synagogue, having weathered the process themselves with their own children, had done what they could to facilitate matters. They offered the following guidelines to aid the bar and bat mitzvah child in the preparation of the *D'var Torah*:

1. *Summarize your biblical portion in one or two paragraphs. Keep this simple: No need to enumerate, for example, the number of goats in the entourage or to recite the genealogy accompanying a given character.*

2. *Relate some point in the passage to some aspect of your own life. For example: "Abraham's worship of idols reminds me of the*

time when I wanted to play Nintendo and didn't want to do my homework. Just as Abraham eventually realized there was one God, I eventually learned that doing my homework was more important than Nintendo" (Alan Goldberg's D'var Torah, *September 1999). Please notice the parallel structure. Idols are to Nintendo as homework is to one God. Ask your parents to help you outline your portion so that you can see the logical structure more clearly and better organize the lesson you want to discuss.*

3. *Thank those involved in the making of this sacred and joyous event. Keep this to the basic groups: Mom and Dad, Grandpa and Grandma, siblings, rabbi, and cantor. An influential teacher or relative can also be added, but if you start naming your friends, you'll never get to your party.*

4. *Explain your intentions for charity* (tzadakah): *i.e., where you will donate a portion of your bar or bat mitzvah gift money. Please note that a charity is a nonprofit organization for the public good. It does not include such organizations as the National Football League, the fines accumulated for your overdue video rentals, or Abercrombie and Fitch.*

Uncomplicated as this template might seem, it did not, unfortunately, solve the problem. Fits of rage and frustration ensued as children were asked to summarize the densely irrational biblical passage, to extract a lesson that was not utterly unrelated to it, to thank an abhorred sibling, and to negotiate how much money from their bar mitzvah stash would go to the Jewish Federation or the American Cancer Society (groups that to the child seemed to have been designed to cheat them out of the little money that would be left them once Mom and Dad had put the rest away into the alleged college fund).

Most children had the whole thing flogged out of them

through threat and bribe, though not without scenes, biblical in size and intensity.

Stephanie was no exception.

Her portion involved Joseph's interpretation of Pharaoh's dream. Mark had thought this a great windfall. "I can't tell you how lucky you are!" he exclaimed. "My portion had to do with hygiene. There was a whole section about menstrual fluid—not the kind of thing a thirteen-year-old boy finds inspiring, at least not in front of his elderly relatives. Your passage is great. The seven fat kine and the seven lean kine—kine are cattle, by the way."

"Duh," said Stephanie.

"Joseph and the pharaoh—man, are you lucky!" Mark waxed on. Joseph's story had always held a place in his affections. As a boy, he had fantasized about being like Joseph and interpreting the dream of a pharaoh, who in his imagination looked a lot like Mr. Rooney, his junior-high-school principal.

"The story is dumb," said Stephanie sulkily. "Joseph has all these bad things happen to him, then he interprets the pharaoh's dream and everything is fine. What's that supposed to mean?"

"Maybe it means that life can surprise you," noted Mark. "You can be down in the dumps one minute and things can suddenly change and put you on top of the world."

"I think that's a dumb moral," said Stephanie. "Everyone knows sometimes good things happen and sometimes bad things happen. Who cares? I'm not going to write that."

"You don't have to," said Carla reassuringly. "Daddy's only trying to give you some ideas."

"Think about something else in the story, then," suggested Mark. "Maybe you want to talk about pharaoh's dream. It's a puzzle, isn't it? Lean and fat kine, fertility and famine. Joseph was a problem solver. You always liked to solve problems. Think of how good you are at Scrabble."

"Scrabble isn't a problem, it's a game," said Stephanie.

"You know what I mean—figuring things out, putting things together, that sort of thing."

"No," pronounced Stephanie. "Joseph wasn't problem solving. He was just lucky. Everyone knows that dreams can't tell the future."

"But this is the Bible," Carla pointed out. "All sorts of magical things happen."

"Well, if it's magical, there's no lesson to take out of it. God just made it happen. He wanted Joseph to be right. Can't I say that?"

"No," said Carla, who had begun to realize that her daughter actually had the argumentative abilities of a Talmudic scholar with regard to not doing what was expected. "You have to find a lesson."

The problem was duly brought before the rabbi a few days later in the pre–bat mitzvah interview. Rabbi Barry Newman was a very young man who had lately been catapulted into the position of senior rabbi when that personage, in the throes of a midlife crisis, had suddenly resigned to lead a congregation in Australia.

Newman, who had actually been hired a month earlier as assistant rabbi and had expected to spend years doing relatively nothing, had at first not known what to make of his sudden elevation to eminence and responsibility. During his first few Sabbath services, he had gazed out at the prosperous doctors and lawyers in the congregation, wondering what in the world he could say that they would want to hear. Fortunately, the cogs of the synagogue wheel had ground forward, carrying him along. He had met with the board for a pep talk, consulted some sermon crib sheets on the Internet, and been generally buoyed by a reflexive attitude of respect from congregants who had never noticed him before. He was working on counteracting his callow appearance with the growth of a small beard and the cultivation of a furrowed brow, and the general consensus was that he was "coming along nicely."

"Okay, what have we here?" said the rabbi to Stephanie now, lowering his voice and trying to sound rabbinical.

"Joseph interprets the pharaoh's dream," said Stephanie glumly.

"And what do you think of Joseph's interpretation of the pharaoh's dream?" asked the rabbi. He had discovered that by asking questions that piggybacked on his respondent's previous statement he eventually arrived somewhere.

"Not much," said Stephanie.

"Okay," said the rabbi, holding, if falteringly, to his method, "why not much?"

"Because dreams can't tell the future," Stephanie reiterated. "My dreams are always about things that don't happen. Like being in Disney World with my friends or getting a real Kate Spade bag for my birthday."

"Hmm," said the young rabbi, taking this in. "Dreams can't tell the future in your experience, but in Joseph's they do. What do you make of that?"

"I make of it that it's a story and not real life," said Stephanie with dry clarity.

"Hmm," said the rabbi, chewing his lip, "And why do you think the story is told that way?"

"I suppose so Joseph can get in good with the pharaoh," said Stephanie.

"And why does he need to get in good with the pharaoh?"

"So he can get powerful and his brothers will come to him for help."

"And why do his brothers need to come to him for help?"

"So he can forgive them."

"And why does he need to forgive them?"

"To show that he's a bigger person."

"And there you have it!" sighed the young rabbi. The twenty-questions technique was supposed to work, but when the thing dragged on one could begin to have one's doubts. Fortunately, he had now hit pay dirt. The idea of forgiving a sibling for a misdeed was as tried-and-true as anything in the bar mitzvah lexicon. It would yield a predictable but charming anecdote of how said sibling had stolen something (a Nintendo game, a favorite hat, a Smash Mouth CD) and had been forgiven by the noble bar mitzvah child. To be sure, this was straying from Joseph's interpretation of dreams and encroaching onto the passage of the following week, but these kids weren't Sigmund Freud, and one made do.

"Okay, there's something to work with," pronounced the rabbi with relief. "Can you think of a time when you were the bigger person and forgave your brother when he acted badly to you?"

"No," said Stephanie truthfully.

"Think about it," said the young rabbi. "I'm sure if you try, you will." He nodded to Carla, as if to say the ball was now in her court. "Bring in a draft next week for the dry run," he told Stephanie. "We can put the finishing touches on it then."

"I don't want to think about it anymore," complained Stephanie to Carla in the car on the way home. "I wouldn't forgive Jeffrey if he sold me into slavery in Egypt and that's final."

"Well, maybe you can think of another lesson from the story," said Carla wearily. "You still have a week to write the draft. Let's talk about it later."

Chapter Thirty-seven

*H*al had BEEN IN A STATE OF EXULTATION EVER SINCE Margot had announced she was coming to Venice. He felt sure they had made some kind of connection in his classroom, and was looking forward to building on that connection during the long plane trip they were now fated to take together.

But his expectation of a warm welcome was disappointed when they met at the airport. Although Margot had temporarily thawed toward Hal during her visit to the school, she had soon had a change of heart. She realized she had been thrown from her original intention by the sight of his receptive students and his line about respecting her mother's wishes. It was just the sort of softening up that opposing attorneys tried to do in the courtroom to sway a jury in their favor, and which she had always been adept at counteracting in her closing arguments. Here, to her retrospective mortification, she had been bested by a middle-school teacher.

At the airport, therefore, she greeted Hal coldly. And once they boarded the plane, she turned her face to the window to avoid conversation. Jessie, however, who was seated between them, seemed content to ignore her daughter and chatter happily to Hal about the prospect of seeing her old home again.

"Just don't get your hopes up," said Hal, stealing a wistful glance past Jessie to the back of Margot's head. "I returned to my old neighborhood in northeast Philly a few years back and there was an ATM machine where our house used to be—a particularly brutal reminder that you can't go home again. In your case, we're talking four hundred years. A lot can change."

"Don't worry so much," said Jessie, patting Hal's arm.

In fact, he did worry—that the trip might tire her and that she would be disappointed in her quest. Hal had developed a feeling for Jessie beyond his academic interest in what she could uncover.

He must have looked depressed, because Jessie began taking snack items out of her carryall and offering it to him. In this area she conformed to the profile of the conventional Jewish mother, believing that any show of nerves, discouragement, or depression could be treated by food. She pressed on Hal an apple, a juice box, some saltines with peanut butter (nicely prepared in sandwich form), and several varieties of sucking candy.

Margot, though she appeared to be indifferent to these proceedings, was in fact feeling rather left out. She watched out of the corner of her eye as Hal accepted each of her mother's offerings— he was now sucking on one of her sour apple candies. It occurred to her that she would like one too. Not, of course, that she would stoop to ask.

"So when do we go to look for the house?" Jessie asked Hal now. "Can we go as soon as we get there?"

"I think we should wait until tomorrow," said Hal. "It's a long flight. I want you to be fresh."

"But I don't want to wait," said Jessie petulantly.

"It will be too dark for you to see anything anyway," said Hal firmly. "We'll walk over in the morning."

"I was just hoping to have a look first thing."

"Jessie, you've waited four hundred years, you can wait one more night."

"I suppose," she sighed, "you know what's best." She patted Hal's arm again, then pushed the button to recline her seat, closing her eyes as she did so.

"You and Mom seem to get along well," said Margot once Jessie had drifted off to sleep. She had turned from the window and was addressing Hal for the first time since her chilly reception at the airport. She hadn't been able to ignore the ease and affection with which he talked to her mother. Despite herself, she was touched.

Hal experienced a surge of pleasure. Being with Margot made him feel as if he were Stephanie's age again, oddly excited and worried about what to say and how to say it. "I'm very fond of your mother," he replied, trying for a casual tone. "My own died sixteen years ago, when I was in college, and there's a sense in which Jessie fills a gap for me, I admit. I also know you think I've been a bad influence with this Shakespeare business"—he spoke haltingly, wanting to get across the full range of his feelings—"but you have to understand how extraordinary her knowledge of the playwright and of the social context of that period is. Really—it's unprecedented. I know you disapprove, but I can't honestly help being carried along by what your mother says."

Margot noted the sincerity of his tone and, again, felt herself soften. "It *has* led rather far afield," she said dryly, "but I have to admit that the whole thing has made her more, well, interesting— and brought back some of the zest she used to have for life."

"She's a delightful woman," said Hal. "Shakespeare or no Shakespeare."

"So what's with your name?" asked Margot, suddenly changing the direction of the conversation. "Don't tell me that your parents actually named you after Shakespeare's Prince Hal."

"Not intentionally," said Hal, pleased by her knowledge of Shakespeare's history play, and even more pleased by her effort to be friendly. "But it really is my name—or at least my genuine given nickname. I come from a long line of Henrys, and each of us got a different nickname in some vague effort at individuality. When it got down to me, Hal was pretty much what was left, even though the name had been tainted by that psychotic computer in *2001*. It's been made worse recently, I should add, by that awful and unfortunately titled movie *Shallow Hal*, in which Gwyneth Paltrow wears a fat suit. Unfortunately, few people know Prince Hal these days—with the exception of my students," he noted rather proudly. "And you," he added.

"Don't tell me you're also the fifth Henry in your family," declared Margot.

"As a matter of fact, I am." Hal laughed sheepishly—this parallel to Shakespeare's Henry V had been a subject of lively discussion between Hal and his friend Gabe Stern when they were about twelve years old. "But as you see, there's no prospect of a crown in store for me."

Margot smiled, then ruminated: "I don't suppose your father or grandfather's nickname was Hank?"

"My father's was, yes."

"Aha!"

"What?"

"Have you ever noticed that *Hank Pearson* is more or less an anagram for *Shakespeare*, give or take a few more N's and a few less E's? But they dropped the E's rather capriciously back then, anyway, didn't they?"

Hal took a moment to think this over. "Boy, you *are* sharp!" he finally concluded admiringly. "I can't say I ever made that connection. Thanks for pointing it out."

There was a pause as they looked at each other, but before either could come up with something else to say, the stewardess began handing out the airline meals. Jessie roused herself from slumber to wave hers away with contempt, and seemed appalled when Hal and Margot each took one and began eating the meal with gusto.

"How can you eat such *chozzerai*?" she asked. "I have a nice turkey sandwich and a potato knish if you want some nourishment. The knish is cold, I grant you, but it's not bad cold. Your father used to like it that way," she said, addressing Margot.

Hal explained that he had always looked forward to the airplane meal. "When you're boxed in at thirty thousand feet, a piece of stringy beef and some soggy potatoes au gratin have an appeal that's hard to explain."

Margot agreed. "I always feel a sense of irrational anticipation when they start rolling that cart down the aisle. It just proves how human beings can adjust their expectations to the circumstances. Everything is relative."

"It's like the Yiddish story my friend Gabe's father used to tell about the family in the shtetl who goes to the rabbi to complain that his house is too small," noted Hal.

Margot laughed. "You know that story?" She picked up the thread (her father used to tell this story on a regular basis): "'Rabbi,' he says, 'my wife and four children are so crowded we don't know what to do. What do you advise, Rabbi?'"

"'I'll tell you what to do, Shmul,'" replied Hal, assuming a rabbinical tone. "'Do as I say. Bring the goats into the house.'"

"'The goats in the house?'" Margot rejoined. "'Rabbi, what are you talking? We're already crowded to death as it is and you say we should bring the goats into the house too?'"

"'Do as I say, Shmul. Bring in the goats.'"

"So he brings in the goats. And the next day, Shmul goes back to the rabbi. 'Rabbi,' he says, 'it's worse than ever. Now we can't even turn around with the goats in the house. What should we do?'"

"'Shmul, listen to me, bring in the sheep.'"

"'Bring in the chickens.'"

"'Bring in the'—what else is there?"

"Cows."

"'Bring in the cows!'"

"'But, Rabbi, now we can't move. We can't breathe. We can't get a wink of sleep.'"

"'All right—now, I tell you what you do—take the goats, the sheep, the cows, and the chickens and put them out of the house.'"

"And so they did—and what a difference," finished up Margot. "So much space, you wouldn't believe—at least for a while!"

Hal and Margot seemed momentarily overwhelmed by the hilarity of this anecdote, which they felt they had recited delightfully and with excellent Yiddish accents. "It must be that Jewish blood way back on your mother's side," noted Margot.

"Probably," said Hal, "You know your mother says her Will claimed to have Jewish blood too, on *his* mother's side."

"That's what they all say to get into the good graces of a Jewish woman," noted Margot.

"No doubt," said Hal.

"In any case, you have a good ear for ethnic cadences. You should have been an actor."

"And who says he wasn't?" interjected Jessie peevishly, having followed their exchange with less amusement. Then, she settled back in her seat, closed her eyes, and fell asleep again.

Chapter Thirty-eight

For the REST OF THE FLIGHT HAL READ *TEACHING AP-proaches to As You Like It*, while Margot read McCullough's biography of John Adams. Jessie dozed, worked on a sweater she was knitting for Jeffrey, and thumbed through a copy of *Gourmet* magazine. When they finally touched ground at Marco Polo Airport, she had been sleeping deeply for some time and woke with a start. "Where am I?"

"Venice," said Hal.

"Home," said Jessie. She had turned chalk white and was shaking slightly.

"Mom, are you feeling well?" asked Margot, concerned. Her mother rarely was sick or displayed nerves.

"I feel so . . . strange," she said.

"No need to be nervous," said Hal, taking her hand.

"It feels . . . like stage fright," continued Jessie. "Not that I've ever been on stage, but he used to describe it. Your heart starts thumping and suddenly you don't remember what you're supposed to do."

"You don't have to do anything, Mom," Margot reassured her. "Just relax and enjoy yourself."

"No, no," said Jessie irritably. "I have something I have to do."

She paused as if trying to recollect what. "There were other loves, you know," she murmured. "Will was a great love, but there were others."

"Sure, Mom," laughed Margot, "we all know, thanks to Uncle Sid, that you were a 'hot tomato' like me."

"No need to think about that right now," said Hal more seriously. He assumed she was thinking of Milt. After all, wasn't this trip, an excavation of earlier love, a kind of imaginative usurpation of that later relationship? He could understand if she were suddenly feeling guilty. "Just take a few deep breaths and clear your mind," he counseled.

Jessie didn't respond, but made her way out of the plane into the airport, leaning on Hal's arm, her lips pressed together. She didn't speak until they had claimed their luggage and walked outside to catch the *motoscafi* that would take them across the lagoon, up the Grand Canal, to their hotel. As the boat approached the bank, she lifted her head to the sky. "That smell," she said.

Margot sniffed. "It smells rather vile."

"It was worse in the summer," murmured Jessie. "Rotting garbage." She waved her hand in disgust.

The boat let them off at the foot of the hotel, where they climbed up the stone steps, through a discreet entrance, and into the lobby, a magnificent room with gold damask wallpaper, blue velvet curtains, and a polished red and beige marble floor. The room was decorated in antique furniture and hung with tapestries and old paintings. A harpsichord stood in the corner near the reception desk.

"Wow!" exclaimed Hal. He had been to Venice before, but had stayed in a modest if quaint bed-and-breakfast.

"Stunning!" breathed Margot.

"*Vanitas vanitatum,*" murmured Jessie.

"What?" said Margot.

"It's Latin. It's what Will used to say whenever he saw how some of them lived. I can't remember what it means."

"'The hollowness of vanity,'" translated Hal.

"Yes." Jessie took this up. "It's the idea that everything passes— even the rich and powerful ones die," she said wistfully, "which makes you wonder what the fuss is all about."

"'Dust to stop a bunghole.'" Hal nodded. "Food for worms."

"Enough already!" said Margot. "Would you stop being morbid and let me enjoy this place!"

But Jessie wasn't listening. She had paused near the center of the room and was gazing around with a look of recognition on her face.

"What is it, Mom?" asked Margot.

"I've been here before."

"You remember the room?"

"Yes. I was here with Poppa when I was thirteen. We came to see the Popish ambassador to work out the negotiations about the new trade routes. I sat over there in the corner and played checkers with the doge's son. I remember: He was stupid but a nice boy. I let him win."

Margot laughed. "That sounds like you, I'll admit," she said, for the first time appearing to enter into the spirit of her mother's story. Then she took Jessie's arm and pointed to the elevator. "Why don't we go to our room and get settled? You can lie down."

"I don't want to lie down," said Jessie testily.

"It was just a suggestion," said Margot in a conciliatory tone. "You don't have to lie down if you don't want to."

"At least see your room and freshen up," said Hal gently. "I'll tell Anish that we're here and you can meet us downstairs in the bar in half an hour—if you feel up to it."

Jessie seemed agreeable to that, and now followed Margot to the elevator without protest.

Once in the room, she changed into her best dress, a blue crepe that she had last worn at Milt's funeral. She told Margot to change too. "Wear the black one," she ordered with surprising vehemence.

It was a little black dress that Margot had bought at Loehmann's a few years ago and that Jessie had insisted she pack. It was nothing special—it had cost $39.99 on the clearance rack. But it had always been one of Jessie's favorites and, truth be told, cheap clothes generally looked as good, if not better, on Margot as expensive ones.

Margot put on the dress. It had a scooped neck and empire waistline, and it draped in simple folds around her body. "Why do you like this dress so much, Mom?" she asked.

"Because it looks good on you—and he would like it." (Margot did not bother to ask who *he* was).

Jessie had taken out her jewelry case as she spoke, and now handed Margot a locket.

"It's beautiful," exclaimed Margot. "Where did you get it?"

"At the jewelry store in Haddonfield. It was on sale." (Jessie could never resist boasting about a good buy.) "It opens, you see." She pointed to the groove on the side of the locket, and Margot pressed the latch so that the two halves sprung apart on the little hinge. "You can put pictures inside," explained Jessie, "maybe of Stephanie and Jeffrey. Or your own children, if you have any. A lock of hair is nice, too."

"I'll keep that in mind, Mom."

"Or you can have something written inside. That's what he did. He gave me one like it once—put in a line from one of his poems." She paused, gazing at her daughter, who had fastened the locket around her neck, then added an uncharacteristically philosophical aside: "Probably things reappear all the time, only we don't recognize them. We're too caught up in what's going on at the moment to feel the past right there in the present." She grew silent, then resumed her more usual, straightforward tone. "Anyway, I think you look beautiful. Just like I did when he took me on the canal the first time and kissed me."

"Mother!"

Still, Margot had to admit that she felt good wearing the dress and the locket. The room itself was a jewel box—with its gold-leaf wallpaper, antique desk, and canopied bed, its velvet curtains swagged along the casement windows. They were overlooking the canal and could see the magnificent façade of a church across the way.

"The Church of Salute," said Jessie, gazing out at the edifice. "Very grand."

When they went down to the bar, where the group had congregated for a late-night snack, everyone turned to look at Margot.

"The locket is a gift from my mother," she said, embarrassed. "She bought it because it reminds her of one she said *he* gave her." Margot's voice had only a trace of mockery in it; she could feel herself falling under the spell of Jessie's fantasy.

Hal stared silently, but Anish was quick to express admiration. "You look like a Gritti princess, or at least a Franco Zeffirelli Juliet. All you need is your devoted Romeo, a role that I slavishly beg to occupy."

Margot laughed and gave a regal bow of her head.

Anish proceeded to introduce himself and his colleague, Felicity Gardencourt, a very thin, pale woman who looked as though she had spent too much time eating tuna fish sandwiches in library carrels. Felicity was the product of a New England family, straight out of a Hawthorne novel, for whom sublimation was as much a part of the family inheritance as the pewter cutlery and the drafty, large-shingled house on Cape Cod where the Gardencourts congregated each August for uncomfortable family gatherings. Like Anish, Felicity was an assistant professor at Yale, respected for her excellent monographs on the Italian Renaissance, though not for her teaching style, which tended to be short on the kind of animation required to keep undergraduates awake. In the words of the *Yale Student Course Review Guide*: "This woman needs to get a life."

Nonetheless, as a Renaissance historian with a thorough grasp of the minutiae of her field, she could certainly be useful in tracking down a lost manuscript from that era.

Hal immediately began interrogating Felicity on specific historical points. Jessie had said she was thirteen at the time she visited the palace with her father to meet the Vatican ambassador, which would have put her visit at around 1588 or '89—since she first met Will, she said, when she was seventeen, in 1593. Did Professor Gardencourt know what the palace was being used for in 1588?

Felicity seemed well versed in the subject. "Doge Andrea Gritti built this palace for himself in 1525 and continued on as doge until 1534," she explained. "After that, the building was used for a variety of diplomatic purposes, including the housing of the Vatican ambassadors, frequent visitors to the region."

Hal and Margot looked at each other. "Would there ever be occasion for a Jew to meet with the Vatican ambassador?" asked Hal.

Felicity responded without a pause. "The Vatican negotiated with the doge and the Venetian trade council on a variety of matters. Since the Venetians relied on trade with the Ottoman Empire, who in turn used the Jews as intermediaries, the Vatican was obliged to deal with them as well."

"So you're saying that Levantine Jews occupied a role of importance in Venice?" asked Hal.

"Yes," replied Felicity. "Of course, the debacle involving Joseph Nasi set things back a bit, but that happened earlier than the period you're referring to."

"Nasi," said Jessie. "Poppa said he was a *meshuggener*."

"*Meshuggener?*" queried Felicity. Yiddish terms had apparently not penetrated her library carrel.

"It's Yiddish for a crazy person," elucidated Hal.

"I don't know that that quite captures the nuance of the word," protested Margot in a sudden renewed desire to place Hal in the wrong.

"It's the gist," intervened Jessie.

Felicity nodded in apparent agreement and proceeded to elaborate: "Joseph Nasi was a member of the wealthy Mendes banking family of Lisbon and Antwerp—a Marrano who ingratiated himself with Suleiman the Magnificent and his son and heir, Selim, rulers of the Ottoman Empire in the mid-sixteenth century. He was briefly named ruler of the island of Naxos and hoped to become king of Cyprus. His attempt to drive the Venetians from Cyprus failed, however, when the Turks were defeated at Lepanto, after which there was a backlash against the Jews in Venice. Talmuds were burned and Jewish movement in the city was closely monitored for several years afterward."

Everyone in the group had begun to shift restlessly. Felicity's tendency to deliver long expositions in a relative monotone, with no sense that her audience was falling asleep, was notorious at Yale. Some of her more inventive students had taken to imagining her in black leather holding a whip. But mental imagery could go only so far, and most ended up with their heads on their desks.

Fortunately, Jessie intervened again. "When we first came here, Poppa had a time cleaning up the mess that man Nasi made. Not that I remember; I was still a baby." She paused. "Kit said Nasi was the subject of his play."

"*The Jew of Malta*," clarified Hal for the company.

"Thank God Poppa and his cousin came along to set a good example and make things right with the doge."

"His cousin?"

"Daniel Rodrigues, a nice man but also a wheeler-dealer. Used to bring me gold bangles from the Orient. Said I shouldn't say where I got them."

Felicity took this up. "Daniel Rodrigues was another wealthy Marrano, but one who maintained good relations between the Venetian state and the Ottoman Empire. He eventually opened up trade routes to the East, convincing the trade councils of the feasibility of ignoring and, in some cases, countermanding Vatican law."

"Yes," said Jessie, "he and Poppa did all that."

"And your father's name was?" prompted Hal.

"Avram Rodrigues. But she wouldn't know about him." Jessie nodded toward Felicity. "He didn't like to put himself forward.

He used to say, 'Let Daniel get the *covet*, make the appearances. Me, I'm content to stay in the background.'"

Felicity took out a pad and began taking notes. "It's something to look into," she observed. "Other family members may well have been involved in some of Rodrigues's trade negotiations; there may be no record of such involvement, but it would be interesting to search the annals for possible references."

"Well, I think that's enough background for now," said Hal. He had noted that Jessie had begun to look tired. "We all need to be fresh for our adventure tomorrow. Let's get an early start and agree to meet for breakfast at seven. As for you"—he looked at Jessie affectionately—"you need to get a good night's sleep. I'm counting on your daughter"—he glanced quickly at Margot and then, just as quickly, looked away—"to see to that."

Chapter Thirty-nine

The next MORNING AT SEVEN THEY ALL GATHERED FOR breakfast in the hotel's lavish dining room. Hal and Anish, both excited about the forthcoming adventure, were in high spirits and launched into a debate about literature—more or less a standing argument they had had since college. It was Anish's view that James Joyce was the beginning of the end of western literature, while Hal was Joyce's energetic defender.

The debate flared up now as they stood selecting from various delicacies at a central buffet table. Hal argued that Anish was too deeply "colonized" to recognize revolutionary genius and innovation. "Let's face it, as the product of cultural imperialism, you've come to identify with the oppressor. It's the Patty Hearst syndrome."

"Spare me your PC posturing," responded Anish irritably. "We're not undergraduates anymore. Why are you American-born liberals allowed to have free will and I, an Indian-born conservative, am not? It sounds to me like classic colonialism masquerading as moral righteousness—just another turn on white man's burden. As for my openness to new ideas, I'm the first to recognize originality when there's something more to it than gimmickry. Mrs. Kaplan's thesis has captivated me, for example. I see a basic intellectual design to the thing, which is more than I can say for your Mr. Joyce, who merely opened the door for every posturing fool who could concoct nonsense and call himself an *artiste*."

"But Joyce *was* a great artist and a great innovator," protested Hal. "He was trying to encompass the entire history of civilization, of language, of meaning itself within the frame of his literary enterprise."

"Well, then, he was trying to do too much," pronounced Anish dismissively. "Give me Jane Austen's fine brush any time."

"And what about Milton, Tolstoy, Melville? What about our own fellow, Shakespeare—they all took up rather a large canvas, wouldn't you say?"

"You confuse epic scale and imagination with babble and pastiche. That pantheon—and I am not prepared to grant them all equal greatness since, as you know, I feel there's been a sad falling off since the age of Samuel Johnson—but at least those you mentioned were determined to communicate with some semblance of clarity and logic. No, it's these gibbering monkeys of modernism and postmodernism that I have no use for. They think that by speaking nonsense they speak all tongues—that the less clear they are, the more they say. And there are always snobs and suckers—forgive me if you fall into those categories—willing to agree."

Margot, who had been standing nearby next to the trays of Parma ham and fresh fruit, intervened at this point: "So, Anish, if you're so opposed to Hal's views, how come you continue to be friends?"

"Views have nothing to do with it," responded Anish with surprise, as if it would never have occurred to him to think that they did. "Our friendship is based on character, not opinion." He had entirely changed his tone, dispensing with "views" and warming to the idea of praising his friend. "Hal is someone I respect and trust—indeed I love. He is the *honnête homme*, as Molière's Alceste called his friend Philinte. I hold him in my 'heart's core,' as Hamlet held Horatio."

"That's right," joked Hal, "I'm the hero's best friend. Always the bridesmaid, never the bride." He darted a glance at Margot.

"Hal is comfortable with ambiguity," continued Anish, determined not to let Hal's jokes get in the way of his exposition. "Look how he's managed to deal with your mother's situation. He neither believes nor disbelieves; he accepts. There's a bit of the Zen master about him."

"*Ommm*," said Margot, putting her hands up in yogi fashion and making everyone laugh.

"Enough already." Hal cut short the conversation. "I can see that our guide is restless and eager to be on her way."

In fact, Jessie had barely touched her breakfast and was sitting at the edge of her chair, staring into space. She had slept soundly, but had awakened with a premonition of something momentous about to happen.

They caught the *vaporetto* at the steps of the hotel. It snaked up the canal, eventually arriving only a few blocks from the ghetto. Hal, who was holding the map, led the way as they walked through the cobbled streets. At one point Jessie paused and stood stock-still. She pointed to a small stone building. "There," she said, "was where Jacopo Robusti lived. Poppa thought he was a great genius."

"The home of the painter Tintoretto," clarified Felicity, nodding.

They proceeded onto the little bridge that led over the canal to the area of the ghetto. A carving of two lions marked the arch leading into the area.

"The lions of Judah," noted Jessie, peering up.

"In actuality," corrected Felicity, "the lions were the insignia of the Brolo brothers, who originally developed the area before it was made into a settlement location for the Jews. But the later inhabitants appropriated it as the expression of their own identity," she added, as though giving Jessie permission to have made this historical error.

Having crossed the bridge, they entered the large campo of the so-called Getto Nuovo, or New Ghetto (though actually the first one settled). The stone houses were built very high. Although the general effect was picturesque, one had to consider that living conditions were not very pleasant.

"It's where the poorer ones lived," explained Jessie. "We didn't mix with them much, except for the shopping. You could get some good buys if you knew where to look," she said to Margot.

Felicity pointed to the top of one of the buildings. "That's the Scola Grande Tedesca on the top floor. It's the German synagogue, and the oldest in the ghetto." Everyone craned their necks. They could make out a Hebrew inscription. "There are two other synagogues in this part of the ghetto." She pointed to the upper levels of two other buildings in the square.

"Yes, they built them on the top to be closer to God, as they liked to say," said Jessie, "but really where else could they go? There was no room. But this isn't where we lived. We want to go this way." She had gotten ahead of Hal, and now led them through a narrow, cobbled street into a smaller area.

As they arrived into this small square, Jessie breathed a sigh. "Here we are."

Everyone stopped and looked around. Jessie had an expression of excited recognition on her face. It was the Getto Vecchio, or Old Ghetto, named for the old foundry that had once been there.

"It looks the same," she said, "but without the decorations. We used to have flowers in the windowboxes and brass plates on the doors. Sometimes there were banners hanging for the festivals or to announce the special programs. Always they were giving lessons or having meetings: concerts, lectures, talks, you name it. And so much noise: people playing instruments, arguing philosophy, gentiles walking around in fancy clothes with their servants. But now it's quiet, like ghosts live here."

Felicity stepped in with the supporting commentary. "There were six thousand Jews in the ghetto during the sixteenth century.

Half were killed by the plague in the seventeenth. Centuries later, those who remained were destroyed during the Holocaust. Only about six hundred Jews live in Venice today, with perhaps sixty living in the ghetto area."

"There's our synagogue," interrupted Jessie, pointing to a large yellow stone building.

Everyone turned to look.

Then, suddenly, Jessie's eyes began darting back and forth as though trying to locate something. She grasped Margot's arm and seemed for a moment to lose her footing.

"Are you okay, Mom?"

"Yes, yes. It's over there." Jessie had grown quite pale and was shaking. She pointed to a building in the corner of the campo, and the group followed as she made her way toward it.

As they approached they could see the words GAM GAM on a sign at the front of the building. Closer inspection revealed it to be a restaurant, apparently the only one in the ghetto. A small placard in the window pronounced that it was run by the Chabad of Venice and offered glatt kosher food, from lunch to dinner, Sunday through Thursday, and on Friday, from lunchtime to two hours before the advent of Shabbos. A small note indicated that it also offered Shabbos dinner, free of charge, to interested visitors.

"There must be a big demand for kosher food," noted Margot, "given they're almost always open."

"Unfortunately, they're not open now," said Hal, looking at his watch. It was only nine-thirty, and the sign said the restaurant would open at twelve-thirty. He had been in a state of barely suppressed excitement as they entered the small campo, and to have this final lap of his journey delayed was clearly a source of frustration. "We'll need to kill a few hours and come back," he said, trying not to sound disappointed and smiling reassuringly at Jessie.

"So what do you want to do?" asked Margot, glancing at the group around her, though avoiding eye contact with Hal.

"Felicity and I noticed a bookshop we passed on our way from the *vaporetto* stop," said Anish. "It seemed to have some interesting reference works on the city that Felicity, with her eagle eye, thought might be useful. I'm keen to have a closer look. What do you say we meet back here around one? It says twelve-thirty on the sign, but in Italy, you have to allow leeway for picturesque tardiness."

"I'd like to take a gondola on the canal," said Jessie softly. "I think it would be a nice way to pass the time."

Hal nodded agreeably and took Jessie's arm, while Margot shrugged and followed behind them. They made their way out of the campo to the side of the canal and hailed one of the more brightly painted boats, replete with a dark-eyed, striped-sweatered gondolier, who kissed his fingers at them, his eyes lingering predictably on Margot.

It took some maneuvering on the part of both Hal and Margot to get Jessie comfortably settled in the front of the boat. They then took their places opposite her, as the gondola began its slow sweep up the canal.

"Very nice," sighed Jessie, "just as I remembered. The buildings, though"—she pointed across to the rows of stone buildings at the edge of the canal—"they don't seem as high."

"They say Venice is sinking," noted Hal. "Lately, an inch or more a year. If the process dates back to your period, I can imagine you'd notice a difference in the size of the buildings."

Jessie did not seem interested in dwelling on this observation. She had been gazing around her, the soft splash of the oars appearing to lull her into a dreamy state. Margot and Hal sat quietly next to each other, taking care to look scrupulously at the sights and not at each other. Riding in a gondola in Venice was the most clichéd of tourist activities, and yet both felt moved by the experience. A slight shiver passed through Margot. It was December and there was a chill in the air, but she was not so much cold as possessed by the eerie romance of her surroundings. She could feel the slight brush of Hal's jeans against her leg.

"Are you cold?" he asked. "You could take my jacket."

"No," said Margot. "I'm just kind of taken with being in this place. It's so beautiful and so old. I feel as though the mantle of time were wrapped around me." She stopped, wondering if she sounded pretentious, but saw that Hal was looking at her with great seriousness.

"Who's that?" said Jessie suddenly. She had been leaning back, her eyes, half-closed, scanning the streets on the edges of the canal.

Margot and Hal turned to where she was looking. A group of tourists who had been traipsing along the cobbled street in front of them was now rounding the corner and passing out of sight.

"It looked like a tour group," said Margot. "I didn't get a chance to see them clearly. Do you think you recognized someone?"

"Yes," said Jessie, "but I was wrong. He wouldn't be here."

"Not in this life," laughed Margot, assuming she was speaking of "Will." "Unless you count his reincarnation in our friend." She gave Hal an amused glance, and he laughed too.

"No, no," said Jessie irritably. "Not Will. I mean the other one. He's probably dead too."

"I didn't realize you had that many admirers," said Margot, speaking lightly, though struck by her mother's wistful tone.

"Milt, for example, is gone," continued Jessie dreamily. "He was a fine man, you know, your father. I never regretted marrying him."

"I should hope not," declared Margot, "especially given the excellent progeny that resulted."

"You and Carla are good girls." Jessie nodded. "I wouldn't have had my life any different, believe me." As if putting this topic to rest, she now shifted her attention to the gondolier, who had been quietly whistling a tune while continuing to stare appreciatively at Margot. "And what's your name?" Jessie asked the gondolier. "I used to know one who looked like you named Roberto. He was very nice about taking Poppa and me around the city, even after hours, when we were supposed to stay put. I won't deny that he liked me." She looked a bit superciliously at Margot and Hal, as if to say that they didn't have to wink about it.

"My name is Giancarlo, and it is my pleasure to show charming ladies my beautiful city," said the gondolier, smiling.

"Why don't you take us to shore now," said Margot, afraid that her mother would begin to confuse the gondolier, or that his appreciation of herself might become more pointed. She had noticed that Hal seemed annoyed by the man's admiring gaze. "We can walk back to the ghetto from here. By that time, the restaurant should be open."

They all agreed that this was a good idea. The gondolier deposited them on the little pier about a quarter of a mile beyond the ghetto, and they walked back slowly, taking time to peek into a small church, unassuming in outward appearance, that happened to house a Bellini in one of its corners. "In Venice, you stumble on a Bellini the way you might stumble on an Elvis poster back home," noted Hal. "It's a fundamental difference in cultural density."

As they left the church, Jessie announced that she was hungry—not surprising, since she had eaten almost nothing for breakfast and it was almost noon. She pointed to a small restaurant on the side of the canal, where they took a table by the window and shared a large platter of fresh mozzarella and tomatoes, along with a loaf of freshly baked Italian bread.

"I don't understand why this tastes so much better than it does at home; it's only cheese and tomatoes," observed Margot.

"It's the sun," said Jessie knowingly. "It falls at a different angle."

Margot and Hal looked at each other, amused. It was unusual for Jessie to admit that anything she had not prepared herself was actually tasty, but she was clearly enjoying this meal. She dipped her bread into the little ceramic bowl of olive oil on the table. "You can't get olive oil like this anywhere," she explained, "even at Whole Foods."

After they had eaten, they stopped at a shop that sold souvenirs made of Venetian glass. Margot bought Stephanie a brightly colored glass pen with a little bottle of red ink to go with it. It was

Hal's suggestion. He said Stephanie would like to use the pen and ink for her "process journal."

"I have them write down their thoughts about literature as these come into their head," he explained. "Stephanie always has lots of good insights—but she's also into fancy notebooks and pens. She says that the tools sometimes *do* make the carpenter. It's the kind of reverse cliché that the young are fond of, and which, I've learned, generally contains some truth."

Margot also bought a pair of glass beads for Carla and wanted to buy another pair for her mother, but Jessie said no—she had always found Venetian glass too bulky for jewelry. "For a window or maybe a lamp, yes, but who wants to wear glass around your neck? I'd rather have a nice silver locket." She glanced approvingly at the one she had given Margot. "And at my age, a string of pearls is best." She patted the pearls she had on. They had been a gift from Milt on their thirtieth anniversary.

By the time they reached the ghetto again, it was one o'clock, as planned, and they saw Anish and Felicity waiting for them as they entered the little campo. They could see that Gam Gam was now open; a few people were going inside.

They were about to cross over to the restaurant when a group of tourists began leaving the yellow stone synagogue that Jessie had pointed to earlier and were congregating rather noisily a few yards away. Their voices identified them as Americans, and a young man, speaking in English with a thick Italian accent, was trying to shepherd them into some semblance of order.

Jessie, Hal, and Margot, with Felicity and Anish behind them, began to walk forward in the direction of the restaurant.

As they moved, the tour group began to move as well. They had obviously completed their visit to this portion of the ghetto and were on their way, possibly to the other ghetto or to other sites in Venice. Their young Italian guide was pointing out architectural details of the buildings they passed, while they chattered among themselves and called out questions. As they approached, Jessie appeared not to see them and indeed walked straight ahead so that the group was obliged to part for her.

"So she can't step aside?" One of the women in the group spoke up loudly to her neighbor.

"Some people have no consideration," said the other woman. "They think they own the sidewalk." She cast a disapproving look toward Jessie, who continued in her obliviousness, incensing the women still more.

"It's how they were brought up," said the first woman more loudly.

"That's hardly an excuse," said the second.

As they were voicing these sentiments, a man who was part of the group and whom several other women were trying to engage in conversation turned his head, his attention drawn to Jessie. He stared for a moment and then suddenly stopped in his tracks and exclaimed: "Jessie Lubenthal!"

At this point the two groups had intersected and were about to pass each other. Jessie, however, hearing her name, also stopped where she was. Her gaze, which had been directed at the restaurant, shifted to the person standing directly in front of her.

He was a man of about seventy-five, wearing a tweed cap and a light raincoat. He looked, quite frankly, like an average elderly Jewish man. sparse gray flyaway hair, middle height, soft sagging gray eyes, a slightly hooked nose, and a stoop.

But Jessie looked at him with an air of surprise. She had now taken a few steps forward, as had the man, so that the two had separated themselves from their respective groups, meeting, as it were, like two dignitaries, with their entourages behind them. The man's group consisted of about twelve people, mostly women, but with a smattering of men—all apparently in their sixties and seventies with the exception of the local guide, a handsome youth who was eyeing Margot with some interest. Jessie's group, meanwhile, was waiting for her to finish the encounter so they could proceed to search for Jessie's lost sonnets.

"Saul Millman!" exclaimed Jessie as she stared back at the man. "It *was* you! I thought I was dreaming when I saw you from the gondola a few hours ago."

"Jessie Lubenthal!" Saul exclaimed again.

"Kaplan," she corrected gently.

"My mistake," said Saul. "How's Milt?"

"He passed away two years ago," said Jessie softly. "And Frieda?"

"Gone," said Saul.

"I'm sorry."

Saul tilted his head slightly forward in acknowledgment, but his eyes did not leave Jessie's face.

"It's been a hundred years," she said, putting out her hand.

"More," said Saul, taking it in both of his. "Not that I haven't thought about you. Every day."

Jessie blushed but did not withdraw her hand, which he continued to hold with no apparent intention of letting go.

"I'm told you moved to North Jersey and made a fortune," she said.

"A fortune, I don't know, but I'm comfortable," said Saul. He paused, then felt obliged to clarify. "Video rentals. I knew right away, it was the future. Movies in your own home: How could it miss?"

"You always liked movies," noted Jessie.

"But I wasn't so creative—just practical. I figured: I'm lazy, so is everyone else. Video is the way to go. So I took a chance and I was right."

"Milt didn't have such good business sense, I'm afraid."

"But he had something better."

Jessie blushed again but said nothing.

"I thought I'd take a little time off," continued Saul, trying to cover up the awkward silence. He gave a nod in the direction of the group behind him, though still not taking his eyes off Jessie. "A JCC Seniors tour. We already did Florence, and we're on to Rome tomorrow—very educational."

"Aha!" said Jessie, as though this detail did not much interest her.

"I have a chain of stores now," Saul continued, returning to the topic of his work. "Mostly my son takes care of things, but I keep my hand in. Videos Unlimited—that's the name of the company."

"Videos Unlimited!" exclaimed Jessie. "Didn't you just open a store in Cherry Hill?" Videos Unlimited was where Hal had gotten her *The Merchant of Venice* tape.

"I did!" said Saul. "Do you live in Cherry Hill? I thought you were still in Vineland. I didn't want to pry, you know."

"I left Vineland almost a year ago. It was lonely after Milt died. I live in Cherry Hill with my daughter now," said Jessie. "Not this one"—she motioned to Margot—"the other one."

"This one looks like you," noted Saul, glancing at Margot. "Of course, I like the original."

Jessie didn't answer.

"You haven't changed," said Saul.

"Don't be a fool."

"I'm serious. As beautiful as ever. More beautiful."

Jessie waved her hand. "You always knew how to flatter."

"Not enough, I'm afraid."

"Oh, more than enough," said Jessie with a trace of rancor. "You flattered me plenty and then took up with Sara Feld."

"What are you talking?"

A floodgate of emotion seemed to open for a moment in Jessie. "You kissed her on the sidewalk after you dropped me off that night after the movie."

"A fabrication!" exclaimed Saul, turning bright red. "A bald-faced lie!"

"You didn't kiss Sara Feld after you dropped me off?"

"Kiss Sara Feld? Are you crazy? Whoever told you such a thing?"

"She did."

"The *mishkeit*. I could wring her neck."

"She's already dead," sighed Jessie. "I read it in the *Vineland News*. She passed away last month."

"Good riddance to her."

"Saul!"

"Excuse me, but she cost me the woman I loved."

Jessie and Saul stood silent for a moment, contemplating this statement. Then Saul exclaimed again: "Jessie Lubenthal!"

And this time, she didn't correct him.

Chapter Forty

Mom," *said* MARGOT, APPROACHING THE PAIR AFTER waiting what she thought was an appropriate interval. Saul had continued to hold Jessie's hand, and Jessie had made no effort to take it away. The members of Saul's tour group were engaged in steady chatter that made them oblivious to the passage of time, while their guide, apparently smitten with Margot's appearance, was engrossed in sending her facial signals, by turns lascivious, pouting, and plaintive in the manner of an accomplished mime.

On Jessie's side, Felicity and Anish were deeply engrossed in the reference book they had found in the bookstore up the street. It dealt with the archival material housed in the doge's palace.

Hal and Margot were the only members of either party who seemed aware that the clock was ticking. They had been watching Jessie and Saul Millman with a certain fascination but with growing impatience. What was going on here? Although it was rather moving to see the look of surprised affection on the two faces, it also seemed slightly embarrassing for people of this age to be looking at each other like that. And it was, quite frankly, a detour from the established itinerary. They were nearing the final object of their pilgrimage. To be stalled now in the middle of the campo as Jessie greeted some *alter cocker* from the past was, to say the least, an annoyance.

Thus, Margot finally stepped forward to intervene: "Mom, we ought to get moving."

Saul looked up as she addressed her mother, though Jessie continued to look at Saul.

"So this is your daughter," he said, smiling. His smile, Margot noted, was very nice. "They told me you were the spitting image of your mother when she was young, and they weren't off base on that."

"This is Saul Millman," said Jessie, finally looking up at her daughter. "I knew him in my youth. What a coincidence to run into him here."

Margot, growing more annoyed by her mother's insistence on prolonging this casual chitchat, spoke in a rather peremptory tone: "It's a pleasure to meet you, Mr. Millman. I'm sure Mom will want to be in touch. But now, I think, we ought to be on our way."

"We're staying at a very nice place," said Jessie, still not letting go of Saul's hand.

"The Gritti Palace," said Margot, hoping this information might facilitate a leave-taking.

"We're at the Danieli," said Saul. "Very fancy too. Do you remember, Jessie, the winter dance in the tenth grade? How they decorated the gym with gold streamers? You wore the pink gown with the crinkly skirt. Like a fairy princess."

Margot, now losing all patience, shot Hal a look. He came forward, nodding politely to Saul and then turning to Jessie. "Don't you think we ought to get going?" he asked in his soft, teacherly voice.

"I don't want to keep you from your tour," said Saul in an unconvincing tone.

"He owns the new video store in Cherry Hill," said Jessie to Hal, "the one where you got that *Merchant of Venice* tape."

Hal nodded. "A fine store—I commend you. I'm Hal Pearson."

He put out his hand. Saul, who had continued to grasp Jessie's, seemed momentarily at a loss. He finally let go and shook Hal's hand. Jessie seemed upset, and Hal hurriedly addressed himself to Saul on her behalf. "Maybe you can stop by the hotel later for a drink."

"I'd like that," said Saul. "What time should I drop by?"

"Around five. We should be back by then."

"I'll be there, with bells on," said Saul, inching back toward his group, which immediately swallowed him up and began to move forward, the young Italian guide sending a sad Pierrot look to Margot as they went.

Jessie, Hal, and Margot were now left together, standing in the middle of the campo.

"Are you all right?" asked Hal, noting that Jessie had a rather blank expression on her face. "Do you want to sit down and rest for a while?"

She shook her head.

"Okay, then," said Hal, "let's get on with it. As Hermione said to Paulina in *The Winter's Tale*: 'There is no lady live / So meet for this great errand.' We're at your service. Lead us forward, lady."

Chapter Forty-one

B *ut somehow* THE SPIRIT OF THE EXPEDITION HAD CHANGED. As Jessie moved toward the Gam Gam restaurant, her face had lost all its eager intensity. She might have been walking through the Cherry Hill mall for all the excitement she showed.

Entering the restaurant dampened their spirits still further. They realized immediately that it had undergone a thorough renovation.

"Shit!" exclaimed Hal, in a rare show of temper.

"No hidden sonnets here, I'm afraid," said Margot, trying to sound flip, though there was a catch in her throat.

But Jessie looked strangely unfazed. "Oh, well," she said, "let's take a peek anyway. It's been a long time, after all."

They walked around the restaurant where several tourists were busily eating blintzes with sour cream. The manager, a young man with a black hat and *pais*, turned out to be from Brooklyn. He was a member of the Lubavitchers, a Hasidic sect that had become a presence in the ghetto and even held services in some of the synagogues. After passing out Lubavitch pamphlets along with the menus, he seemed pleased to show them around.

They climbed the steps to the upper floors of the building.

"This was where I slept," Jessie said matter-of-factly when they arrived at the third floor. "I believe my bed was over there. But you see they've changed everything. They've put in new floors—much easier to clean, I should think."

"So I don't suppose we could pull up this—what is it, linoleum or something?—to look for the sonnets." Margot turned to Hal.

"I don't believe we could," said Hal. He seemed to be perusing the pamphlet, but Margot could see that he was upset and trying to get a handle on himself.

Everyone seemed at a loss as to what to do next. "I don't suppose you're hungry?" asked Hal, turning to Jessie. She shook her head. The salad at the little restaurant on the canal had been enough for her.

"There's a museum in the Getto Nuovo," suggested Felicity. "It has some interesting artifacts dating back several centuries."

Everyone gamely trooped back to the other ghetto and into the small museum that Felicity had mentioned. They began to look at the items in the display cases along the walls, artifacts from the ghetto's history. Most of what was preserved was from the eighteenth and nineteenth centuries, though a few scrolls and candlesticks, and one magnificent menorah, dated from an earlier period.

The museum curator, a young Italian woman with excellent English (she'd gotten her Ph.D. in art history at Stanford), explained that the menorah was from the sixteenth century, or perhaps earlier.

"Maybe it looks familiar," said Jessie.

Hal asked the young curator if she knew when the building in the other ghetto, where the Lubavitchers had their restaurant, had been renovated.

"Six or seven years ago," responded the woman.

"No letters or papers found there, I suppose?" asked Hal.

"I'm sure we would have heard if there were," said the woman.

They all stood looking around, not sure what to do. Finally Jessie spoke: "Do you think we could go back to the hotel now?

I'm feeling a little tired. I'd like to lie down for a while before Saul drops by."

Margot took her mother's hand and led her down the stairs and out the door of the museum. She didn't wait for Hal. She sensed he wanted to be alone.

Chapter Forty-two

*I*t *was* ODD. THE MEMORIES THAT HAD ONCE BEEN SO PRESS-
ing on Jessie's consciousness had begun to fade. First, it
seemed that she was only tired and less interested in the subject of
that other life. Then, as she and Margot took the *vaporetto* back to
the hotel, she began, quite simply, to forget. It was as though her
mind were a delicate archaeological excavation: Some strange shift
in the terrain had opened up a crevasse where one could glimpse
something extraordinary about the past. Now another shift had
begun to cover over what had been briefly revealed.

"You know I'm not a literary person," Jessie said to Margot as
they took the elevator up to their room. "What do I know from
William Shakespeare?"

"You knew quite a bit an hour ago," said Margot, feeling angry
and frustrated. She had, in a short period—dating from exactly
when, she couldn't say—come to feel invested in this cockamamie
scheme. What had originally seemed like an absurd delusion now
seemed like a wondrous fairy tale. She wanted to shake her mother
and say, "Don't you remember—you're the Dark Lady of the sonnets, the model for Jessica in *The Merchant of Venice*!"

Margot had also noted Hal Pearson's expression as he looked
up at her from the Lubavitcher pamphlet. The sense of loss was

palpable in his eyes. She suspected that it was not just the loss of the sonnets that pained him; it was also the loss of someone who had had at her fingertips knowledge of a vanished world and a cherished author.

Anish was also disappointed. He could imagine his report on the aborted expedition to the grant committee: "Site of lost sonnets converted into glatt kosher restaurant; reincarnated Dark Lady suffers amnesia; no manuscript found."

But Anish was by nature resourceful when it came to burrowing in the mines of academe. If there were to be no sonnets, that didn't mean they couldn't dig up something else of interest for the *Shakespeare Biannual.* Thus, he and Felicity went off to explore the archives in the doge's palace.

Hal, meanwhile, had decided neither to go with Anish and Felicity nor to return to the hotel with Margot and Jessie. He remained behind, after everyone had gone, and then walked out of the ghetto, without thinking about where he was going. He walked in a kind of daze, taking no note of the time, until he suddenly realized that it was getting late and he turned around and walked back. When he arrived again at the ghetto, it was night, and the tourists had left the area. The glatt kosher restaurant was closed—locked and dark.

But Hal, for some reason, stepped up to the door of the building and knocked loudly. He didn't expect anyone to answer. He simply wanted to knock on the door that he still believed had once been knocked on by the greatest writer in the English language.

Surprisingly, his knock was answered. The door opened, and an old woman in a black shawl, obviously the caretaker or the concierge for the building when it was not in use, stood before him.

"Excuse me," he said slowly, sensing that this person was not fluent in English. "I have a friend who lived in this building once, a long time ago. Would you mind if I come in?"

The woman did not seem to mind. She was so old that perhaps the notion of minding anything had fled. She led Hal up the stairs to the second floor and then into a small alcove that had not been visible to them when they had visited the rest of the building earlier in the day. The room felt more like a cave than a house. It was perhaps the one area that had not undergone renovation.

"You are the caretaker?" asked Hal.

The woman's head moved slightly under her shawl.

"How long have you lived here?" he asked.

She shrugged. "*Sempre.*"

"And have you ever"—he wasn't quite sure what it was he wanted to ask, but he spoke the words that came to mind—"have you ever—found anything?"

She did not seem surprised by the question but went to a drawer and took out a small metal box. She opened it carefully. Inside was a locket. It was very old and very tarnished, but, to Hal, it resembled the locket that Margot had worn the night before. He took it in his hand.

"*Aperto,*" said the woman, reaching out and pressing the little latch so that the locket opened on its hinge. Inside was inscribed in tiny scroll script the following words: "Let me not to the marriage of true minds / Admit impediments."

"*Inglese,*" said the old woman proudly, "*antico.*" Then she kissed the locket gently and replaced it in the box.

Chapter Forty-three

*W*hen Hal RETURNED TO THE HOTEL, IT WAS LATE, BUT Anish was waiting for him in the bar, looking surprisingly awake and excited.

"I was worried you might have thrown yourself into the canal," said Anish. "After all, it's pretty disappointing to see 'this insubstantial pageant shot to hell, with not a frigging rack left behind'— to very loosely paraphrase the Bard."

"Maybe a rack," murmured Hal.

"Then again, maybe a rack!" said Anish gleefully, oblivious to Hal's comment because so clearly intent on imparting something of his own. "Actually, I haven't been waiting up for you out of concern for your well-being. I know your capacity to survive painful experiences. Remember that girl in English 89 who put you through the ringer, quoting Keats every bloody minute of the way? And remember the time you broke the record for cheeseburger consumption at the Yankee Doodle in New Haven, a feat that you paid for by retching your guts out half the night? If you survived those ordeals, you could survive anything. No, I stayed up because I wanted to relay a nugget that I thought you might find of interest. Felicity, dear, industrious soul that she is, had the brainstorm of looking through the archival records in the doge's palace for reference to an Avram Rodrigues. And wouldn't you know it? Her experience hunting the hare of historical minutiae panned out. After much sifting, we did find an A. Rodrigues in the trade record for the year of 1595, listed as responsible for bringing a considerable amount of English wool into the country."

"That would have been the year that Jessie said she and her father went to London at Shakespeare's instigation," noted Hal.

"Bingo!" exclaimed Anish. "It does fit nicely with her story. Not enough in itself to substantiate anything, but Felicity plans to do more digging into the matter of English involvement in Venetian trade in the 1590s. She has some grant money of her own, you know. Who knows what she may turn up?"

"Did you tell Jessie?" asked Hal. He was wondering if he should mention the locket and perhaps bring Jessie to see it tomorrow.

"I did, but I'm afraid she didn't seem much interested. She told us she was glad that we didn't think the trip was a waste of time but that it had all begun to blur for her. She wanted to go back to her room and take a nap, so she'd be fresh for her gentleman caller."

"Oh well," said Hal.

"Yes," said Anish, "I believe your source is now definitively not a source, though she gave us a good run for our money when she was."

"'Now my charms are all o'erthrown, And what strength I have's mine own,' murmured Hal. It was from Prospero's speech at the end of *The Tempest*, when he broke his magic staff, and it seemed to fit the mood of the moment.

"Precisely." Anish nodded. "But you know, I can't say I care. There's something to be said for falling back on our own subjective powers. I'm excited by what Felicity may turn up on the English wool, but I've gained more than that," he observed thoughtfully. "A new perspective on the plays. The idea of Jessica and Miranda emanating from the same essential source—it's a compelling one. Nothing objective there, of course; no hard data to support it. But it's got me thinking about the limitations of hard data. I'm even considering striking out in a new direction. My mind's been opened. I may even go back and read James Joyce with a fresh eye."

Hal nodded. "It's the gift I receive from my students every day. They're constantly seeing literature and life with fresh eyes: uncovering patterns and relationships that never occurred to me."

"Then I suppose I can finally understand why you do what you do," said Anish. "Not that I'd ever want to do it myself." He paused and gave Hal an inquiring look. "Is there anything you want to tell me?"

"No," said Hal. He had decided to keep the discovery of the locket to himself. If the record of English wool was a material fact, the locket seemed part of the baseless fabric, best left to melt into air.

After the meeting with Anish, Hal wandered out onto the veranda of the hotel, where, at a corner table overlooking the canal, sat Margot. He had somehow felt she would be there and experienced a leap of joy at seeing his intuition confirmed. She was wearing a coat over a flimsy white garment that might have been her nightgown; she still had the locket around her neck. It was, he saw now, amazingly similar to the one he had seen—or thought he had seen—just an hour or so ago.

"So where were you?" she said. It was a genuine question, not mocking but irritable. It was the sort of tone, Hal noted with secret pleasure, that a wife might use with a husband who had come home later than expected.

"I've been wandering around the city," he said, "and thinking."

"Did Anish tell you about the English wool?" she asked.

"He did."

"It's promising, I think."

Hal smiled to himself but didn't ask her what she meant by "promising."

"But you know," she continued softly, "my mother's more or less forgotten everything. On the way home from the ghetto it all began to go, and after she met her friend Saul for a drink—and, I should add, a very long subsequent dinner—it disappeared from her head entirely."

"I know," said Hal. "Anish told me. It makes sense, though. It takes a lot of concentration to love someone. You can't have too much getting in the way."

"Sometimes you have to throw out the clutter to see what's there to love," said Margot.

She looked at him then, and he looked back, but they didn't say anything. Finally she got up. "Mom and I are taking an early fight home tomorrow. She wants to get back to be with Stephanie for the few days before the bat mitzvah. So I changed the tickets. We'll be taking the *motoscafi* to the airport at five A.M., so I better get some sleep." She stood there for a moment, her nightgown fluttering in the chill Venetian breeze.

And then she was gone.

Chapter Forty-four

*O*n the MORNING OF THE BAT MITZVAH, STEPHANIE ROSE early to review her haftorah portion. Hearing the sweet voice emanating from her daughter's bedroom, Carla momentarily forgot to worry about her *D'var Torah*. Of course, a few minutes later, she remembered and began worrying again.

The issue of the *D'var Torah* had not been resolved—at least not to Carla's satisfaction. Stephanie had prepared a draft of the speech for her meeting with the rabbi the week before, but Carla had not had a chance to review it. She had been in a state of distraction when she dropped Stephanie off for her appointment with the rabbi and rushed to the airport to meet her mother and sister's flight from Venice. Then, after depositing Margot at her apartment in Center City and Jessie at home, she had returned to the synagogue to find her daughter waiting placidly in front of the temple door.

"So how did it go?" asked Carla.

Stephanie seemed extremely pleased with herself. "He liked it," she said.

"Really?" said Carla. She couldn't imagine what her daughter had finally written, after resisting every possible idea that she and Mark had offered on the subject. "I'm sure it's very good," she said, trying to keep the note of doubt out of her voice. "When we get home, I'll take a look and we can polish it up."

"No," said Stephanie. "I like it the way it is and so did Rabbi Newman. I don't want you to read it. You'll hear it at the bat mitzvah."

"Honey," said Carla, "I really don't think that's a good idea."

But Stephanie was adamant, and Carla, worn down by the events of the past few months, eventually gave up trying to change her mind. Nonetheless, she remained in a state of trepidation about what her daughter was going to say. That Rabbi Newman liked the speech did not in itself seem a powerful recommendation. Rabbi Newman was very green. No doubt he was easily pleased, or at least willing to accept anything that did not seem utterly off the wall or flagrantly heretical. What did he care if the child appeared simpleminded? She was not his child. But Carla was Stephanie's mother. She knew that Stephanie was a bright girl, and, furthermore, that relatives and friends, who had traveled long distances at great expense, would be judging her daughter—and herself, as the one principally responsible for shaping her. For Carla, the stakes were higher.

Yet nothing could be done. Stephanie had dug in her heels, and Carla, recalling the admonitions of Dr. Samuels, decided to back off and let things take their course.

At eleven A.M. on the day of the bat mitzvah, she took Stephanie to the local beauty salon for the bat mitzvah coiffure. This was de rigueur. Having one's hair done professionally was as important a mark of initiation for the adolescent female as the religious ceremony itself. The hair had to be teased and twisted into some kind of serpentine style that screamed "special occasion." Stephanie had made an earlier pilgrimage to the crafts store, and bought an array of sparkles and small silk flowers for insertion into the lacquered hairdo. The hairdresser, a blasé, gum-chewing young woman named Angela, was, as a result of her Cherry Hill clientele, an expert on the bat mitzvah coiffure. She looked at Stephanie with a serious gaze, cocking her head to one side and popping her gum.

"I recommend an upsweep with a few tendrils and maybe a few

of these sparkles," she concluded after some deliberation. "My thinking is, trash the flowers. You want to look fun, but also sort of spiritual. The flowers are too, you know, prom queen."

Stephanie listened and nodded. She put the flowers back in her purse (perhaps to be resurrected for the seventh-grade dance) and gave herself over to Angela's ministrations.

The final result was, Carla had to admit, decidedly fetching. Her daughter had an excellent face: the striking Lubenthal features softened by less intimidating contributions from the Kaplan and Goodman sides of the family. It helped as well that Stephanie seemed to like the way she looked, turning her head this way and that and smiling with pleasure. It occurred to Carla that the greatest beauty enhancement to an adolescent girl was a smile.

They returned home for a light lunch of smoked turkey and hard-boiled eggs that Jessie had prepared, in between ironing her new dress and creaming her face and hands. Carla had never seen her mother so concerned about her appearance. She put it down to the fact that Saul Millman would be attending the bat mitzvah.

Jessie had talked to Saul every night since her return. Although he had continued with his tour of Italy and had not returned to the States until yesterday, he had called like clockwork, calculating the time difference with great care so as not to disturb what he called Jessie's "beauty sleep." The bat mitzvah would be the first time they would see each other since meeting for drinks and dinner at the Gritti Palace the week before.

When Margot had called from Venice to report that Jessie's delusions had vanished, Carla had been surprised to hear a note of disappointment in her sister's voice. "But it's wonderful news!" exclaimed Carla. "It means we have her back again."

"I suppose," said Margot. "But to think that she no longer wants to talk about Shakespeare and the lost sonnets."

"Are you crazy?" said Carla.

"I suppose I am," Margot sighed.

"Mass hysteria; group delusion; *folie à deux*. I read about that stuff in my abnormal psych course in college. But I never thought that my rational sister would be party to it."

Margot said that she had surprised herself as well. "It's odd, but the trip changed me somehow. I feel sad about not finding the sonnets but glad to be coming home. You know, I've actually been thinking that maybe I should move out of the Rittenhouse apartment and nearer to you and Mom in Cherry Hill."

"What?" said Carla. "Don't tell me you're having the delusions now!" She had always supposed that Margot would want to move to New York or possibly Paris—but to Cherry Hill, never!

"I feel somehow drawn to the place," continued Margot. She spoke in her usual facetious tone, but her sister, who knew her better than anyone, discerned an underlying seriousness. "Maybe it's the way Mom felt for a while about the ghetto in Venice. Places like Cherry Hill are probably scattered all over the world, where 'our people' feel instinctively at home. In any case, I have the oddest feeling that I'm going to end up living in Cherry Hill, or its facsimile, sooner or later."

"In one of those mock-Tudor developments or hacienda-style mini-mansions?" asked Carla.

"Yes, with the two-story foyer and the Palladian windows," laughed Margot. "But you know, suburbia gets to look better and better the older you get. You develop a sort of yen to make cupcakes for a kindergarten class and trade in the sports car for a Volvo."

"And there's always the consolation of getting a Jaguar later on," noted Carla. "When the kids are grown and we move down to Boca, Mark and I definitely plan to acquire one. My instincts tell me that we will."

"And what do your instincts tell you about me?" asked Margot.

"I don't know. I wouldn't really recommend Cherry Hill if you're single, which at the moment you are—though somehow my crystal ball tells me that condition will be altered. Perhaps, if I might speculate, you're thinking of altering it soon?"

"Don't be silly," said Margot, reverting to her usual flip tone. "I was only pulling your leg."

Chapter Forty-five

Two hours BEFORE THE BAT MITZVAH, JESSIE HAD TAKEN the curlers out of her hair and applied a generous amount of eyeliner and mascara.

"You're really putting on the ritz," noted Mark. "Perhaps you have someone in mind to impress?"

Jessie waved her hand coyly.

Meanwhile Jeffrey had come downstairs in a straitjacket-like suit bought for him at one of the outlet stores that specialized in "formal boyswear," an oxymoron if there ever was one. He looked extremely uncomfortable, though he perked up when everyone exclaimed at how handsome he looked. In no time, he had shoveled down most of the smoked turkey and three hard-boiled eggs, and had gotten a large mustard stain on his tie. Carla applied some spot remover and deposited him in front of the television with the express admonition that he not eat another thing before the ceremony.

The phone rang. It was Susie Wilson.

"Don't tell me that Mr. O'Hare won't wear the tux," said Carla with exasperation, not waiting to hear what Susie had to say. "Tell him he has to; I won't stand for it otherwise. He's a fundamental part of this occasion and, even if he's in a wheelchair, I consider him an usher and so he has to dress accordingly. And make sure that Pinsky remembers to zip his pants. You know he has a problem with that."

"It's not about the tux," said Susie quietly. Carla didn't like the tone of her voice. "It's Mr. O'Hare," said Susie, after a moment's pause. "He passed away this morning."

Carla took the phone away from her ear, then brought it back. "What?" she said.

"Mr. O'Hare died this morning," repeated Susie.

"That's impossible," said Carla. "He couldn't have."

"I'm afraid he did," said Susie.

"But he's got to be at the bat mitzvah! He was looking forward to it. It's important—that he have the experience."

"I think he got a pretty good idea of what the experience would be like."

"But you don't understand," cried Carla. "I wanted him to hear Stephanie chant her Torah portion—and see the flowers and the mashed-potato sundae bar. He could have eaten that."

"I know," said Susie gently, "but sometimes things are better when they're left to the imagination." Her inclination to see the bright side was kicking in. "This way he's taken his own idea of the occasion with him. It's more—poetic, in a way. And he was eighty-nine, after all. He had a long run."

"Yes," whispered Carla, trying to get her bearings. "Is there going to be a Mass?" She knew O'Hare was Catholic—she had seen him with a rosary and they had once talked about the consolation of belief. "I'm sure we go to the same place," he had told Carla, "only the scenery is different, which makes a lot of sense when you think about it. God doesn't want to go to the same goddamn play every night." Carla had thought this was rather a profound way of looking at the idea of religious diversity.

"Yes," said Susie, "Mass will be on Monday morning. It's at Our Lady of Good Counsel. I'll pick you up."

"All right," said Carla.

"I know how you must feel, but this mustn't spoil your celebration. I'll be there and so will Mr. Pinsky—I'll be sure to check his pants. O'Hare will be there too, in spirit."

"I know," said Carla, wiping her eyes. "But I so wanted him to see the hors d'oeuvres stations."

"He'll see them," said Susie. "He'll have the best seat in the house."

Chapter Forty-six

*A*fter Carla HAD REDONE HER MAKEUP AND PUT ON THE overpriced mauve silk suit of the conventional mother-of-the-bar-mitzvah-child variety, she went to check on Stephanie. She knocked softly on her daughter's door. The Bloomingdale's dress—especially the sleeves—flattered Stephanie's slim, adolescent frame. Margot had come by early to do her niece's makeup, and had managed to convince her that a light touch would show her hair and dress to best advantage. What it really highlighted, of course, was Stephanie's face—a face that was open and fresh, with nothing yet to harden or disappoint it.

"You look beautiful," said Carla.

"So do you," said Stephanie, and they hugged, taking care not smear each other's lipstick.

After leaving Stephanie, Carla looked in on Jessie, who was sitting quietly in her new blue dress (very much like her old blue dress) in the armchair in her room. "Are you all ready, Mom?" she asked.

"More than ready," said Jessie.

"You look happy."

"I am, dear. It's not just meeting Saul again, though I must say that's given me a lift. It's everything that's happened in the last few months. It's been—exciting. And it's helped me see what a blessing my life has always been. Full of joy and surprises—and to still have surprises, at my age, that's saying something."

"It is," agreed Carla.

"And today is Stephanie's bat mitzvah. What *naches* for our family. I only wish your father could be here to see it. He would have been so proud."

Finally, Carla went into their bedroom to see how Mark was doing. He had finally broken down and purchased a tuxedo. His new career in the media spotlight made the acquisition of this garment a necessity, since he was now being invited to black-tie events on a regular basis. Yet the outfit was still a novelty, and he was struggling with the studs for the shirt, muttering under his breath that studs were absurd, labor-intensive ornaments, and that the word "stud," when you came to think about it, was an obscene term to apply to a button on a man's shirt.

Carla watched for a moment, then quietly took the studs out of his hands and put them into the shirt for him. "You're upset," she said. "You're remembering your own bar mitzvah."

"Yes, the *D'var Torah* about menstrual fluid."

"Poor boy," said Carla, kissing his cheek. "But I'm sure you handled it well. And you look very handsome now."

"I do?" Mark turned to admire himself in the mirror.

"The tuxedo looks good with your haircut," noted Carla.

He looked for a moment at his reflection and then turned back to her. "You know—I ought to confess something."

"Oh?"

"I've never told you this before, and it may come as a shock."

"I'm listening."

"I actually enjoyed my bar mitzvah. In fact, it was one of the best days of my life."

"Of course it was," said Carla, straightening his bow tie complacently. "I never doubted it for a moment. And this is going to be one of the best days of your daughter's life. But enough talking. Let me put in your cuff links so we can get this show on the road already."

Chapter Forty-seven

The Goodman BAT MITZVAH WAS HELD IN TEMPLE B'NAI Or, a spacious Reform synagogue in the developing suburbs of Cherry Hill—once the boondocks of the area, now the site of multimillion-dollar high-concept homes, upscale multiplex movie theaters, and synagogues in the Frank Lloyd Wright architectural style. B'nai Or, which vaguely resembled Wright's Falling Water, was one such relatively new congregation that already boasted about five hundred families. This was large, by any standard, though certainly not exceptional in Cherry Hill, where there were several Reform and Conservative synagogues twice the size.

Normally temple services were not heavily attended, but for certain occasions the parking lot was full. This was during the High Holy Days of Rosh Hashana and Yom Kippur (which often featured sermons in which the frustrated rabbi berated the congregation about their failure to attend the rest of the year) and at bar mitzvahs and weddings. Indeed, on Saturday, the synagogue was never empty, since a morning and an evening affair were usually held back to back, forcing rival caterers and florists to brush elbows. Angry skirmishes, one involving a serving fork, had been known to occur during this interval.

Because of the size of the congregation, children were sometimes forced to pair up for bar mitzvahs—a "double" being a result of only so many Saturdays in the year. Stephanie had drawn a solo evening ceremony, making her one of the lucky ones (or unlucky, as the case may be, since some children enjoyed the comfort of the buddy system). Of course, it had only been possible to assure a solo date by scheduling the bat mitzvah rather far afield from Stephanie's actual birth date—she would not turn thirteen for another month. (Carla had put aside some of the bat mitzvah booty for presentation when the actual birthday arrived. She knew that thirteen-year-olds were prone to literalness in such matters.)

The whole ceremony would take perhaps an hour and three quarters. One of the boons of Reform Judaism was the shortened service. A Conservative bar mitzvah was likely to run nearer to three and a half hours, which meant that guests invariably knew to arrive late and were liable to come and go throughout the ceremony. Carla remembered her experience as a child in an Orthodox synagogue, where the tendency to move around during a service was even greater—the women and children often spending most of the time in the coatroom trading recipes and gossip. She recalled this scene as great fun as well as oddly infused with spiritual feeling. The Reform synagogue, by contrast, was more exacting in its view of attendance. Perhaps because congregants had moved further from the fold, they behaved more properly on the occasions when they actually made it to the temple.

But whatever the denomination of Judaism and however long or short the service, the bar mitzvah was, in the final analysis, one of those rituals—part rote, part festivity—that assured that the religion would live on. Everyone liked a good bar mitzvah, and many non-Jews, invited to one as children, had shed their suspicion of this alien religion by virtue of the fun they'd had doing the limbo.

It was impossible, in short, to overestimate the public relations value for the Jewish faith of the bar mitzvah ceremony and celebration. It was here that one saw the full vitality of the Jewish people—their love of family, food, talk, song, and dramatic festivity. Here were all the excesses endearingly displayed, an event so full of energy and glitz as to disarm all but the most puritanical Puritans and the most snobbish self-hating Jews.

For Stephanie's bat mitzvah, everyone was present in his or her expected place as the designated starting time for the ceremony drew near. There, in the front row, sat the immediate family: Stephanie between Mark and Carla—their precious jewel, her curls sparkling, her face radiant. Beside Carla sat Jeffrey, showing promise that he would one day be able to pass through this ritual himself by the simple fact that he was now capable of sitting still. Next to Mark sat his parents, Rose and Charles Goodman, a well-brushed and handsome couple. Charles, a retired furniture salesman, had the slightly smug look of a seventy-three-year-old man with a nice pension, good eyesight, and a full head of hair (attributes that made Rose the envy of all her friends).

Seated next to Jeffrey was Jessie, looking like the aging beauty she was, but with an added quality of youthful anticipation and excitement in her posture. She had been turning around, ever since she arrived, glancing toward the door of the sanctuary until Saul Millman finally entered, at which point she waved her hand shyly and appeared almost inclined to blow a kiss. He entered the synagogue in a tallis and skullcap of richly embroidered material, a kind of proclamation of his business success, and put his hand to his heart in an unabashed expression of devotion. Jessie blushed and turned away, but only to turn back at regular intervals to smile and nod again in his direction.

Margot sat next to Jessie, looking, as always, show-stopping. She had tried, to her credit, to play down the effect of her appearance in deference to Stephanie's designated role as the center of attention. She was wearing a suit (less expensive and a shade lighter than the mother-of-the-bar-mitzvah-child suit) that did not succeed in damping down her luster. As already noted, it was a paradox of Margot's appearance that in dressy clothes she looked striking, while in more understated ones, she looked more so. Uncle Sid, now fully recovered, was sitting in the row behind and announcing to everyone in the vicinity that Margot was a "Jewish Sophia Loren." (Margot told Carla that she wished Sid would update his references; Sophia Loren was rapidly disappearing from cultural consciousness. "The Jewish Madonna would be better, or maybe the Jewish Catherine Zeta-Jones." "I've never seen anyone so picky," noted Carla; "you even critique your compliments.")

Stephanie's friends, a swarm of gabby seventh-graders, were seated at the left of the *bima* under the stern eye of the Sisterhood member assigned to keep them in order. The problem of the bar mitzvah child's friends was a much-discussed topic of the Education Committee. How was one to control the hysterical giggles that tended to erupt when some fifty twelve- and thirteen-year-olds were clumped together to watch a friend perform in another language for long, boring intervals? A number of suggestions had been proffered by way of solution. One was to forbid the children to sit together. When this idea was implemented, however, the result was worse: The giggles grew louder and the gestures broader, as friends attempted to communicate across the vast space of the sanctuary. Another suggestion—to distribute a printed sheet explaining rules of behavior—also backfired: The children crumpled the sheets loudly or configured them into airplanes to be sent with messages back and forth across the room.

The committee had finally settled on installing a special bar mitzvah guard, drawn from the ranks of the Sisterhood. It was agreed that not just any Sisterhood member could serve in this capacity. The woman had to have a proven reputation for ferocity—an ability to take on the thirteen-year-olds without fear. A group of candidates had been assembled for this purpose, and since these women were outright scary ("Jewish ballbusters," as one board member had whispered to another), behavior had markedly improved.

Now, a woman in a tartan skirt and high heels was parading

back and forth, shooting withering glances at the children whenever they began to act up. The girls in the entourage were all dressed alike: even the non-Jewish ones had on the requisite skimpy dress with cover-up (to be removed during the party), the bangles and chains, the Nine West heels, and fake Kate Spade bags. The boys wore suits or sports jackets (generally too small or too large). Unlike the girls, who were busy sizing up each other's outfits and reapplying their lipstick, the boys were concentrating their minds on the first-rate spread that they knew was awaiting them once the service was over.

Stephanie, seated between her parents, was of course the focal point of her friends' attention, and she was continually darting glances and making faces at them when she was not trying to assume the pose of being above the fray and ignoring them entirely.

The doctors and nurses from Mark's hospital were also seated in respective clumps near the back of the synagogue. The doctors, mostly Jewish, felt at home. The nurses, mostly not, did not—they had a look of petrified formality on their faces, wondering what to expect.

Margot continued to look back toward the sanctuary door, and seemed relieved when finally Anish, Felicity, and Hal entered. Jessie had insisted that they be invited. Fortunately, there were a number of last-minute cancelations from Florida, the result of phlebitis flare-ups and hip replacements, to accommodate them.

Jill and Adam Rosenberg sat amid a group of Carla's friends. Jill was busy regaling everyone about her success at preventing the residents of the Golden Pond Geriatric Center from being thrown out onto the streets of Cherry Hill. Adam was sitting quietly beside her, his eyes half-closed, like a dog before the hearth.

On the other side of the synagogue sat Dr. Samuels and his wife, Sylvia. Samuels regularly attended his patients' bar mitzvahs, both to have a handle on what they would subsequently be talking to him about and because, as he put it, "nothing beats a good bar mitzvah." As always, Samuels had a way of stripping things down to their most basic and, ultimately, appealing form. "It's a headache to plan," he said, "but in the end, it's a sacred ceremony of initiation and a hell of a party. What's not to like?"

Near Samuels, the Brooklyn Katzes, wearing boas and yellow cummerbunds, were vying with the thirteen-year-olds in the amount of noise they could make. And near the door, in case a quick bathroom trip was necessary, sat Mr. Pinsky next to Susie Wilson.

The service began. Rabbi Newman, only months earlier a mere assistant rabbi, had made great strides in his appearance and manner. His beard had come in and his voice had assumed a pleasant, steady timbre. He seemed to actually enjoy reciting the prayers, so that the congregation was inclined to enjoy them too. Best of all, he did not speak too much or have too many opinions. It was therefore concluded, in that most desirable of all descriptive phrases, that "he has a nice way about him."

Stephanie, when she came up for her recitation of the *V'ahafta*, was nervous, and the first few lines were hardly audible. Carla tried to gesture for her to raise her voice, but Stephanie would not look in her direction. Fortunately the young rabbi now showed his mettle. He got up and whispered magisterially in Stephanie's ear to take it up a notch, which she did to surprisingly good effect. Her voice was clear and sweet, and as the congregation grew quiet listening to her, she gained in confidence and sang even better.

Her Torah and haftorah portions were subsequently performed beautifully.

"The voice of an angel," whispered one of the cousins from East Brunswick with typical overstatement.

But it was true that Stephanie sang her portions very well and that even her friends stayed put rather than recess to the bathroom as they normally would at this juncture in the service. When she was done, there was a murmur of admiration. A child with a decent voice and some feel for the melodies had the ability to create a profound response to these age-old tunes. Nor was it Stephanie's rendition alone that the congregation was responding to. Her performance brought to consciousness the rich cultural legacy obscured by the routine and bric-a-brac of daily life. Indeed, even where kids mangled the melodies and mispronounced the Hebrew, some of that cultural meaning always came through, lifting the event, if only briefly, into the realm of the sacred. A sense of wonder for the fact of the child turning into the adult, for the idea of family reaching back generations, for the religion that had endured despite persecution and hardship, for the sense of shared community—all this was present in those ancient melodies.

"And now," said the young senior rabbi, "the bat mitzvah, as is customary, will offer her own interpretation of her Torah portion. For those not familiar with our vocabulary," he added sagely, "we use the term 'bar or bat mitzvah' to refer to our young initiates as well as to the ceremony in which they are engaged." (This explanation was later deemed by the board to be a nice touch.)

The rabbi now nodded to Stephanie, who took out a folded sheaf of paper from her imitation Kate Spade bag and wobbled to the lectern in her Nine West heels.

She placed the speech on the lectern and then took a sip from the glass of water that the rabbi had placed there for her.

Carla held her breath.

"My Torah portion deals with Joseph's interpretation of Pharaoh's dream," Stephanie began in the familiar adolescent singsong. "In my portion, Joseph is called out of prison by the Pharaoh who has heard that Joseph has the power to interpret dreams. He, the Pharaoh, tells him, Joseph, his dream. He says he dreamed about seven fat kine and seven lean kine—kine meaning cattle"—she shot Mark a look—"and Joseph tells him that this means that there will be seven fertile years in Egypt followed by seven lean years. The Pharaoh then rewards Joseph for his interpretation by giving him an important position in his government. Joseph then goes on to take care of things for the country. He makes sure that the country puts enough grain away during the fertile years so that they won't go hungry during the lean years.

"My Torah portion is about interpretation. Joseph interprets Pharaoh's dream as telling the future, and he turns out to be right. I think this portion can be understood to show the power of interpretation. When we read a play or a story, there isn't a set meaning to it. We interpret it according to who we are and what we think. It's not always a matter of its being true or false but of its making sense and helping us to see things that we didn't see before. We can't really tell the future and we can't really understand the past—but we can find ways to interpret them that help us live our lives better.

"I can relate this to my own life. Recently, my grandmother had some strange ideas. She thought she had once lived in Shakespeare's time. I don't know if she really did or not, but her feelings about what happened helped me and other people see that time in a new way and read Shakespeare's poetry in a new way. It also helped us see my grandmother differently. Sometimes you see people only in the ways you are used to. So your mom is just your mom and your grandma is just your grandma. But there's more to people than that, and when something weird happens, it can make you look at them differently. My grandma is still my grandma, but I also learned that she's a very interesting person.

"I think this is what happened with Joseph and Pharaoh. Pharaoh was used to seeing things a certain way. When Joseph came, he interpreted Pharaoh's dream and gave a new perspective on how to deal with his country's food supply. Maybe Joseph was lucky and it happened that there were seven fertile years and seven lean years. Or maybe it was only a way of saying that when there's a fertile time it's good to plan for when there's a lean time—that would make the story more like a metaphor. But maybe it was just that Pharaoh's life had gotten really boring and he needed a new perspective on things. Joseph came along and gave him that. He helped make Pharaoh's life better and also more interesting.

"The lesson that I get from this is that we should be open to new influences that can make us see things differently. Also, that interpretation is very important and we should all do more of it.

"I want to thank everyone who has helped me with my bat mitzvah. This includes my mother and father, who are the best parents in the world, even though they sometimes get on my nerves [laughter], my Grandma Rose, my Grandpa Charles, and my Grandma Jessie, who are the best grandparents, my brother Jeffrey, who is annoying but is getting better [laughter], and the rabbi and the cantor who have been very patient in helping me learn my Torah and haftorah portions. I'd also like to thank my teacher Mr. Pearson for teaching me about interpretation.

"I would like to give part of my bat mitzvah money to the American Heart Association. My Grandpa Milt died of heart disease and I know this is a good cause that will help many people.

"I am very happy that my friends and family could come and celebrate with me today and that I have finally completed my bat mitzvah."

Everyone laughed, as was customary when the bar mitzvah child expressed relief that the ordeal was over.

But Carla bowed her head and cried with joy. It had struck her forcefully that Stephanie had said something worth saying, and that, suddenly, things seemed clearer and simpler than they had ever been before. She thought of her father and Mr. O'Hare, men she had loved who had passed on. And she thought of her mother and Stephanie, both, despite the vast difference in their ages, embarking on something new. She thought of her heritage, reaching back, generation upon generation, and of herself, one link in that chain. She knew things would go wrong again. She would be disappointed and irritated, stressed and unhappy. But right now she was experiencing life at its best, and she was grateful. "*Dayenu*," she thought to herself in the words of the Passover song. This moment, which would soon pass into history, was enough.

Chapter Forty-eight

After the SHORT *HAVDALAH* PRAYER, IN WHICH THE LIGHTS in the synagogue were dimmed to dramatize the transition to evening, the service ended, with the children, as was customary, throwing candy at Stephanie. Rabbi Newman, who remembered being hit in the eye by a gumball at his own bar mitzvah, had ruled, among his first edicts, that bar mitzvah candy be of a consistency that would not cause bodily harm. A candy-vetting committee had been duly formed to assure this. As a result, all the candy that was thrown at Stephanie was of the soft Chuckles variety.

Everyone recessed to the cocktail area directly outside the sanctuary. The synagogue had been built with a large, cavernous space that could be partitioned for various occasions. On High Holy Days, when the place was packed, all the partitions were opened and folding chairs were set up reaching to the back of the room. For bar mitzvahs and weddings, the space was partitioned into thirds. The front area, which included the *bima* and the built-in wooden pews, was where the ceremony took place. The second space, directly behind the site of the ceremony and relatively narrow, was used for cocktails and hors d'oeuvres. The rest of the space was where the tables were set up for the sit-down dinner.

The idea was to funnel the congregants out of the ceremony,

coop them up for an hour or so to gorge on a variety of hot and cold hors d'oeuvres until, schmoozed out and with the edge taken off their appetites, they would be allowed to spill into their seats at the designated tables in the remaining portion of the space. The whole process had been worked out at some antecedent time (possibly fifty years ago by a manager at Leonard's of Great Neck) as the most efficient and psychologically effective way to handle things. No one was known to have deviated from it since.

In the case of the Goodman bat mitzvah, Moishe had set up three hors d'oeuvres "stations" in the narrow cocktail space. As O'Hare and Pinsky had recommended, one was a mock-sushi bar, a favorite among the hipper guests; one a roast beef carving station, in which the carvers, wearing white chef hats and brandishing large knives, seemed to take an inordinate interest in the thirteen-year-old girls; and one a mashed-potato sundae bar in which, as O'Hare had surmised, the mashed potatoes were treated in the manner of ice cream with topping choices of gravy, faux cheese, mushrooms, and so on. This particular station had been the brainstorm of a caterer in Bayonne, New Jersey, some ten years ago, and the general consensus in the industry was that, if catering concepts were so recognized, he would be the recipient of a Nobel Prize.

All the stations were a big hit, a credit to Mr. O'Hare's excellent judgment. Pinsky had favored a station featuring caviar rather than roast beef, but O'Hare had argued that beef was important to the men and boys and only goddamn snobs like Pinsky wanted fish eggs. He was right.

In the center of the room was a vast table of artfully arranged crudités, a concession to the anorexic women, always well-represented at bar mitzvahs. In the midst of it all, waitresses carried trays with the various hot and cold hors d'oeuvres: phyllo pastries with spinach, potato knishes, stuffed mushrooms, and so forth. There was also, of course, an open bar, around which the Brooklyn Katzes had congregated.

The general impression was of a cornucopia of culinary delights—the kind of thing that non-Jews, unaccustomed to what was possible in the way of hors d'oeuvres, tended to find mind-boggling. Indeed, it was a general rule of thumb that it was best not to dwell on the prospect of the meal to follow, since this was liable to inhibit the pleasure of gorging unrestrainedly on what was at hand. Besides, everyone knew that however good the bar mitzvah dinner, it would never hold a candle to the hors d'oeuvres.

As the congregation retired to the cocktail area, much congratulation ensued. Uncle Sid made a point of kissing all the women.

Mark's parents, Charles and Rose, quickly commandeered several of the small cocktail tables in order to hold court for their Florida friends. After some preliminary *mazel tovs*, they all settled down to gossiping about those who hadn't come.

Dr. Samuels and his wife sashayed through the throng, pressing the flesh. At any gathering in the Cherry Hill area, there were always sure to be a lion's share of Samuels's patients present, giving him the status of a foreign dignitary at a state dinner. Although the event was not, strictly speaking, about him, he always felt he could take a certain credit for its success. Carla had briefly pigeon-holed him after the ceremony to report triumphantly that Jessie was now back to normal—the whole Shakespeare *mishegoss* dissipated.

"I told you," said Samuels, waving a baby lamb chop for emphasis, "she just needed to find another outlet." He looked across the room to where Jessie had her head close to Saul Millman's as they surveyed the phenomenon of the mashed-potato sundae bar. "And love is certainly the best outlet. Still, it's a shame in a way," he added, taking a bite from the lamb chop and ruminating on this for a second. "That was one gold-plated fantasy she cooked up about being Shakespeare's girlfriend. Can't say I won't miss it."

"It certainly made life more interesting for a while," said Carla doubtfully. Whatever Margot thought, Carla was more than relieved to have her mother give up her fantasy life for something more down to earth.

"And your daughter put one hell of a spin on it in her *D'var Torah*," said Samuels.

"The speech was very profound," interjected Sylvia Samuels. "It reminded me of the philosophical ideas of Jacques Derrida." Sylvia was known to be cutting-edge not only in art but in everything intellectual—a compensation, presumably, for her culinary incapacity.

Carla thanked them both. Secretly, she did think Stephanie's speech was profound and that it had helped explain her mother's foray into irrationality more fully than anything anyone else had said.

During the hors d'oeuvres, Margot had been busy with relatives—or at least pretended to be busy with them, making a concerted effort to avoid Hal.

He, meanwhile, had been surprised, immediately after the ceremony, to have Anish take him aside to discuss his revised opinion of *Ulysses*: "An astonishing feat of a book; Shakespearean in ambition!" Anish exclaimed, shaking Hal's hand as if congratulating him for having stood by Joyce. "I stand corrected in my judgment."

Before they could discuss this revisionary perspective further, however, Hal was spirited away by Jessie to meet her relatives. Jessie had not lost her feeling for Hal, though she had forgotten most of the details that precipitated it. He was now, quite simply, her granddaughter's English teacher, for whom she felt an intense maternal affection. He was duly introduced to the sedate Westchester Lubenthals and the rowdier Brooklyn Katzes. Hal found himself quite at home with the latter, who bore a striking resemblance to his mother's side of the family (in which lurked the alleged Jewish blood). Although the Dellons (a name of dubious ethnic provenance if there ever was one) hailed from northeast Philadelphia and the Katzes from Brooklyn, the general tenor of their talk, which revolved around the plight of labor unions and the great buys to be had at BJ's, was the same.

Every once in a while, Hal's eyes darted about the room, settled on Margot, and darted away again. He had a very nervous, excited feeling that he tried to subdue but that kept returning, despite his best efforts.

Perhaps the most eccentric interaction during the cocktail hour was between Felicity Gardencourt and Jill Rosenberg. Seeing Felicity standing alone near the mock-sushi station, Jill immediately descended to rescue her—an operation that was akin to saying that a raptor rescues a mouse when it swoops down upon it. Jill had discerned in Felicity's dowdy, uptight appearance an implicit cry for help. After a brief interrogation into Felicity's background (the idea that she was a scholar of Renaissance history interested her about as much as if she were a window washer), Jill determined to introduce her to a distant cousin on Long Island who, she said, also did something with books (though whether he wrote them, sold them, or took bets in them was not clear). She would first, of course, have to do a complete makeover on Felicity, who seemed surprisingly accommodating to the idea. Such was Jill's Svengali-like effect on certain people; others, of course, fled her like the plague.

Chapter Forty-nine

inally, Moishe's EMISSARIES MADE THE ANNOUNCEMENT that dinner would now be served. The partition was removed with all the flourish that a five-hundred-pound folding wall allows, and the guests, suitably weary from trying to make sure that they had grabbed a sampling of hors d'oeuvres from the trays before the miniskirted waitresses had passed on to the other side of the room, stumbled to their designated tables.

Carla had worked very hard to arrange the tables so that like-minded people would be seated together. In some cases, this posed definite strategic problems. The Brooklyn Katzes, for example, could not be seated with previous spouses for fear of a scene. At one family member's bar mitzvah a few years back this had involved the throwing of a baked potato by Murray Katz's ex after she referred to his new wife as "that chippie."

"A little of the chippie wouldn't have done you any harm," Murray had said, after which he turned to the table as a whole and asked: "Twenty years with this battle-ax and who wouldn't want a chippie?" At which point, the potato had been thrown.

Other seating arrangements were easier. There was a Florida table, a doctor's table, a nurse's table, a table of Stephanie's former baby-sitters, a table of Mark and Carla's college friends, and a table of their present friends, presided over by Jill Rosenberg, where Mr. Pinsky and Susie Wilson were also seated, under the assumption that Jill, for whom everyone was viewed as an extension of herself, would assimilate them into the general tenor of the company.

The "Shakespeare table," as Carla called it, was smaller than the others and consisted of Hal, Anish, and Felicity. Dr. Samuels and Sylvia were also placed here, as Carla thought that they would appreciate the intellectual banter. Indeed, Sylvia proved an adept literary critic and was soon pontificating on Joyce's "modernist aesthetic."

A last-minute addition to this table was Carla's cousin, Natalie Katz, whom they hadn't expected to attend and who didn't seem to belong with the rest of the Katz clan ("a stray Katz," as Mark put it). Natalie Katz was an assistant professor of women's studies at Montclair State College, and though one might have expected putting her at the table with Anish to cause problems, the results turned out to be surprising. As Natalie pontificated on the necessity of purging all "DWEMS" from the literary canon (DWEMS, as Sylvia explained to her husband, referred to Dead White European Males, whom academic feminists felt ought to be jettisoned from the college curriculum so that society could be free of the legacy of patriarchal oppression), Anish made no strong effort to oppose her. He was, quite simply, enthralled, whether by Natalie's bushy locks, flashing dark eyes, or substantial cleavage, it was hard to say. "Not Shakespeare," he finally pleaded, after listening to her argument for some time in a state of bedazzlement: "Leave us Shakespeare, at least. Shakespeare is really a feminist. I can prove it."

Natalie, not averse to entertaining proof (a clear sign that she found Anish attractive), threw her hair out of her eyes and leaned forward, thereby exposing even more of her substantial cleavage.

"I never thought I'd be arguing for Shakespeare as a feminist," Anish whispered to Hal. " 'Do I wake or sleep?' "

"Maybe the bat mitzvah is the Forest of Arden," Hal whispered back. "Everything is possible. All are reconciled." He then drifted off into a reverie.

Meanwhile, the Joyce discussion had taken off in a new direction. Anish, given his recent rereading of *Ulysses*, had queried the group as to whether Leopold Bloom, the Jewish protagonist of the novel, had been circumcised.

"Funny you should mention it," said Samuels. "I just came across a letter from a urologist in the *New England Journal of Medicine* on that very topic. According to the writer, there are indications he wasn't, though Joyce is characteristically oblique." Much discussion ensued on this topic, pro and con.

Griffin, the entertainment motivator, had now introduced the Goodman family in suitably imperial style, and they had taken their seats at the head table. Mark was mortified by this, but fortunately the whole ordeal had passed quickly, and before he knew it, he was dancing to "Sunrise, Sunset" with Stephanie. She looked so happy and so beautiful that he couldn't even feel embarrassed by the conventional nature of the moment.

"And now, for the hora," announced Griffin, his two entertainment facilitators grabbing everyone within the vicinity of the dance floor and hurling them into the semblance of a circle. The klezmer band took over here in a rousing rendition of that traditional, much-performed staple of ethnic festivity. Felicity Gardencourt and some of the nurses had somehow become sandwiched in among the Brooklyn Katzes, forcing them to a level of energetic exertion they might otherwise not have known how to experience. The whole thing left everyone breathless and exhilarated as they sat down for their salad.

It was now time for the candle-lighting. The candle-lighting is always the high point of the bar mitzvah reception—an expression of banal but heartfelt sentiment that goes to the very root of the bar mitzvah ethos. Stephanie, with Carla's help, had written rhymes for each member of the family, which she now recited as, one by one, they came forward to light a candle on the thirteen-pronged menorah that Moishe had set up in the center of the room.

> Florida is where they stay,
> They love me and they're lots of fun,
> I'm very glad they're here today,
> Will Grandpa Charles and Grandma Rose light candle number one.

Mark, who had been against the whole candle-lighting thing as an exercise in doggerel, smiled and laughed along with the rest as his parents walked proudly up to light a candle. Carla elbowed him and whispered, "You see, it's adorable." Mark, who wouldn't go quite so far as that, was diplomatic enough not to respond.

> She cooks and cleans and works so hard,
> She really is like very few,
> She even thought she knew the Bard,
> Will Grandma Jessie come light candle number two.

Everyone laughed, and Jessie, casting a shy glance back at Saul Millman, went up to light a candle.

> He really bothers me sometimes,
> And many times we disagree,
> But as a brother he is fine,
> Will Jeffrey come light candle number three.

And so it went: through Margot, Uncle Sid, Aunt Edie and Uncle Fred, Aunt Rachel and Uncle Bart, Cousins Mindy, Tasha, Bethany, Sara, Ari, and Carlotta (one communal candle), her camp friends (one candle), her school friends (one candle), and her Hebrew-school friends (one candle). A memory candle for Grandpa Milt. And finally, the thirteenth candle:

They have their faults,
They sometimes scream,
But they are just the best there is,
I love them though I say they're mean,
Will Mom and Dad please light candle number thirteen.

"Wow," whispered Mark, "we got an extra line of doggerel. That must really show she loves us." Carla gave him a look. They went up and stood on either side of Stephanie, as the photographer snapped their picture ("in the manner of a Best Picture Academy Award shot, Mom and Dad as Producers"—as Cass Sunshine explained, directing in the background). Everyone applauded. Indeed, it was right that they applaud, thought Carla. Stephanie *was* their product—at the same time that she was her own unique person. A welling of love for her daughter, her family, her friends, and her religion passed over her in a great wave of happiness.

They began the meal. The matzo-ball soup was a big hit with both the adults and the kids.

Then the deejay did a game and gave out a CD.

The sherbet course was served to cleanse the palate, while the klezmer band played some authentic Jewish songs.

Then the deejay played some Motown and led another game—with the distribution of the hula hoops and sparkle rods.

Then the main kids' course was served—the kids lining up for their buffet of faux cheese steaks, nuggets, and pasta, after which more kids' songs, games, favors, and CD prizes.

The adult main course was served. More klezmer. And then some oldies by the deejay for the oldies.

Saul Millman came over to the head table and asked Jessie to dance. Everyone watched them silently for a few minutes.

"She looks happy," said Mark.

"She's in love," said Carla.

"Who would have thought it?"

"On the contrary. After hearing her talk about being in love with William Shakespeare four hundred years ago, being in love with Saul Millman from Vineland seems a very normal sort of thing."

"You have a point there. But how do you think she knew all that stuff about Shakespeare? It got pretty detailed for a while."

"I think that she remembered," said Carla. "And then, when things happened for her again in the present, she forgot."

Meanwhile, Margot had been flirting with Uncle Sid, trying not to pay attention to anything going on in the room around her. A number of Mark's colleagues from the hospital had already swept her up for the Motown tunes. Now that the deejay had segued into the ballads—they were playing Sinatra's version of "Witchcraft"—she expected one of them back by her side, intent on holding her closer than she liked.

Feeling a presence near her chair, she assumed it was the allergist with the earring. When she turned, her brow was slightly furrowed.

But it wasn't the allergist. It was Hal. He was standing with a look on his face that she couldn't quite make out. Was it fearful, expectant, assertive, desiring?—it was, she felt, a combination of all these things. She stood up and he took her in his arms. She felt suddenly weak. What was happening to her? She had, she realized, been waiting for this all day. She had been waiting to dance with Hal Pearson—and now she was.

"I'm sorry about the sonnets," she said.

But he didn't respond. Instead, he continued to look at her in a way that made her at once uncomfortable and extremely happy.

"I don't really care about the sonnets," he finally said.

"You don't?"

"No." He cleared his throat and recited softly, "'My spirits, as in a dream, are all bound up.'"

"That's from *The Tempest*."

"You do have a retentive mind."

She looked up at him as they danced and moved closer.

"You're teasing me," he said.

"Why do you say that?"

"Because—I'm not good enough for you. I teach middle school. I don't work out. I haven't got much money."

She drew him to her, pressing her body against his, and murmured, "'My affections are then most humble. I have no ambition to see a goodlier man.'"

"Look, at that," said Saul Millman, who had deserted his place at the table with the Brooklyn Katzes to sit beside Jessie. "Your daughter is kissing that Shakespeare teacher. I thought she didn't like him."

"Oh, no," said Jessie, smiling knowingly, "Margot and Hal were made for each other."

Acknowledgments

I would LIKE TO THANK MANY PEOPLE WHO PUT THEIR TWO cents, or more, into this book. First, the early readers of the manuscript: my mother-in-law, Gertrude Penziner (how was I blessed with such a mother-in-law?), my husband, Alan S. Penziner (whose wit and weird erudition never ceases to amaze me), and my daughter, Kate Marantz Penziner (who is *not* Stephanie but who did help with Stephanie's dialogue). I also want to thank my delightful research assistant, Irina Teperman, who hunted down background material and served as a touchstone for my ideas.

Other thanks go to those who served as informational resources. On literary and pedagogical matters: Rosetta Marantz Cohen and Sam Scheer. On Philadelphia geography: Barbara Coleman and Sue and Phil Lipkin. On the Venetian ghetto and sundry Italian details: Lauren Weinberger, Fred Abbate, and Mort and Annette Levitt. On Jewish law and lore: Phyllis Markoff. Special thanks to Rabbi Ramy of the Chabad of Venice, who answered my e-mails and whose responses I hope to have accurately incorporated.

I am also grateful to Rosemary Abbate, who never ceased cheerleading for this book, to Albert DiBartolomeo (aka Liza), my literary therapist, and to the conversational and culinary support of my dear friends Mark and Vivian Greenberg. Others who have provided support and advice include Bella Stander, Karen Simonides, Carolyn Hessel, Don Riggs, and Marsha L. Mark.

I could not have written this—or anything else—without my family. The influence of my father, Murray S. Cohen, and the memory of my mother, Ruth Marantz Cohen, inform everything I do.

I count myself blessed to have Felicia Eth as my agent and the brilliant Hope Dellon as my editor.

Finally, I want to thank Drexel University, where I have taught for over twenty years. Early portions of the novel were presented at the Honors Research Forum for the Drexel Pennoni Honors College, the Writing Gala for the *Drexel Online Journal* (*DOJ*), and the Betty and Milton Shostak Lecture for Drexel Hillel. I am grateful to my academic mentor, Dave Jones; to my supportive department head, Abioseh Porter; and to the university in general for allowing me to range so widely in my work. Most of all, I want to thank my Drexel students, who have helped me stay fresh as a teacher, thinker, and writer.

READING GROUP GUIDE

1. How do you view Jessie Kaplan's ideas about her past life? In what ways are they creative and/or therapeutic for herself and for her family? Does it bother you that her ideas are never fully explained?

2. How is Carla's reaction to her mother's behavior at once logical, loving, and selfish? How do you view her handling of her daughter? Discuss the stresses of Carla's position as she struggles to do the best for her family.

3. How do Margot and her mother resemble and differ from each other? How does Margot reflect the gains that feminism has made possible for women as well as some of the losses that accompany those gains?

4. Discuss the different views of religion held by Carla and Mark. What do these differing views reveal about the temperament and nature of these two individuals?

5. Discuss Stephanie's initial response to her Torah reading and then look at her final *D'var Torah*. In what way does her response reflect a synthesis of Carla and Mark's views of religion?

6. The gap between appearance and reality is a major theme in Shakespeare's work. Discuss what it means to look below the surface of things and how this theme functions in the novel.

7. Discuss the idea of interpretation (the theme of Stephanie's *D'var Torah*)— as it relates to Jessie's notions of her past life, as it relates to Hal's role as a teacher and critic, and as it relates to Margot's abilities as a lawyer and as a woman seeking a soul mate?

8. Discuss the methods of Dr. Samuels. Is he a good therapist, in your opinion? Would you like to consult him? Why or why not?

9. Discuss the statement made by Mr. O'Hare: "I'm sure we go to the same place…only the scenery is different, which makes a lot of sense when you think about it. God doesn't want to go to the same goddamn play every night." How does this statement relate to the lives of the characters in the novel? To your own life and beliefs?

For more reading group suggestions visit
www.stmartins.com/smp/rgg.html

🦁 St. Martin's Griffin